Trust Me

Trust Me

by LAURA FLORAND

Chapter 1

Lina was fighting a dragon.

You'd think a dragon would know better than to mess with an international heroine who could take terrorists out with a bucket of liquid nitrogen, but no.

The damn thing was smirking at her.

She revved her chainsaw. *You sure you want to take that tone with me, lizard?* Ice shards flew as she took her saw to the curve of its neck, the cold in the room trying to overwhelm her body heat even through her gloves and hoodie.

Why the hell she had wanted to learn to ice sculpt, she did not know. It had seemed like a fun new challenge when she first took her motorbike out to Brittany to talk a famous sculptor there into teaching her his tricks— after all, she got to wield a chainsaw—but then hell had exploded in the Au-dessus kitchens, and now she was still on the hook for next month's contest and likely to humiliate herself by coming in last place, at the rate she was going.

Of course she'd probably be excused for giving up, in the circumstances. Backing down.

Letting the bad guys win.

She narrowed her eyes at the smirking dragon and revved her chainsaw menacingly—

And a big figure moved in the doorway of the freezer.

She swung violently, the chainsaw slicing straight through the dragon's neck. Ice shattered on the floor around her boots.

Size, danger, violence, freckles, and all her adrenaline shooting into her bloodstream ready to fight him—

1

Freckles?

Oh.

It was him. The mountain lion.

Jake. Friend of Chase "Smith", Vi's ridiculously over-confident new boyfriend. (Vi had the *worst* taste in men, honestly.) The man who was always leaning in the doorway of Chase's hospital room, watching Lina as she left the elevator with her police security and went into Vi's hospital room. Watching her when she came down the hallway to check on Chase.

Watching her now.

Long, lean, powerful. Hazel eyes, red-gold hair clipped short. Hard jaw. Controlled movements. And as far as she could tell, covered all over in freckles. This thick, golden-brown layering of them, as if every mote of sun that had ever had the chance to touch his skin had clung to him, unwilling to let go.

Greedy sun, just wanting to get its hot little rays all over that life of him. Would he have the same freckles on those broad shoulders? That hard, flat belly? That tight butt? His...did freckles go to...that is, she'd never seen a freckled man without any clothes before, was it possible that he'd have freckles on his...that the sun would have gotten all hot and greedy with his...

Are you turning into a nymphomaniac in some kind of post-traumatic stress reaction?

Probably worse things she could become. Scared. Weak. Paranoid. *Yeah, all the other options made nympho sound pretty enticing.*

She cut off the saw and set it on the steel table by the destroyed dragon, then bent to pick up the biggest two chunks of the decapitated head in her gloved hands. Totally ruined. After all that work. Her fingers cramped around them suddenly, in a spasmodic urge to throw them across the room, to scream, to grab the block left and just batter it to the floor.

She took a deep breath and let it out, setting the chunks down, pulling off her thick gloves, pushing back the hoodie of her sweatshirt, pulling out her earplugs. "Little life tip. Never sneak up on a woman fighting a dragon with a chainsaw."

From the subtle amusement in Jake's face, he probably took out six crazed chainsaw-wielders with a toothpick before breakfast every morning. "You know, it does seem as if my training should have included more practical tips like that. I'll have to tell my old instructors they missed a situation."

"They probably counted on you to have common sense."

He cocked his head and considered that a moment. "A group of wild teenage males who thought they could become the biggest bad-asses on the planet? I doubt it."

True. In her eleven years in top-notch kitchens, she'd dealt with more than her fair share of teenage males wielding lethal objects. Common sense didn't come into it.

"The real question is how *do* you approach a woman with a chainsaw?" Jake asked. "Any tips?"

"Very carefully. So you don't lose your head."

"Ah." Something about that steady gaze of his calmed her nerves the longer he studied her. How did he manage that? He'd come to most of her interviews with the French counterterrorist units, leaning against a far wall and watching without input, making her afraid he was there as some kind of shadow enforcer, primed at any moment to grab her by the neck and throw her into some interrogation chamber, on the grounds that she was Muslim and all Muslims were responsible for all acts of terrorism. Even acts turned against them.

But then, once in a while, during the two days of interviews, he'd disappear and come back with mint tea and maybe a little quiche from the nearest bakery. The mint tea was the crappy kind that came out of a police station's machine, but the gesture had made her feel as if someone was on her side. Cared about her. Sure, mint tea was a stereotype, but she actually did like mint tea—

3

her grandmother always made it for them—and at least it meant he was trying. And even though she knew from movies that his trying might be part of a good cop-bad cup routine, a way of getting her to trust him and lower her guard, well…it had still worked. She'd drunk the tea.

"You know, I've always wanted to meet a woman who could slay her own dragons," Jake said quietly.

She'd always wanted to be that kind of woman. What no one had warned her about was that most dragons were hydras.

"Here." Lina dropped the head into his hand. "I even brought you back its head as a trophy."

Jake considered the ice dragon's head a long moment. "I'm overwhelmed."

The weird thing was that he really sounded as if he was.

"Did you need something?" She made her voice brisk.

An odd expression flickered in those hazel eyes, as if he was considering whether he should just go ahead and tell her exactly what he wanted.

More leads on her cousins' friends? To sweep her away to some secret CIA prison for further interrogation? She was pretty sure her sudden international heroine status would mean the Americans couldn't get away with that one, but all she had known about it until a week ago was what Americans got away with in their own Hollywood films, and that was pretty scary stuff.

Merde, had her life ever been fucked up and turned on its head. Kind of like that time she'd spent thirty-six hours, no sleep, constructing the most fantastical, wonderful sugar and chocolate structure for the international pastry title and, as they transferred it to its base, her sous-chef tripped, and the whole thing went crashing upside down to the ground. Like that, only in this case, the sugar structure was her life, and she'd been working on that for the past twenty-six years.

Beautiful, ambitious...and it turned out, a lot more fragile than she had thought.

"I just wanted to check on you," Jake said. He still blocked the doorway, gazing down at her. "Vi worries, which makes Chase worry, and both of them are stuck in hospital beds. So here I am."

Okay, that was all plausible, in fact she knew quite well that Vi was climbing the walls, but somehow it didn't ring true. He wasn't telling her something.

Probably his secret orders to lure her into compliancy or something. Even though she'd *been* as compliant as she could be, but her grandparents had immigrated from Algeria back in the sixties, so she was never going to be just French. She was always going to be Arab-French. And a little bit suspect.

Although given that her own cousin was an actual terrorist, she supposed she should cut them some slack on that one. Damn Abed. What a way to prove to the family she was right when she insisted he was a creepy little turd.

Well, nothing for it. It wasn't as if she could start giving up in challenging circumstances *now*. When that sugar structure had crashed, she'd picked up the pieces and started over with the thirty minutes she had left before the bell.

She walked on past Jake as if she could walk right through him, which was pretty much the only way to deal with a man twice your size who carried himself as if a crazed woman wielding a chainsaw wouldn't even ruffle his nerves. She'd been asserting her space around and eventually imposing her will on over-macho men since she was...well, born, really, but definitely since she was first apprenticed at fifteen. She knew how to do it. But even she had never run up against a will quite so firm and controlled as Jake Adams'.

He wasn't flamboyant about it, like his friend Chase. Not cocky and flashy with his confidence. It was just *there*, bone deep inside him, as if he didn't give a damn how much people noticed it because it was so solid and sure in him he didn't need that attention.

He stepped back so she could leave the cold freezer. Really stepped back—leaving her a perfectly respectful amount of space, far more than she was used to in crowded, busy kitchens.

So either she could still assert her space, or he was just fundamentally courteous and had only needed a little nudge to realize he'd been blocking her. Or maybe both were true? Her strength and his courtesy.

"You can tell them both I'm fine," she said. "Although I stopped by already today. They can see for themselves."

"Maybe they worry you're putting on a good face for them at the hospital," Jake said. "And that the truth will show up better in your natural environment."

Lina threw him a sharp glance. Was that, maybe, something that the counterterrorist team thought? That some other *truth* would show up if they just watched her until she let it slip? Or was she just paranoid?

It was so hard to tell. Like, *Yes, you are paranoid but quite possibly because your own cousin, the one your family always claimed you were being over-paranoid about, did just try to kill you.*

And kill all your team. And your best friend.

Yeah, if she could get her hands on Abed again, she'd dip his freaking *dick* in liquid nitrogen and watch him scream.

"I've told all the truth, the whole truth, and nothing but the truth," she said wearily. But her skin was golden, so Jake and his ilk were probably never going to believe that.

"You're really fine?" He had come to stand on the other side of the counter that was her workspace. Courteously leaving that barrier between them. Not crowding her, as if he understood the crazy edge of paranoia that kept her awake at nights and tried to crawl its way into the light of day.

6

"My own cousin just tried to kill me and my best friend and everyone who helped us get where we are because he hated us so much for being successful, happy women," she said very lightly. "Of course I'm fine. Who wouldn't be?"

Jake reached across the counter and closed his big hand gently around hers. Callused hand, covered with freckles and little nicks and scars. She stared down at it a long moment and took a slow breath, careful with that breath so that it wasn't shaky. She couldn't handle sympathy right now. She might curl up in a fetal ball.

She cleared her throat and pulled her hand away, setting a copper kettle on a burner. It was warmer in this part of the kitchen, but not warm enough. Still, she unzipped her sweatshirt and pulled it off, maybe so she wouldn't huddle in its pretend protection.

Or maybe because the goose bumps that rose on her bared arms could be an invitation to Jake to rub those callused hands right up them and...

She caught that thought and stuffed it back down in a box called *behave yourself* and pulled out a pot. "Tea?" she asked him, filling the teapot with green tea and mint leaves and sugar. After all, he'd offered tea to her, when she needed it.

And sometimes being the one who offered the tea was a far greater need than actually drinking it.

His face relaxed in that infinitesimal way it did, a slight softening around the eyes and the corners of his mouth so that she could see the lines left from long narrow looks into the sun. He nodded.

"How long before you're ready to go?" he said, while she made the tea. "Maybe I'll hang out here until then and see you home."

Oh, hell, that would be nice. It was going to be her first night sleeping alone. She'd spent the first few days huddled with her family while journalists had gathered outside the gates and her parents' neighbors glared over the wall.

Her mother had hardly let go of her for three days straight—just grabbing her whenever Lina got anywhere near her, or anywhere too far, pulling her back in and holding on tight. Her father had paced the floor and muttered and gestured. And her grandmother had made du'a, praying for her and even for her cousin, and also a *lot* of mint tea. For the first four days, Lina had only left her parents' house to talk to police and to visit Vi in the hospital, but she'd been going crazy that way, and she'd forced herself back into her kitchens two days before. Tonight, she was going to take one more big step toward reclaiming her life. She was going to sleep in her own apartment again. Alone, with monsters in her closet.

She eyed Jake.

Maybe...now here was a thought...maybe he wasn't here out of suspicion of her but to help keep her safe. Had she been getting more death threats? Probably. She'd cut off all contact with social media a week ago, leaving it all in her poor publicist's hands, but the counterterrorist teams were still monitoring all her accounts and trying to follow threats back to IP addresses to see if that gave them any leads. Or any warning, if someone tried to make those threats a reality. She used to just dismiss misogynistic messages on social media, but now that a misogynist had burst into her kitchens with an AK-47 and a suicide bomb, she had a very different perspective.

Some people brought their hate to fruition.

"The police will escort me," she said. She had four officers guarding her right now, two of them currently stationed outside each entrance to Au-dessus. Her president would consider it a national failure if anything else happened to *"les héros d'Au-dessus"* under his watch. "But I appreciate it."

Even though she knew Jake Adams might not even consider her on his side, she still felt safer around him. He emanated toughness and control.

He shrugged. "Nothing better to do today."

8

Doubtful. At the very least, he could choose downtime. Play a video game. Watch a movie. Pursue bad guys instead of...well, her.

"Unless..." He eyed her speculatively. "You wouldn't be interested in getting me into your gym, would you? I hear you box, and I'd love to get a workout in."

Chapter 2

You're such a damn masochist. Jake gripped Lina's punching bag, for no reason whatsoever except that he wanted to feel every blow she gave it vibrate through his body. The gym smelled of grime and old sweat, a real boxing gym. And she hit that bag with blow after blow, too hard, wearing herself out on anger, passion, hurt, and her attempt to beat her life back into shape.

Every single blow aroused the hell out of him.

Not her fault she's everything you've been craving. Leave her alone.

Fine time to hit on a woman, a week after she'd nearly gotten killed, while one of her closest friends was still lying in the hospital. No, it was better to let her hit on him instead.

One way or another.

"So you ready to go a few rounds?" she said, with a gleam in her eye. Her dark curls were caught in a ponytail, but two had escaped to cling to her temples. She shrugged up a shoulder to wipe away the sweat that trickled.

Really? "Do you think you're up to my weight?" he said, warmth moving through him unexpectedly. Not quite amusement, not quite indulgence, but it carried with it a desire to lift his hand and tuck those curls back into her ponytail holder, to cup her cheek. He dug his fingers into the bag. He had volunteered for this, to be the guy on their team who kept an eye on her, but he might have taken on more than he could chew.

Or nibble. Or very, very gently nip...and taste...and—

She shrugged one shoulder. "If I can kick the ass of a black ops guy, imagine my street cred."

"Civilian." Was she testing him? Seeing what he did when she laid herself open to harm from him? He met that glint in her brown eyes with one of his own. "You sure you want to mess with me?"

She pivoted in a kick up high near his head and landed in a fighting position. "You sure you want to mess with *me*?"

"Yeah," he said with perfect honesty. "I do want to mess with you."

A lot.

Like, cuddle up in sheets and get messy as hell.

"It's amazing how many men do," she said and jabbed the air, right and left. "And they're *always* sorry," she warned him.

Oh, she was still using him as a punching bag. Proving to herself she could handle whatever any man threw at her.

Okay.

"Well, it's my first time," he said, wrapping his hands. "So be gentle with me."

"First time in a mixed-martial arts ring?" Lina said, surprised.

First time in a ring with a woman. Ever. He had never in his entire life even pretended to fight against a woman. "First time messing with you."

She relaxed into a kind of fierce, defiant arrogance. Spirit. That was the word. Fierce spirit. "Yeah, that is always a tough first lesson for a man."

Damn, he liked her. He pulled on his gloves and prepared to have one hell of a good time.

God, he had fun, sparring with her. She threw herself into it, and he couldn't, not the way he was used to—his particular challenge here was making sure he didn't hurt her while still giving her a decent opponent. More dodging and blocking on his side and punching to a point a couple inches shy of her, rather than through her, and making extra sure he didn't time it wrong so that she ran into one of those punches.

He had expected that he would find this sparring arousing as hell, but he'd still underestimated how much so. Grappling with and responding to every move her smaller body made, like an aggressive, passionate dance. Not that he knew how to couples dance, hell. He knew how to instruct newbies in combat training, though, and he used that—drawing her out, responding to the flicker of her eyes, opening himself up, closing a trap, feinting, engaging, taking all she could give him.

Yeah. Give it to me, honey.

He loved the way the curls clung black to her forehead as she sweated, and the way that sweetheart face could keep making him underestimate her determination, over and over, a lesson she kept teaching him every time she connected.

By the time they were done, she was actually grinning, as if for a moment she had cleared all memory of the attacks out of her soul.

"Thanks for the sparring," he said, on the walk back to her apartment, after they'd both showered at the gym. Her police guards accompanied them. All the Au-dessus kitchen staff had been assigned guards for six months, to protect them from any possible vengeance attacks or other kinds of crazies. "Happy to hit a boxing gym with you any time. If you need an outlet."

The glance she sent up at him flashed with so much—relief? Gratitude? His fingers curled into his palm so he wouldn't just take her hand and squeeze. "Thanks," she said. "I—thanks."

Yeah, he wasn't a firm believer in trying to articulate all his emotions either. Sometimes there just weren't the right words. "I'll see you up to your door."

A flicker in her eyes, the smile fading. "I've got the guards." She threw a *thank-you-guys* smile over her shoulder at them.

"I know. But I'm a control freak."

12

"Like to make sure everything's done right?" Lina said, unexpectedly rueful.

Exactly. He nodded.

She smiled. "Me, too."

That was funny. So if he could be patient while she was traumatized, and wait, and build this attraction into something *stable*, damn it, would that mean they would fight not over whether the toothpaste cap was on or not— it would always be on—but what side the toothpaste was on the sink and whether it should be in a vase or flat on the counter, or—

What the fuck is wrong with you? Quit imagining long term. Why do you do this to yourself?

He spent half his life deployed and another fourth training all over the world. Long term didn't exist for him.

A pile of flowers and stuffed animals and letters had collected by the door to her apartment building, all addressed to her. Jake glanced at the police guards who nodded to confirm to him that they were safe. Not only had the police provided bodyguards to Lina and the rest of the staff, but they also were maintaining security over the Au-dessus restaurant and the apartment buildings where people lived, and in the cases of those who had drawn the most dramatic international attention—Lina and Vi—of family members, too. So the gifts to her were verified before anyone was allowed to deposit them, and the letters—lots of adoring children's drawings—had to be open rather than sealed in an envelope.

They were an effective counterbalance to the ugly craziness that came at the two women—but particularly Lina—online, which they let their publicist handle and tried to pretend didn't exist. Even though they couldn't help knowing it did.

Lina picked up the top drawing. A child's hand. *I love you.* And a carefully drawn black-haired circle that might have been Lina's face, except the child had drawn an arrow to it that said, ME. Lina's face crumpled a little, a sheen of emotion in her eyes.

Journalists kept at a distance by the police snapped pictures of the moment. *Damn it.* But there was nothing to do but ignore them and try to function normally. Jake scooped up the stuffed animals and flowers and handed Lina a particularly nice floppy dog, angling his body to shield her face from cameras.

Lina took it and rubbed its glossy, furry ear between her fingers. "Why stuffed animals, do you think?"

"Because they're kids," Jake said. "And they want to comfort you." Probably plenty of adults had thought of stuffed animals as gifts for her, too. He kind of thought it was one of those secret advantages women had that they didn't understand, that even as adults they were allowed to seek comfort in a stuffed animal without anyone calling into question their strength and courage.

But he was pretty sure there was no worse way to shoot himself in the foot than to start a debate on female privilege with a strong-minded woman he was trying to impress, so he kept the thought to himself.

Stepping into her apartment was a blast of unearned intimacy. He took a breath of it, the warm golds and ochres and rust-red tones of her comforter as he peeked under her bed, the scent of *her* as he opened her closet door to see a row of jackets—leather, a long wool coat, denim—and on the floor a neat line of boots and pretty heels and flat, comfortable street-styled black tennis shoes.

He checked the view from her windows, compulsively, even though he knew Elias's men had the apartment watched, and then turned to nod to her, struggling to crush the sudden urge to kiss her good night. *We weren't just on a date. Jesus, talk about a desperate soldier. Can you not act like a pathetic stereotype?*

"Satisfied I'm not harboring terrorists under my bed?" she demanded, very dry. She was trimming the ends of the stems of the bouquets and putting them in a few inches of water in her sink. She'd passed out a big batch to random lonely people in the hospital the day before, when she visited Vi.

Harboring? Weird word choice there. Maybe his French wasn't up to some nuance. Or maybe she was just being ironic. The whole freaking culture seemed to consider irony the essence of communication. "I'm just compulsive," he said truthfully. Yes, he knew the police were keeping an eye on her to make sure she was safe, but he was never comfortable until he checked over important things himself. There were only a handful of people he'd trust to pack his parachute for him, for example, and he'd been through blood and fire with all of them.

"My dad used to do that," she said unexpectedly. "Check for monsters under my bed and in my closet to prove to me they weren't there so I could go to sleep."

He smiled down at her. "How old were you before you got a bat so you could go after them yourself?"

"Eight. He gave it to me."

Jake thought he might like her dad. Of course, a smart dad might give her a bat to use against him, too.

"Well," he said, profoundly reluctant to go. He'd feel so much better about things if he could at least sleep on the couch. Guards or not. "Good night."

The instinct to kiss her surged up high in him again, and he tamped it down hard. *Get a grip. Jesus.*

"*Bonne nuit*," she said. And just for a second, something flickered in her eyes, a fear of the dark he was about to leave her in that wrenched out his heart and fed the craving in him to stay.

But her father had been a smart man, giving her that bat and that belief she could handle whatever she had to. Turned out she'd needed that strength, when no one had been there to save her but herself.

"The guards are right here," he said. "And you've got all these locks." He ran his hand over the door on which, just like most city residents, she had three separate locks, and an alarm system Elias had made sure to have installed. He hesitated, wondering how long it had taken her dad to force himself to give her that bat instead of handling the problem himself, just because he knew she was scared. He was pretty sure she didn't trust him enough for this, but... "Do you want me to stay? On the couch, I mean."

Her chin went up, her ponytail swinging with the motion. "I am *perfectly fine.*"

He took a deep breath. "I know." Or at any rate, she would be. If he would just leave her alone and let her confidence grow back.

He took a step back. Controlled one last time the urge to kiss her good night. "*Bonne nuit,*" he said and closed the door firmly between them.

Damn.

In the hallway, the two guards studied him with suspiciously neutral expressions. "I know," Jake said tightly. "I know. You've got this." He meant to run downstairs, but instead he looked up at the ceiling. "Think I'm going to go sit up on the roof for a while." He warned them so nobody accidentally shot him.

One of the so-neutral guards let his lips kick up in a subtle, slanted sympathy. Yeah, okay. They had a protective instinct, too. Jake nodded at them and jogged up the next flight of stairs, then unlocked the roof access and climbed out.

He took a long, slow breath as he settled on the roof, tension easing. He'd always liked to be up high, where he could survey all his surroundings. He excelled as a sniper. It was just...

That intimate moment, when he held a human being in his sights and drew a breath and let it half out and squeezed the trigger...and that human being jerked and died...

Maybe Jake was getting old. Eleven years of this. He still got the adrenaline rush in a firefight, and it was still kind of addictive, but he wasn't sure agreeing to go into sniper training had been a good choice for him. It gave

16

him too much time to wish that he knew another way of saving lives that didn't require him to kill so many people.

Lives spread out all around him here. Sparks of light everywhere. When that Eiffel Tower over past the Seine lit in its sparkle dance, he wondered if that was why Parisians had made it sparkle—the lights on the Tower represented the life in every person who looked at it. In which case, it made sense the Tower had gone dark a time or two these past few years, in grief. But mostly, it kept stubbornly sparkling. Just like Lina. *You can't put us out.*

***

"*Ça va, ma puce?*" Sofia Farah asked over the phone.

Lina peeked over the edge of her bed at the windows. "I'm fine, Maman. You know I've got the police guards."

"Do you want us to come in?"

"It's an hour drive, Maman. I'm *fine.*" She couldn't tell her mother this, but her plan was to indulge in sexual fantasies until she fell asleep. Jake Adams was going to come in very handy.

She stretched down and checked under her bed again, holding her phone to her ear. Still no monsters under there.

She sat back up, pressing her back to her closet door. She'd already checked in there once—just in case Jake had missed a fang gleaming in the dark—and she was absolutely determined not to check again.

"It would be no problem, *pucette.*"

Pucette. Lina had gotten about twenty years younger in her mother's eyes the instant someone had tried to kill her. It might be her mom was calling her every hour not for Lina's sake but for her own. To make sure she was still okay. "I'm still okay, Maman," she murmured. "I worked on my ice sculpture today."

"Yes?" An encouraging murmur.

"I'm going to do a dragon."

17

This time, a warm, fierce sound of approval. Actively lured over from Algeria by the French government to help factories desperate for workers, her mother's parents had ended up stuck in the terrible conditions of the Nanterre shantytown, where Sofia had been born. When the public outcry had pushed the government to build better lodging, the family had been moved into the HLM where Sofia had grown up and near where Lina herself had grown up. Sofia should, in theory, have been too young to remember much of the shantytowns, but she'd grown up a fiery activist. Missing 1968 by a decade—as far as Lina was concerned, her mother would have made a *perfect* student protestor—Sofia had instead become an ardent feminist and a teacher, determined to change all the lives she encountered, all the time, and insisted they stay in their bad *banlieue* so she could better do that. But when Lina's father, who had started work at fifteen just like Lina had, had therefore been eligible for retirement at fifty-five two years ago and sold his little *épicerie*, Lina had finally talked her parents into moving with her grandmother into a better *banlieue*.

Where the next door neighbors glared at them, but anyway...

Lina's fiery, vibrant, warm mother was going to wrap those neighbors around her finger in the end, Lina was sure of it.

"But I keep cutting off its head," Lina said.

Her mother laughed. Lina relaxed a little of the pressure she was putting into making sure the closet door behind her stayed closed.

"Seriously, Maman, you guys need to go ahead and leave on your vacation. You know if you wait until August 1, you'll be stuck in traffic for hours getting away from Paris."

"Well, you come with us," her mother said stubbornly.

"Maman. No. Vi's still in the hospital. I'm not leaving her there."

"And I'm leaving you here and going off to fight police officers over burkinis?"

Lina gazed beseechingly at the ceiling. Her mother didn't even wear a hijab and had spent her student years refusing to even don a bra, that "symbol of the patriarchy," but of course she was going to wear a burkini at the beach to make a statement, now that some beaches had been outrageous enough to try forbidding them. Her mother's main cause was girl power, and this battle was a *don't tell us what to do with our bodies* one. She was dying to get a picture of herself in the papers with a couple of (ideally male) police officers looming over her on the beach, forcing her to remove a burkini.

"Maman, you do know anything you do now will be amplified a million times, with all the media focus on us." Particularly on Lina, but since Lina wasn't giving media interviews, television crews kept trying to feed their audiences by hanging out around her parents' house, too. But even that was *nothing* like the numbers of journalists and crazy people hanging around her aunt and uncle's building; their situation was *terrible.*

On the plus side, the numbers Lina could see hanging outside her apartment building and restaurant halved each day, proof that no matter what happened, media attention just never lingered long.

But her mother getting arrested in a burkini would probably pull it right back. "It's an opportunity to make a stronger statement," her mother said firmly.

Her mother's own way of trying to find a damn silver lining.

"Go make that statement, then. I'm fine, Maman."

"I know you're fine, *pucette*," her mother said. "You're going to be just fine."

She sounded like she had all those times when Lina skinned her knee as a child or struggled with some social situation as a young teenager—hugging her, rocking her if she was little enough, consoling her, and

19

communicating her absolute certainty that Lina could handle anything she had to.

"Anyway, I haven't actually figured out where to buy a burkini yet," her mother said. "I think I'm going to have to buy one online."

Lina's face slowly split into a grin. She really loved her mother.

"The only one I saw in a store made me look fat," her mother said, and Lina laughed. A political activist did have to draw the line somewhere.

Oh, damn, it felt good to laugh. She unfolded herself from the floor behind her bed, hesitated, peeked inside the closet quickly one last time, and then climbed onto her bed, stretching out her legs. She'd be fine here in this bed. There were police officers outside.

Hell, her mother had survived being born in a shantytown, and her grandparents had survived living and working and trying to raise a child in those conditions. Lina was going to do *just fine*.

"Thanks for calling, Maman." Lina turned off her light. Hesitated. Then got up and turned on her bathroom light and cracked the door ajar. There, that worked. She pulled the covers over her, but didn't cover her head. Monsters loved it when people hid their heads in the sand. "Tell Papa and Djadeti I love them."

Her mother's voice was warm and strong. "We love you, too, *ma puce*."

So Lina was smiling and feeling as strong as she could when she disconnected. But she still had to stare her way through a long, long, long dark night. *Thank you*, she thought to the police officers. To people like Jake and Chase. *For being out there, keeping me safe.*

***

A couple of rooftops over, a man in black ran along the peak of the roof. Jake watched as Elias jumped and swung up to the roof three meters above him, ran along that, dropped and rolled, and then slowed, walking panther light up to Jake and dropping beside him.

20

"Did you go into RAID just for the patch or what?" Jake said. RAID was one of France's elite counterterrorist units, and its patch was a black panther. Tall, black-haired, bronze-skinned, Elias was Jake's team's liaison with RAID. Capturing Al-Mofti had been a politically delicate joint operation, with Jake's team here unofficially as far as the general public was concerned. Both countries had agreed on the goal of eliminating Al-Mofti, so it had been better for all concerned to coordinate their efforts rather than for the U.S. to keep going it alone, in secret, in an allied country where there would be outrage at discovering U.S. black ops were active.

"What, you think the patch suits?"

"Man, you could practically graft a black tail onto your body."

Elias laughed and settled down onto the roof beside him. "Want to explain what the fuck you're doing here?"

"Not really," Jake said. Enjoying the lights. Reassuring himself that a certain dragon-slayer was safe.

Made for kind of a good evening.

Elias looped an arm around an upraised knee. "Just to clarify my understanding of American dating practices, was taking her to a boxing gym your idea of flirting?"

Jake sighed. This was the freaking problem with knowing a Frenchman.

Elias pressed his lips together to try to contain himself, but it was clear from the smirking that kept escaping at the corners that he was boiling with hilarity. "Did, ah, she respond well to that approach?"

"Well, she did hit me," Jake said.

Elias laughed.

"Several times in fact."

Elias just grinned and shook his head.

21

"But she didn't beat me up and throw me in the river, so I think I'm doing better than Chase."

Elias gave a shout of laughter that echoed over the upside down stars of the city and clapped his hand to his forehead. "*Bordel, ces Américains.*"

"Also, I didn't hurt her, and since she's had men in her life who were willing to do that, I figure it's just as well to demonstrate early on I'm not one of them."

Elias cocked an eyebrow. "So rather than hitting her over the head and hauling her off to a cave, you demonstrated your worthiness by grunting and posturing in front of her but not actually doing anything?"

"Oh, fuck you," Jake said. Frenchmen. Well, he only knew one that well, but Elias was annoying enough to stigmatize his whole nation.

Elias grinned and shook his head. "When they told me I had to babysit a bunch of Americans and make sure you behave—"

"*Babysit?*"

"I never guessed it would be this much fun."

Chapter 3

Lina thought she was used to pretty much all ways males of the species could be annoying, but the human mountain lion prowling constantly around her kitchens for the second day in a row was making the nape of her neck prickle.

If he could just...*go* somewhere. Or sit still. Or stop prowling in a way that made her want to reach out and sink her fingers into his ass to feel how those muscles flexed in that long, smooth, silent stride of his. She liked the flame deep in him, burning and secret and guarded, as if no sudden wind could put it out.

I know what you're doing, she told herself sternly. *Trying to hide in thoughts of him rather than deal with real life. Well...real death.*

Sexy guy prowling around her kitchens. *Not* the blood she and Adrien had only yesterday washed off that counter he was just walking by.

Not the bullets flying out of nowhere into her beautiful world, shattering everything. She'd thought she'd made her life so strong and glorious and *hers*. And all that time, it had just been blown sugar that anyone could break.

Wrong. They didn't break us. We fought and we won.

Jake turned at a corner and prowled back. He was a hard-muscled man, but not bulky in that way of men whose workouts focused on bulk. His muscles had clearly developed to a purpose. Survival emanated from his every pore.

Yes, he was very stubbornly, very indomitably *alive*.

And *merde* but those freckles killed her. For example, his butt. Would he have freckles on his butt? A woman needed to *know* these things. The curiosity was

23

killing her. Would they be fewer, would the skin between them be paler? Would that hard, tight ass feel like—

Her hand squeezed on the torch, and her attempt to give her dessert a delicate golden-speckled complexion overheated and the sugar blackened and smoked.

Merde. Survive one damn terrorist attack and it turned you back into a rank apprentice with nymphomaniac issues.

The mountain lion prowled back.

Her skin prickled all over again.

"Is it supposed to look like that?" Jake asked, nodding to her blackened dessert.

Lina's teeth clicked together. "No. Don't spoil my concentration."

"So it's leftover?" he said.

She paused. Well, there you go. She'd known *somebody* was filling this room with hunger. She'd been worried it was her. "The sugar's burnt," she said. "You can't eat that." Not in *her* kitchen.

That tiny, compressed curl of his lips that meant he was amused. She thought. He had a secretive way with his amusement, as if he didn't think she deserved to be in on the joke. It made her want to upend a bowl of custard on his head.

But it tickled her middle, too.

"You've never tasted an MRE, have you?" he said.

A what?

"Meals ready to eat. For when we're in the field."

She looked at the over-blackened sugar globe that was her earlier attempt to turn the traditional crème brûlée into one that could give the visual impression of floating off the plate, entirely cased in that famous burnt-sugar crust. When you tapped it with your spoon, all the cream inside would spill lushly out in an orgy-like glorification of what a crème brûlée should be.

"Did you just compare something I made to military rations?" She was a two-star pastry chef with eyes on a third star. Military rations?

"*Favorably,*" he said. "Definitely favorably."

"I can see why Vi tries to kill Chase on a regular basis." Violette Lenoir was the head chef of this two Michelin star restaurant. She and Lina had been close friends ever since they were teenagers growing up in a sketchy outskirt of Paris and fighting to make their way in a male-dominated profession. *Together against the world.* Then Chase had burst into Vi's life only a couple of weeks ago. And now both he and Vi were lying in hospital beds, thanks to Lina's cousin.

And maybe jokes about killing someone weren't funny, once someone actually did try to kill you.

"She should make the attempts more irregular," Jake said. "Spontaneous. Keep him on his toes. He'll enjoy it more."

Lina couldn't stop her lips from twitching. Extroverted, cocky, larger than life Chase probably would, at that. Maybe Vi's attempts to "kill" Chase were still a little funny.

"Of course, Chase is a trouble-maker," Jake said. "Adrenaline junkie. Me, I'm more the calm, quiet type."

Lina took a moment to look that lean, powerful body up and down. (Nobody could blame her for taking her time with that, could they? Not every day a woman got a chance to eye a body like that so slowly and then pretend she was dismissive of it. All those thoughts that didn't want to behave bumped against the lid of that box she was trying to keep them in.) "...Right."

That tiny, secret curl of his lips again, like he would just *never* let her in on the damn joke. "Patient," he said. "Thorough."

Okay, her mind just went somewhere dimly lit and horizontal where he could be *patient* and *thorough* as he...

She scrubbed her face and frowned at the black globe of sugar. "I'll make you another one. Don't act desperate."

Hazel eyes held hers a moment, faintly narrowing. "...Desperate?"

"You can't be that hungry," she clarified.

"I'm guessing you don't know much about hunger."

For some blasted reason, that did a whole *tumult* of things to her middle, as if a slumbering volcano had just rolled over in her belly and thought about waking up.

Jake picked up the spoon she'd used a bit earlier and eyed the blackened sugar globe as if planning his attack on it.

She grabbed his hand and pressed it down to the counter. "Will you wait one minute! I'll make you a good one."

His gaze dropped to her pale gold hand on his darker, freckled one, hazel eyes hidden by stubby, sandy lashes. His hand was large and warm under hers. Her callused, capable hand looked suddenly absurdly small.

She pulled it back so it could go back to looking its capable, strong self again.

He flexed his hand carefully. "I could eat both. There's no point this one going to waste."

"Shh," she said, and his lips curled again.

She had made a dozen sugar globes for experimental purposes, because she was trying to be normal again. Just *be herself.* Even if "Lina Farah" felt like an alien, someone she couldn't recognize in her own mother's photos of her, she could at least *try.* Follow the recipe of who she was. Make desserts and pretend she could make her world secure again.

On Vi's desk, she had piled today's tribute left at the restaurant door—more stuffed animals and drawings, including one where the kitchen staff was lined up like superheroes for a movie ad, with her and Vi leading the charge, holding hands, one blonde stick figure and one black-haired. *I wish I could be brave like you*, said the drawing.

And Lina didn't dare admit that she didn't feel brave anymore. That it was all an act, around a hollow center, and that center felt as if it would always be hollow, always be echoing inside her performance of strength. But she couldn't tell people that. She couldn't tell herself that. It was exactly like when she'd first stepped in an all-male, high-powered kitchen at fifteen and nearly been overwhelmed and driven out. *Just fake it. Fake confidence and competence and courage until it becomes true.*

So she focused on the second sugar globe. She had been experimenting with this idea the day terrorists changed her life as she knew it. If she could get these crème brûlée sugar globes right, well, then...well, that would be *something*, damn it.

First, and most difficult, fill the delicate blown sugar shell with the custard cream without breaking it. Pose that on the narrow column of very dry lemon-laced *biscuit* or cookie that formed the base. Then a quick brush of the torch.

Better, no? She considered it a moment. Despite how tricky it was to actually make it, it still didn't look as special and fancy as it needed to, in order for the dinner guests to understand how precious it was. She wanted them to take a minute, before they plunged their spoons in and destroyed it. Wanted them to think first about how valuable and fragile and beautiful it was. *Don't just wantonly ruin it.*

Maybe she needed to scatter a few tiny flecks of gold over the sugar before she took the torch to it. Give it something that added texture, like kisses from the sun.

"Now I can?" the hungry mountain lion asked meekly, that sun-loved hand easing toward the edge of the plate. His skin had a visual texture to it that fascinated her. All those burnt-sugar shadings of freckles and tan. It made all other skin tones look boring. Uniform. No wonder the sun liked to kiss him.

27

She was going to need to put some stronger locks on that *behave yourself* box. Those *I'd rather be a nympho on top of my bed than hide scared under it* ideas kept escaping back out. Hell, she'd nearly invited him to stay last night. Sex with a sexy stranger had sounded *so* much better than trying to sleep alone.

She held up a hand to make him wait. In a matter of seconds, working as fast as she would when all their tables were ordering desserts at the same time, she added a burst of beautiful golden spun sugar, sprinkled that with a grating of lime peel so that just a hint of green was caught in it, slid it across to him and turned it precisely as it came to a stop, so that he was facing the dessert exactly as he should. Presented.

Beautiful. Because...it was kind of beautiful, wasn't it? One of the scariest things since the attack was that she seemed to see even her own desserts through gray-tinted glass, so that she could no longer tell.

Jake gazed down at the dessert a long moment, his face tightening. Okay, why? He did the same thing when she brought special treats to Chase and all the guys who liked to fill Chase's hospital room, and it pissed her off every time. He was supposed to just relax into raptures.

If her desserts really were still worthy of wonder. Had she lost her touch? Or was it something else? He spent most of his life surrounded by violence. Did he have a gray wall, too?

He cleared his throat. "That's...ah...beautiful," he said awkwardly. Like someone politely trying to pretend he loved the ugly sweater his nine-year-old niece had knitted him for Christmas. He snuck a sideways glance at the burned, ruined version, as if he would rather have been eating that.

"Oh, just sit down already." She caught a stool and swung it to him.

He'd damn well better not eat one of her desserts standing at the counter like they did in movies in his heathen country. Energy pricked her at the thought, little golden sparks of annoyance that helped make tiny

28

holes in that foggy gray wall between who she was now and who she had been.

"Yes, ma'am," he said meekly, that faint curl back to his lips, and sat down.

But as he gazed at the floating crème brûlée, his face tightened again, and he slid a sideways glance at the ruined one as if asking it to rescue him.

Lina reached out and dumped the ruined one in the trash.

"Hey!" He stretched to save it, too late, and frowned at her. "That was wasteful."

"This one," she nudged the good plate, "is for you."

He took a deep breath. Lifted his spoon. Hesitated.

"I'd do it for you, but you seem like a big strong man, and the biggest delight of a crème brûlée is breaking through the sugar for the first time," Lina said.

A little kick at one corner of his lips, and he glanced at her.

"Go ahead." God knew, maybe a man who spent half his life eating military rations *was* afraid of real food. "Be brave."

He tapped the spoon against the globe.

Hey, it *worked*. The cream spilled out just as she had meant it to, the sugar cracking in pieces, the cream a warm subtle pale gold, a visual explosion of flavor just before the taste hit his mouth.

And his smile for the first time opened up as if he'd forgotten to keep it a secret. He slipped a spoonful into his mouth.

His eyes closed a second.

Now Lina's smile felt like a secret, tucked up behind her lips, as she busied herself with the next plate, trying to figure out the best technique for doing dozens of these a night quickly and efficiently and without shattering the globes over and over in her team's hands. Pretending that, well…that was who she was. A top pastry chef.

29

Delighted when someone took pleasure from slipping a spoonful of her work into his mouth.

Jake ate silently, absorbed, all his focus on the dish. He ate until the tiniest sliver of sugar was gone. He dabbed one finger into the last bits of lime zest and sucked those off the tip.

Now those were the kind of bad table manners a pastry chef could really warm up to. Lina smiled at him despite everything, the pleasure warming her, as if it could thaw out the old her and bring it back to life.

Oh, the old Lina wasn't dead? She was just Han Soloed?

She pulled one of her earlier preparations out of the lowboy and started to finish it off. Pretty, fancy sweetness, as if the doors to this restaurant kitchen had never burst open. As if she could control the raw world and make it beautiful.

Offer it to someone else who had seen raw, ugly things.

She slid the new dessert across to the mountain lion. Jake gazed down at it warily. A bar shape of chocolate, which she had just that instant coated with melted chocolate that gleamed, covering the multiple layers of chocolate mousse and *croustillant* underneath the chocolate coating. One line of a gold sugar baton across it and absolutely nothing else but the deep brown-black chocolate gloss. She loved the purity of this dessert. Nothing to distract. If that gleaming chocolate wasn't the most beautiful thing a diner could see, then he should quit ordering the chocolate dessert every time and experiment a bit.

Live a little, people, she used to say, in complete oblivion to what the antonym of *live* really was. *There's more to life than chocolate.*

"Thank you," Jake said stiffly.

She turned away and watched sidelong under her lashes as he gazed at the dessert as if he and the bar of chocolate were having a battle. Then he slowly brought his spoon down and sliced through the gloss.

Maybe he was in power when he was prowling around, but eating her desserts made him vulnerable? Maybe that was why he braced like that?

Well, and so he should. She gave her dessert a firm nod. That dessert was *powerful*. Men could burst through these doors and spray bullets, and when a woman picked herself back up off the floor and made sure her friends were alive, she could square her shoulders and make *more* fragile sugar.

She could hang her life on it. Keep going forward.

Yeah, you'd better run, evil, you asshole. I'm Lina Farah. And every single beautiful dessert I make says FUCK YOU. I WIN.

"It's really good," Jake remembered to say. He looked up at her. "I mean really."

Right, like *that* was convincing.

As convincing as her *I'm still Lina Farah, top pastry chef* act.

But, "Thank you." Because sometimes manners were like a recipe, too. They helped guide you through the dark moments so that you didn't hurt anyone while you were in them. "I'm glad you like it."

His mouth softened, and he looked back at his chocolate, focusing on it.

He had a very intense focus. As if he wanted to absorb every sensation. And once again, as he finished he ran a finger over a tiny splotch of chocolate on the plate to scoop it up and suck his finger clean. Her mind zoomed immediately in on those lips sucking his finger.

Will you quit? she thought, exasperated. *Can't you prove you're still alive without jumping on the first hot man you see?*

Still, if you wanted to get down to basics, the one time-honored way for life to keep forging forward and producing new life was...

31

Merde, Lina! Pull yourself together.

She cleared her throat. "Don't scrape the plate, Red. There's more in the kitchen."

Hazel eyes lifted to hers. "Is there?"

Of *course* there was. Did he even know who Lina Farah was? (*Lina Farah. Yeah. I'm Lina Farah.*) "Sure. Want something else?"

Come on, want something else. Let me show you who I am.

Let me show me *who I am.*

He pivoted on the stool to face her more fully, resting sinewy forearms on the counter. "Would that be too desperate?"

If they were going to talk about desperate, she was pretty sure she shouldn't throw stones. She gestured to herself. "It's okay if you're desperate for me." Hell, that was like bathing in sunbeams to a pastry chef.

A tiny lift of red-brown eyebrows. "Is it. Good to know."

Ridiculously, Lina started flushing a little. Hopefully not enough to show on the warm tones of her skin. She should be able to beat him in a hide-the-blush contest any day. Right? She eyed the thick gold-dust of his skin again. Maybe not. Maybe the sun had baked the visibility of a blush out of him. Whereas she spent much of her day indoors.

She turned her back and bent to look in a lowboy, just to be on the safe side.

But it felt good to flush. *Alive.*

"This one might take a while longer," she warned. Since the restaurant was still closed, she had very little prepped—just her experiments, produced from a need to get back in here and make these kitchens a place where life was lived and fed and made beautiful again, rather than a place of fear and death. She'd made far too much, but she couldn't stop.

If she stopped, she'd crouch down behind a counter and cower there, unable to drag herself back up. And there was no freaking way she was doing that.

Jake shrugged. "I'm here as long as you're here."

Lina paused. "Are you planning on stalking me indefinitely?"

"You complaining about having a few extra safety measures right now?"

When he said *safety*, tension relaxed across her forehead and down the nape of her neck through her shoulders.

She bent her head, for one moment purely grateful he existed. To keep her safe. Then she took a deep breath. "That's a really excellent 'good cop' technique. Make the person you're interrogating feel grateful to you for keeping her safe, and she's much more likely to tell you things."

That faint lift of his eyebrows again. "You got anything you still want to tell?"

Lina glared at him. "*No.*"

"That's what I thought," Jake said. "Don't start throwing liquid nitrogen on me, ma'am, I'm on your side."

She gave him a dirty look. She'd thrown the liquid nitrogen she was carrying into her cousin's face in her first reflex when the attackers burst into the kitchens. It might be the only reason she and Vi and their Au-dessus team were alive today. And he was going to *joke* about it?

But another little spark got past that gray wall. As if his humor had peeled off a flake of gold leaf from the sheet on the counter and blown it off his finger to float down into her soul.

His secret smile lurked. "I guess you know how to freeze a man's heart, don't you?"

Okay, you know what? She didn't have to put up with this. "Mostly I use nitrogen on men's dicks."

33

He gave a shout of laughter. It slipped out of him, his hazel eyes lighting with it as he pressed a hand to a flat belly as if to hold it in.

Wow, it felt good to have laughter ringing through those kitchens again. She hauled out a can of liquid nitrogen and poured some into a bucket in as villainously menacing a way as she could. The vapor rose instantly around her hands, a delicious chill spreading around the metal bucket. She had always loved liquid nitrogen. It made her feel like some sorceress, bending the world to her wiles. So she pushed memories out of her mind and gave Jake a sorceress's smile over it.

He reached out and brushed a curious finger over the surface of the vaporizing liquid, too fast to cold burn himself. Nitrogen vaporized so quickly at exposure to human body temperatures that you had to sustain contact or expose yourself to greater quantity to end up hurt by it. A bucket thrown on a man wearing a cotton sweatshirt that soaked it up would do it. And punching that soaked sweatshirt repeatedly would leave some burns on fists.

She flexed the knuckles that had been burned, picked up one of the roses she used for one of her desserts, and handed it to Jake.

"Flowers already?" he said. "So you like me better than you let on?"

Oh, were they flirting now? Even if it was part of a good cop routine, it still felt...warm. Hopeful. And fed far too much encouragement to her brain's apparent desire to focus on life in the most primitive way possible, where he was concerned. "Dip it in."

"If this rose is supposed to represent my dick, I'm not sure I'm flattered by the comparison."

She grinned. Oh, yes, she liked the way he beat back bad things with humor. She really did.

Jake dipped the rose in the nitrogen, looking like a fascinated kid as the flower froze instantly. When he lifted it out, a perfectly frosted red, Lina thumped it with her middle finger, and it shattered onto the counter.

"Graphic," Jake said solemnly. "Excellent way to warn a man to keep you away from his dick."

Well, that wasn't...okay, that wasn't quite what she had...but now she couldn't *say* that because it would seem like...(*would* he have freckles there? *Stop wondering that, you idiot. Go Google it, if you want to know the answer that bad.*)

No! Don't Google it! God knew if her computer might be confiscated, and Jake himself would be looking at her search history, with the words *freckles on penises.*

Oh, God. Definitely don't Google it. Not even on your phone. They've got phone hackers these days.

"Don't worry," Jake said solemnly. "I find my frozen dick an uncomfortable subject, too." He gazed sadly at the shattered rose.

She realized how long she had been standing there flustered and glared at him again.

That little smile of his got a tiny bit less secretive. Like maybe, *maybe* she might deserve to be in on the joke one day.

"So you literally blow hot and cold with men, is that it?" Jake asked, nodding to the blowtorch.

She sighed at how pathetic this level of innuendo was. And yet she was enjoying it anyway. It was the most human she had felt in several days. To flirt, you had to believe life would go on, right? Flirting was itself an act of hopeful fantasy.

"Sometimes I freeze a heart *and* melt it within seconds." That was one of the fun things to do with liquid nitrogen. Encase something molten in a shield of mousse, dip the mousse in liquid nitrogen, plate it, and send it to the table, so that the client had the hot and the cold both together.

"I guess a humble boy from the hills would be no match for a sophisticated Parisian player like yourself, then."

35

What? Who were they talking about? "I don't think I know anybody who fits either of those descriptions."

"From where I'm sitting, you look pretty damn sophisticated, sweethe—ma'am."

"*You're* the humble boy from the hills?" she said incredulously.

He inclined his head.

"That humility wore off fast once you left them, didn't it?"

He looked a little confused. What, he thought his prowling, mountain lion presence was humble? That was hilarious.

Of course the idea that she was a sophisticated *Parisienne* was pretty funny, too. She was a working class girl—a chef, for crying out loud—in a neighborhood of artsy diversity. The sophisticated Parisians were the *bobos* over in the Sixth and Seventh and beyond. But hey, if there was one bright side to tourists, besides the obvious economic ones, it was that they thought *all* Parisians were sexy and sophisticated, compared to them. She could go with it.

She tried to stand a little sexier and more sophisticated.

Jake dipped his spoon in the liquid nitrogen and watched the ice crawl up its stem. He touched it to his arm, jerking it back immediately, set the frozen spoon down on the counter, and braced his forearms there, studying her.

Wow. When this man looked at someone, he really *looked.* He could probably see right through to the marrow of her bones.

"Is it true what you told the investigators? That you don't have a boyfriend?"

"*Everything* I told them was true," Lina snapped, temper flaring instantly. She should have known. The investigators didn't believe her, or at least their U.S. counterparts didn't, and Jake was just hanging around to see what else he could find out.

"Kind of hard to credit," Jake said mildly.

"That I could tell the truth?" Lina glared at him. Why, because she was "Arab"? She'd been surrounded by some form of racism all her life, but caught up in her work, in the life of a Parisian, in the diversity of her city and her friendships, it had hardly seemed like the backbone of her identity. But these days, between the rise of fundamentalism in some circles and the anti-Muslim backlash in others, sometimes being just the typical Parisian who barely thought about religion at all felt like being Leia in the garbage disposal unit on the Death Star. Judgment pressing against her from all sides, trying to squeeze the life out of her. And no droid ready to intervene and release the pressure of all that crap either. She'd always thought she was *Lina Farah*, not *arabe* or *musulmane* or *franco-arabe* or *beurette* or *maghrébine* but a top pastry chef. But being the central target of a terrorist attack had shattered the hell out of *that* bubble.

"That you don't have a boyfriend."

Oh. She hesitated, not at all sure how to take that. A test? A compliment? Was he seriously coming on to her? And if so, was it for his sake or for his country's?

"Why don't you?" Jake studied her.

"I can't get anyone to put up with me."

Jake laughed low in his throat, a laugh like that secret smile of his, as if he didn't intend to share it. A sexy rumble that heated her from her toes to the roots of her hair. "Yeah, right."

"I have a very intense career, I'm busy almost every night until midnight, and I don't do that eyelash crap."

"Eyelash crap?"

She batted her eyelashes. *"Ooh, you're such a big, strong, smart man, of course you should decide everything."*

That elusive smile broke into a slow, full grin. "You sound like me."

"I do?"

"Intense job, busy most nights not to mention most months of the year, and I don't do that eyelash crap either."

She gave his stubby, sandy eyelashes a doubtful look.

He leaned across the counter, into and over her personal space, and gazed down at her from under those lashes. *"Ooh, you're such a cute, sexy little thing. Of course I should make everything I am small enough that you can wrap it around your little finger."*

Their eyes met and held. She braced herself against the impact of that hazel. "I have to confess, I'm very disappointed you didn't try batting your lashes, too."

He winked at her and sat back.

Hmm. This man might be trouble in more ways than one. And the last thing she needed in her life right now was more trouble. "So you can't get anyone to put up with you either?" she said dryly.

Ha. He was seriously hot. Women must fall all over him, with that alpha sexy crap going for him. And those freaking freckles. It should be illegal to flaunt those things so close to a woman's fingers.

But his amusement faded. He prodded a thawed, limp rose petal with one big finger and didn't say anything. A hint of grimness to his mouth and eyes.

"Why, are you a jerk?" she asked.

He pushed away from the counter and went back to prowling.

And Lina took a deep breath of...relief? Disappointment?

It's better this way. The last thing you need to do is try to use sex to get over trauma. That can't possibly be healthy.

Plus, she'd forgotten to mention one other reason she didn't have a boyfriend. Lina had not gotten where she was today—independent, in an all-consuming career shooting for the top, not required *ever* to accommodate

a man, to bend to a man, to weaken herself for a man—
by not knowing how to cock block any dominant, sexy,
arrogant guy who thought she was a cute little thing.

Chapter 4

"She likes shy, geeky guys," Chase said.

Jake folded his arms and gave his team buddy an exasperated look. "You couldn't mention that two days ago?"

"Excuse me, but I have been recovering from a terrorist attack." Chase contrived a martyred look.

Yeah, seeing Chase in a hospital bed punched Jake in the gut. But he rolled his eyes anyway. If he got too soft with Chase it would hurt that cocky morale of his. None of them were all that good at acting soft with other guys.

Could he act soft with a woman? Just curve his hand over those glossy curls and say, *It's okay, honey. I've got you.*

Stroke away that frayed around the edges look that meant she hadn't slept in a week. *Shh. I know what it's like to have bullets interrupt your dreams. You don't have to prove you're brave to me, sweetheart, I already know it. Shh. Does this help?*

He frowned. He'd sure crashed and burned on his first attempts to get in closer to her. Her friend Vi might wait until a man was close enough to throw knives at, as Chase had established, but Lina shot men down with *precision.* When they were still a *long* way out.

"Why the hell does she like shy, geeky guys anyway?" Jake demanded indignantly. What did *they* have to offer? Hell, he didn't even know any shy, geeky guys. "I'm reserved." Did that count?

"Mark's shy and geeky," Elias said, amused.

"Damn it," Mark said. Tall and lean, their team leader had a nerdy warrior-philosopher thing going that made some people overlook his intense physical self-confidence. "You guys are never going to let me live that book club down, are you?"

"It gave us a reputation," Ian complained. "*Reading.* You do too much of that and people expect you to start thinking next."

Said the guy who had graduated summa cum laude with an economics degree from Harvard and spent two years on Wall Street before he got bored and ran off to join the Navy instead.

"Now everyone thinks we're nerds," Chase said sadly. "They make me sit at a table by myself at the mess hall. Sometimes they throw spit wads."

Yeah, right. Nobody in the whole world, except possibly Ian, was as overtly cocky as Chase. Big, muscled, gold-streaked brown hair, blue eyes, completely incapable of being serious except in very specific situations that usually involved someone dying. And even then he might say something to make everyone laugh. They *had* gotten a lot of shit about their "book club," but not any more than they'd gotten for that damn charity calendar.

"Americans can read?" Elias said, astonished.

"I have to sound out the words," Chase said solemnly. Chase could read in four languages. But his pronunciation remained Texan to the core. "Which doesn't help me with French because you guys don't know how to spell. Why the hell do you have so many letters in words if you're not going to pronounce them?"

"Thought," Elias said. "Though. Through. Laugh. Ought."

"Cute accent." Chase clutched his heart, going big-eyed. "Say *through* again?"

Elias narrowed green eyes at him. Elias's American was pretty good, but the THR sound tripped him up every time.

"You should take that accent into an American bar," Jake said. "Give Ian a run for his money."

41

Ian had pretty much the whole Atlantic contributing to his genome, and as far as Jake could tell, all those different gene sources had gotten into some kind of one-upmanship contest at his conception. Whatever it was, he'd turned out too sexy for his own damn good, and he only had to stroll into a bar and quirk that grin of his to have women start stripping off their panties.

It was *quite* trying to hit bars with him, to be honest. Jake did just fine, but Ian did better, and that provoked his competitive instinct. All of them had extremely healthy competitive instincts.

"I've reformed," Ian said. "Now I'm shy and geeky."

Jake unfolded his arms in a clear signal: *don't make me punch you.*

Ian grinned. "What? She's cute."

She was more than cute. She was fucking gorgeous. Her heart face, her black curls, her raging courage, her shoulder under her friend's that day as Vi slumped and Lina helped hold her up. She was literally the most beautiful woman Jake had ever seen.

If he told his team that, though, they would roast the hell out of him.

"This city is full of cute women," Jake said. "Go find another one in some bar."

Jake himself was sick of bars. Of how easy it was to pick up hot women and how hard it was to keep them. He was sick to damn death of being a facile sex object, and yet having no one to Skype home to, no one who was glad every day he was still alive, no one he could *count* on when things went south to help pull them back to true north. He didn't want mindless sex, he wanted...something else.

A vision of black curls and a slim, pretty face, of gallantry under fire, of persistence and determination in bad times, of steady friendship and support and courage. A woman who wrestled with dragons.

So close he could touch her, and yet when he'd even hinted at making a move, she'd shot him down so far off he was barely a dot on her flirtational horizon. Picked him off at a thousand yards the first crawling movement he'd made out of his emotional bunker toward her.

"But what if I want *this* one?" Ian said, with a gleam in his brown eyes, watching Jake.

"These hospital windows are pretty small," Jake said. "Be a shame to have to stuff you through one."

Ian stood up, delighted.

"Hey!" Chase protested. "No getting banned from the hospital. This place is killing me."

"Technically, it's *keeping you alive*," Mark pointed out. "But yeah. Let's not get kicked out."

"I have to malinger just the right amount," Chase explained. "I mean, I'm fine, obviously"—this even though he had an IV in his arm and looked like a corpse trying to grin cockily—"but my girlfriend is just down the hall. I need an excuse to stick around."

Chase contrived to look smug about having such a hot girlfriend, but the glitter in his eyes revealed the darkness hiding under that smugness. Vi had been hurt worse than he had, and he was failing quite badly to handle that with the same aplomb with which he handled everything else.

"So you guys have to help me survive it," Chase said firmly.

Yeah. They did. That was what it meant to be a team.

So Ian settled down and Jake lounged in the doorway, keeping an eye on the guards and the elevator and wondering when a certain pastry chef would stop by with special treats. She always brought extras for Chase's buddies.

He'd always liked being the man who kept watch. He trusted himself more than anyone else with that job. You saw trouble a long way off that way.

Sometimes you even saw good things. When he was a kid, he used to lie out on his roof and watch for Santa

43

Claus, determined to be the first to spot a glowing red light.

Of course, it had never worked out for him as a kid. Presents appeared under the tree, the few, very precious presents his mom could afford, but somehow Santa himself never showed.

Just like somehow that magic woman who would love a man through thick and thin never showed. *Besides you, Mom, sorry.*

He sighed. Braced his stomach muscles against defeatism. And kept an eye on the elevator.

***

Lina softened at the sight of Vi in the hospital bed, a feeling she could not get used to. Vi had a spirit that was pure flame, and normally if you got too soft around her, she'd crisp you to an oozing marshmallow. Not in a deliberate attempt to overwhelm you. She was just that powerful a force of nature.

But now Vi lay bandaged and weary and pale, her blond hair lank, shadows under her eyes, an IV in one arm. Lina hesitated under a wash of relief and guilt and rage, and her friend's eyes flickered open. Vi angled the bed higher immediately, trying to get her energy to flare up. Violette Lenoir was not used to dealing with the world when she was down. She never let herself be put down in the first place.

"Lina." Vi looked relieved and happy. Poor Vi. Bored out of her mind but too weary and wounded to do anything. Like being seasick and stuck on the cruise from hell.

"I brought you something." Lina set down the case that carried the desserts and pulled a dart board out of a big plastic shopping bag.

Vi brightened. "Now that's more like it. Although you know I really need my knives."

"It would upset the nurses. This one's magnetic, so you don't have any actual sharp objects flying around."

44

"Hospitals." Vi groaned. "They take all the fun out of life."

Lina grinned. Yeah. That flame in Vi had definitely not been put out, not even by this.

She opened the case. "And I've got something better than hospital food. Can you eat yet?"

"In small amounts." Vi looked hopeful.

Lina pulled out a verrine—a small narrow glass—of mango and passion fruit and a light custard cream, not too rich, nothing difficult to digest or challenging for the liver. And very pretty, if she did say so herself.

"Lovely," Vi said, green eyes happy. "Thank you, Lina."

"Hey, don't mention it. It was my bastard cousin." If Lina hadn't been there as a focal point for Abed's hatred of successful women, he never would have chosen Audessus as his target. Maybe he would have still become a terrorist, since he'd chosen to wallow in hatred, but he wouldn't have focused that terrorism on Lina's people.

"Fucking pathetic little asshole," Vi said.

The two women nodded at each other. That summed it up, and just because Abed had strapped on an AK-47 and a bomb to try to make himself into a bigger man only proved how tiny he had always been. Vi had called him a cockroach when they were teenagers. Too bad cockroaches in human form couldn't be crushed under a boot before they actually committed a crime, even when you knew they were trailing vileness everywhere they went.

And one of the wonderful things about friends was that Vi still saw her as a human being who had had really crappy luck in a certain relative rather than as the Muslim cousin of a terrorist.

"Chase not here?" Lina took down one of the generic hospital prints on the wall and hung up the dart board in its place. Chase had a tendency to sneak into Vi's room whenever he could, to the great distress of the hospital staff, since he wasn't supposed to be out of bed himself. The nurses had been pretty understanding about it overall, though. Anyone could see how much good it did the two of them to be able to touch each other.

"The nurses had to do a few things to me." For a second, Vi looked exhausted. Then she blinked hard and lifted her chin. "He's got company now, I think."

Yeah, no kidding. They could hear the macho shit talk all the way down the hall. Jake Adams had been lounging in the doorway, watching Lina as she came out of the elevator, probably prepared to take out any threat at a distance.

But when his face had relaxed at the sight of her and he'd straightened, Lina had...flushed and hurried into Vi's room. *If you want to indulge in hot meaningless sex in order to get through the nights, do you seriously think a U.S. black ops friend of Vi's new boyfriend is the least complicated person to do that with? Go hit a bar or something.*

Although bars held people. Who could get sprayed by the same bullets, torn into pieces by the same bomb that was meant to punish her. For fighting. For living.

She focused hard on those confident male warrior voices down the hall.

Chase nearly always had company in the afternoon. Those macho buddies of his were *loyal*, that was for sure. Vi had constant visitors, too, from the kitchen staff, her friends, her big family. But her wounds had been more serious than Chase's and she was incapable of admitting she was tired and needed to rest, so Lina and Adrien, Vi's sous-chef, had taken it upon themselves to organize the staff to make sure they paced the visits enough to liven up her days but not so much that she overdid it. Everyone wanted to see her. Vi's team had thought the world of her *before* she fought terrorists on their behalf and won.

"How's the ice sculpting going?" Vi said.

Lina took a dart and threw it at the dart board so hard it bounced off. Oops. "*Why* did I enter this damn contest again?"

"You like to freeze your ass off?" Vi suggested. "Don't you dare back out now. You're practically representing all of Paris at this point. *Nothing makes us quit.*"

Oh, great, layer on *more* pressure. "This morning, just when I was starting to sharpen the teeth, the whole damn dragon nose-dived off the stand. Clearly I gave that thing too much mass in the brain area."

Vi laughed.

Lina smiled, pleased with herself at having helped produce that laugh. Maybe she could put up with a few more ice dragons acting like brats to have stories that made Vi laugh. "And when I stop trying to make it fly and make it curling up around treasure instead, it looks more like a damn cat with cream."

Vi chuckled, looking more and more relaxed.

"Made it," said a cheerful voice from the doorway, and Célie bounced into the room. Célie's burgundy-red hair (her natural brown being not nearly expressive enough for her) was currently at a very unfortunate stage in her attempts to let it grow out to shoulder length, and being crushed by a motorcycle helmet hadn't really helped it. But she brought all her warmth and energy into the room with her, and Lina could feel herself relaxing to it. Unlike Lina and Vi, Célie hadn't been at Au-dessus for the attacks because she worked for Dominique Richard. She had rushed to them as soon as the news started to flash across all the media outlets, devastated and furious, but she still retained a normalcy that Vi and Lina might never have again.

Vi smiled at Célie, too. "Busy day?"

"If you ask me, in times of crisis, people eat more chocolate. Can't really blame them." Célie's boss had been letting her go early every day to come see Vi, but given that Célie was the chef chocolatier for Richard's, sometimes no matter how willing Dom was to cover for

47

her, she couldn't pull herself free sooner. "Speaking of which…" Célie pulled a flat metal box out of her backpack and set it on Vi's table beside Lina's verrine.

"You're the best," Vi said.

"Also for you." Célie handed a box to Lina.

Lina smiled at her, blinking once against the sting in her eyes that had been plaguing her at every kind gesture ever since the attack. *I'm so glad I'm still alive and have such good people in my life.*

"And of course for you know who…" Célie pulled out Richard's biggest box, the one that held one hundred forty-four chocolates. "And for all his 'buddies'."

"That should last them…oh, an hour," Lina said. She had never in her life seen men quite so hungry. Even if a certain Jake Adams did tend to look at her desserts as if he expected them to bite him and not the other way around.

"Hey, thanks for taking care of Chase, too," Vi said. "I know you weren't sure about him when you met him."

"Neither were you," Célie pointed out. "That's why we weren't."

"He still seems like a lot of trouble to *me*," Lina said. "I like shy, geeky guys." *Except for hot, short-term, I'm-still-alive sex. In that case, a shy, geeky guy might get his shy feelings hurt so maybe I'd be better off with someone supremely confident—*She forced her thoughts back into their box.

"You keep saying that, but I don't see you trailing a shy, geeky guy around with you," Célie pointed out.

Lina narrowed her eyes at her. "They're hard to find with you and Vi scaring them off all the time."

"Maybe you should try to find a guy who can't be scared off by your friends," Vi said pointedly.

"Yeah." Célie flexed her biceps. "Because I'm not planning on getting less scary."

Lina laughed. Vi actually *looked* scary—tall, blonde, gorgeous, striding through life in her black boots and leather, wielding knives. But Lina and Célie looked like *cute little things*. So far, in Lina's case at least, no man had proven able to handle the shock of how stubborn, confident, and determined to get her own way she actually was.

Célie looked pleased with herself at the laughter. It had been tough going, pulling a laugh out, those first few days. "Speaking of guys," she said. "Remember those guys who were trying to pick us up in Italy last month?"

"Oh, those idiots." Vi rolled her eyes.

"Well, anyway, I put the photos up so you all can download them." Célie picked up Vi's tablet and clicked on the shared cloud space they used for photos from trips they took together.

"They weren't *that* cute," Vi said.

"Not the guys! They make Joss get very annoyed." The three of them had been taking trips together for years, and even though Célie now had a serious boyfriend, she had declined to bring Joss along to Italy and disrupt a female tradition. Joss had been okay with it—which he'd damn well better be, given that he'd disappeared on Célie into the Foreign Legion for five years—but that didn't mean he loved knowing how many guys had hit on the three women traveling together. "All the photos of Italy."

Célie called up the first one. Lina stared at a photo of three women laughing in an infinity pool overlooking the Tuscan countryside. Wow. Who *was* that oblivious, happy, confident, black-haired woman?

She peered at her through that gray fog, but she couldn't reach her other self. Célie swiped to the next photo, the three of them each with a bright orange spritz, the favorite Italian apéritif, toasting toward the camera as they sat on a restaurant terrace overlooking a vineyard. Laughing. Not a care in the world.

Lina slid a glance sideways at Vi. Did *she* recognize herself?

Vi's glance slid sideways to meet hers.

Yeah. Célie was showing them photos of strangers. Strangers they knew they were supposed to recognize, but somehow that recognition just wouldn't come.

Vi refocused quickly on the photos, grinning for Célie's sake and maybe also for their own, knowing just as well as Lina did that they had to pretend their way back to normal again. Célie looked from one of them to the other and then focused very fiercely on the tablet screen. She shoved her hand once hard across her eyes instead of breaking down, which Lina appreciated. None of them had better start breaking down.

They were tough. Tough was who they *were*. They had to handle this.

Célie's ex-Legionnaire boyfriend Joss came by after a while, to visit with Vi and to give Célie emotional support when she left the hospital room. His big hand closed snug around Célie's as they left, and Lina's gaze lingered wistfully on that hand hold.

Probably not surprising that the thought of having a strong man's hand around hers was enticing right now. And...hey.

Was she actually the only one of the three friends left who *didn't* have a guy? That was going to feel funny when they went out together.

Her lips relaxed. Well, look at that. She'd just imagined a moment in the future. It must be pretty resilient, the future. It kept sneaking back images of itself even when you thought it was shot to hell. She scrolled through a few of the photos Célie had left on Vi's tablet, touching her finger to her own black curls in the image. Then touching her hand to her hair in real life. Same hair. Even if a different person.

Vi was tired and clearly trying not to show it. Lina left her with a stack of the magnetic darts and some fresh movies and went to make sure Chase and his buddies were fed.

Because that was still who she was. The woman who fed people, fed their stomachs, their hearts, their eyes, through the beautiful things she made.

We won, she thought to herself. *Never forget that. We fought evil and* won.

So she refused to start losing now.

Chapter 5

Lina had been surrounded by too much testosterone all her career, but Chase's friends really took the prize. So much testosterone packed into that hospital room that it spilled out into the corridor in laughter and male voices and a dark-streaked golden glow of *I am a badass; however bad you think you are, I've taken out worse than you.*

She liked it. Every rough joke said, *This is how you deal with a life full of violence and death. You look it in the eye and you laugh.*

Her police guards relaxed when they were in the hospital corridor and Chase's friends were around. They chatted with Vi's guards and half of them took a break for coffee. Officially, this was because having both Vi's guards and Lina's stand watch when Lina was visiting her friend was redundant, but Lina figured even the guards were susceptible to that sense of masculine certainty that radiated from Chase's team: *We've got this.*

The guys she spent most of her life around, the Au-dessus kitchen brigades, were extremely physically confident. They could juggle hot pans with their bare hands, slice and dice a quarter of a steer into its separate parts in a matter of minutes, fillet a fish, create miracles, and do it all at battle-speed as orders rushed in and the pressure mounted.

But these guys worked at battle-speed in actual battles, when on every reflex, every split-second decision, hung someone's life. They had never met anything they believed they could not do, because if they could even admit failure was possible, they wouldn't be here.

Chase and his friends had *confidence.* It just strode its way through everyone else's confidence like a lion through a flock of gazelles.

It must take a lot of calories to nourish that kind of confidence, too, because whenever she approached Chase's room with a case of special treats, they gazed at her as if they were famished.

She was used to seeing hunger in a man's eyes—she was a top pastry chef—but there was something about Jake's as he propped himself in the doorway watching her approach that made her want to walk right up to him, put her hands on his shoulders, and go up on tiptoe. Probably a good thing she was carrying a case of desserts and couldn't.

He straightened and stepped out of the doorway. "Ma'am." His big hands closed around hers as he took the case from her as if she, who spent her life carrying giant mixing bowls, might need help.

Cute little thing, am I?

She narrowed her eyes up at him. *I am not fragile.* Even if the fragility of her world did splash across her consciousness in vivid red any time she closed her eyes.

How did he do it? He carried himself so strongly, but he had to know his world was just as fragile as hers was. His friend Chase was lying on that hospital bed, proof in the flesh of how bullets didn't really care if you were big and strong and arrogant or little and sweet and arrogant.

Jake made her shoulders feel straighter just looking at how straight his were. If *he* could be strong and handle this life with grace and humor, then so could she.

She was Lina Farah, damn it.

Jake's mouth curved subtly, a wash of warmth over her, as he studied her lifted chin. Then that hazel gaze drifted to just below her eyes. She touched the sense of heaviness there. Could he tell she wasn't sleeping?

He held her eyes a moment. Then he braced the case in one hand to close the other around hers in a warm, firm, gentle clasp of greeting: *You're strong. You're doing just fine.*

She took a little breath in relief at the message, because she really hadn't felt she was doing just fine.

But he would know, wouldn't he? He wasn't new to this. Her hand tightened a second around his.

"Lina." Sexy Elias, the only Frenchman in the room, moved in to kiss her on both cheeks, Jake holding on a little too long as the other man claimed her attention. Green-eyed and black-haired, Elias clearly had Maghrébin ancestry—Algerian, maybe?—which she probably wouldn't have even noticed two weeks ago but which these days she found vaguely reassuring. Like they were all in this together and she wasn't the Other in the room. "Come to spoil us?"

"Come to spoil *me*," Chase called from the bed, and Lina's face relaxed into a grin. How anyone could not grin around Chase was a mystery to her. "Quit stealing my treats! *You* aren't wounded."

He strove to look pitiful, having no idea how sick and pale he already looked without posing. Chase's belief in himself was too strong to admit his own mortality. Bullets hadn't bounced off him, but he was going to go ahead and pretend to the whole world, himself included, that they had.

"I brought enough for all of you," Lina said. Feeding people. Now *that* felt as if her life was still normal.

Ian stepped in beside Elias and proved he was trying to adapt to local culture by bending down for *bises*, too. Accidentally brushing too close to her lips, he pulled back, looking bashful and awkward.

Hmm. Her previous impressions of Ian had been of extravagant flirtatious confidence, not bashfulness. Of course, Americans were always awkward with cheek-kissing. And then they went around wrapping their arms around people they barely knew to say hello. Their sense of personal space worked in mysterious ways.

Jake was giving Ian a very steely look. She moved to greet Mark and bent down to kiss Chase's cheeks. Chase had taken to cheek-kissing *fast*. "How are you doing today?"

"Bored," he said. "How's Vi?"

54

"Bitchy," Lina said, amused. "She's about to climb the walls, only she's not strong enough to do it yet, so you *know* how that's making her."

Chase beamed. "That's my girl."

Lina sighed. Yeah, Vi probably was his girl. She sure had fallen head over heels for a cocky idiot fast. An idiot who had literally upended her life. *And you wonder why I prefer shy, geeky guys, Vi.*

"Seriously, if he talks about *his* girl one more time in that gloating tone, can I throw him out the window?" Ian said plaintively.

Chase looked delighted. "Jealous?"

From all around the room came several huffs of breath.

"Don't be," Lina said, biting back a laugh. "She's trouble."

None of the men looked scared of trouble.

"It's not jealousy of Vi per se," said Ian. "I mean, myself I prefer brunettes." A sidelong, merry glance at her.

Oh, he did, did he? Lina raised an eyebrow at him.

"But I'd love to be able to call someone *my girl*." He deepened his voice longingly over the words *my girl* in a way that would warm any girl's bones and make her long, too.

He certainly had gotten over that moment of awkward shyness quickly, hadn't he?

Jake was gazing at him as if Ian's life span was shortening dramatically with every word he spoke.

"I mean..." Ian suddenly retreated into bashfulness again, giving Lina an awkward look. "I mean...you know what I mean." He looked down like a shy virgin who would never in his life dare flirt with a woman of her bedazzling beauty.

Lina bit the inside of her lip, and on the other side of her, Jake shifted.

"Hey!" Chase said very loudly. "What did I say? Don't get thrown out. Then I'd have to watch French television again to keep me entertained." He shuddered.

Jake and Ian held each other's eyes a moment longer, Ian's dancing and Jake's inscrutable. A little dangerous.

She focused on Chase, who was easy. Cocky, fun, and taken. "I brought you some movies." So Chase and Vi didn't have to spend a fortune on downloads while they were in the hospital, she and the kitchen team had gone through their old DVDs for favorites.

"*Captain America*?" Chase said hopefully. "The one where he gets to flirt with a beautiful woman in leather?"

Lina pulled out a dozen DVDs from her backpack and spread them out on Chase's table. French films, with artsy covers. Chase's face scrunched. Then he tried valiantly to hide it. "Ah...just what I was wanting to see."

Lina watched him pretend to be enthusiastic for a moment, keeping her teeth firmly on the inside of her lip. Then she opened the DVD cases.

Several James Bond films. *Mr. and Mrs. Smith.* All the good *Star Wars.*

Chase broke into a big grin. "Lina. I am taken, but trust me, if I wasn't, I would love you."

"I'm not taken," Ian said.

Jake released a long, careful breath. Ian grinned.

"If you guys behave, I've brought you something special," Lina said, reaching for the case Jake still held.

He set it down on Chase's table for her, and she popped the clasps.

Having worked part of her teenage years *en boutique*, where much of what they made was catered to location, she had kind of enjoyed revisiting the concept of transportable desserts for these guys. *When things go wrong, go back to the beginning*, a certain Spanish swordsman had once said. Well, boutique work was her beginning. Maybe, if she worked her way right back up through an apprenticeship again, she could turn back into herself.

If only life was like a shattered dessert. You cleared the ruins off your counter and started over, pulling a fresh one together in seconds to make perfection again.

***

The woman was crazy.

The world demonstrated for her—graphically—that it was brutal, full of hatred, and that death stalked life jealously, always ready to snuff it out.

And Lina went to the gym to try to beat the crap out of it in response and then went and made more desserts so delicate and brave that even she couldn't always touch them without breaking them. Jake had seen her shatter the impossibly fragile sugar domes repeatedly the day before, but she'd just kept working on them until she got them right.

A layering of gold and deeper gold in a short glass, cream and...mango? And sugar caramelized golden-brown on top of it.

The guys flocked around her, holding up the glasses she gave them, completely subjugated by this beautiful delicacy in their rough and tumble world. She ought to be careful with that, but she didn't know her own power. How much it meant to them that anyone would do something so special for them. So damn fancy and delicious.

As if they weren't just body armor and nerves of steel and ruthless will and ability, but they had palates. Taste buds and eyes that appreciated beautiful things and the patience to take time and savor it.

It was strange to take that time and savor, he had to admit. He'd been so used to shoving food in his mouth in mess halls and out in the field, indifferent to its crappy taste, just nourishing the machine so that he could keep on dealing in death to save the lives of people like her.

The fact that the enemy was getting more and more skilled at infiltrating behind the lines and still attacking people like her was fucking shitty.

His fingers brushed hers as he took the little glass from her, and they felt too big and rude, crowding out her smaller fingers' space. It wasn't like his fingers were clumsy. He could disassemble and re-assemble any number of weapons blindfolded and under pressure. He could rest his finger on a trigger and gently squeeze just at the right second in the bob of a boat to kill someone at a thousand yards.

So he had a delicate touch, too. It just felt really, really different from her delicacy.

He didn't even have words for the sensations in his mouth, when he took his first spoonful of her dessert. The fresh and the sweet and the cool, the layering of— yes, mango—and something creamier and greener in flavor that he didn't know the name for. It made him think of an oasis. Or of sitting in the shade of a palm tree on a deserted island, with nothing but him and peaceful, warm water as far as he could look.

It made him want to kiss her, to see if she would taste like that, too.

Jake. She's just been through a major trauma and she gave you a hard brushback earlier today. Take it easy.

He knew how to do easy. He knew how to do slow. Not so much with a woman, because for the past ten years, he'd mostly picked up women in bars in under half an hour, but he was a sniper. Slow and easy getting in place without being spotted. Slow and easy sometimes for days under a bush that didn't look big enough to hide a bunny, waiting, keeping his mind calm. Slow and easy on the trigger...

Jesus. No wonder guys had such a hard time adapting back to civilian life. Sure, the skills were *in theory* transferrable, but hell. He looked down at her black head. That wasn't the kind of slow and easy he wanted to do with her at all.

58

And definitely not the kind of slow and easy she might need. It was all he could do to keep his hands curved around the glass and not lift one to cup those glossy curls. *Trouble sleeping, honey? Come here.*

"You don't like it?" Lina said, a little stiffly.

He realized he'd taken only one spoonful of her fancy dessert and not said a word. "Mmm." He quickly took another. Jesus, this stuff tasted dangerous. She could mess a man all up feeding him things like this as if his insides were tender and fancy and fragile. He'd found her a hell of a lot less terrifying when she was wielding chainsaws.

Her expression cooled. "Please don't force yourself." She held out her hand to take his glass back.

He tightened his hand on it. "No, I—really like it." *Like* didn't seem the right word, since the dessert scared the hell out of him, but he'd better not tell her that.

"Obviously." Brown eyes flashed with temper.

"No, it's delicious!" He shoved another spoonful into his mouth. "Yum!"

Lina's eyes shot sparks. She pivoted on one low, chunky boot heel and looked at the other men. God, those jeans loved her ass.

Ian beamed at her. "Ma'am, this must be about the most delicious thing your humble servant has ever tasted."

Oh, for God's sake. Since when had Ian had a Southern drawl? Jake shot him a bird behind Lina's back.

Ian just grinned and focused on Lina, whose chilly look had disappeared for *him.*

"*Délicieux*," Elias said, which was just fucking unfair. *Every*thing sounded more flattering in French. You could cuss someone out in that language, and it sounded romantic. "*Exceptionnel. Vraiment parfait.*"

Of course, Jake spoke French, too, but it didn't sound anything like Elias's French when it came out of his mouth.

Lina smiled at Elias, too.

Maybe Jake would just beat up all the other guys in this room. Take them all together. That would be fun.

"It's wonderful, ma'am," Mark said, and he didn't use his grilled-too-black voice with her. No, he was quiet and a little awkward, *when he knew already she liked shy, geeky guys.*

Seriously, Jake was going to kick all their asses. At once.

He ate his dessert, brooding over how delicious it was and how awkward he felt swallowing and the fact that he was the only man in the room whose compliments Lina didn't lap up as if they were her due.

She packed up their empty glasses and headed out again, glancing up at him once more as she passed him in the doorway. Brown eyes met his for one moment, from too close.

Heat climbed up the back of his neck, but she probably couldn't tell. He used to have the kind of freckles that showed blushes, but after so long in too much sun, the variations in his skin tone now looked more like a very pixelated tan.

Even more importantly, the rest of the team couldn't tell, because they would ride him mercilessly if they could.

"It was really good," he tried again. "Thank you."

She pressed her lips together, pissed off, waved to the rest of the guys—Ian blew her a damn kiss—and turned on her heel, heading back down the corridor.

Elias started to laugh. Gripping the windowsill behind him, his teeth flashing white, green eyes gleaming, a low laugh but one he couldn't stop. "Sorry." He released the windowsill to press a tear from the corner of his eye. "But you guys are hilarious around women."

60

Chapter 6

She kept getting the support too thin, that was the problem. She wanted the dragon to fly free on its own, but every time she made the base too narrow so that it seemed to be flying, the whole thing came crashing down. Lina dumped chunks of shattered ice dragon in the sink and came back out onto the main floor where she could peel off all those extra layers and warm up again.

Jake glanced at her immediately. "Can I see?"

"No," Lina said between her teeth. "Damn dragon."

"Ah." Jake, who had been banished from observing her ice work half an hour ago, went back to prowling.

Should Lina just ignore him? Why did he even keep hanging out in her kitchens whenever she was there? Did he have to keep watch that compulsively?

He was by far the most enigmatic of Chase's brothers in arms. Ian seemed pretty straightforward—he threw down his flirtation like a gauntlet and dared her to pick it up. Mark struck Lina as a philosopher-warrior, intellectually self-conscious about how he fit in the civilian world. But Jake watched calmly in the doorway when she brought them treats, unreadable.

The boxing thing had been almost brotherly. But at other moments, she thought he had that hint of flirtation there, so subtle that she wasn't quite sure what he meant by it. She liked it better than Ian's openness, though—liked the subtly intriguing, liked wondering rather than knowing. Liked being able to pretend it wasn't there if she wanted, or respond if she chose.

Liked the way she could hold him in the center of her mind and let him block out all the violence and fear and blood. He looked at that fear and blood and violence, and it cringed down like a beta wolf before a pissed-off alpha and crawled backward.

Using sex as a crutch is not a good road to go down. Fight off the blood and violence yourself.

With her work. She focused on making a *crèmeux chocolat noir*, a dark chocolate cream she planned to layer into a dessert for Vi and the police officers and Chase and his team buddies.

Jake came to the opposite side of her counter and leaned on it, eyeing the chocolate cream sideways as if making sure it wouldn't bite him.

Why he seemed to think her desserts were the apex predators in this situation was beyond her. "It's not ready." She kept whisking, a curl falling over her forehead. "Be patient."

He said nothing. When she glanced up, he was studying her as if she'd said something meaningful.

"What?" She puffed at the curl to get it out of her eye.

"Patience." He reached out and tucked the curl back into her ponytail, the calluses at the tips of his fingers brushing her skin. "One of my skills."

It was one of her skills, too. It took an incredible amount of patience to make thousands of some impossible dessert turn out exactly right—and to make sure everyone, from a new intern to her temperamental but excellent sous-chef, was as patient and persistent and perfectionist as she wanted them to be. And to be honest it took a great deal of patience to deal with Vi and not kill her. Also a steel will like a quality chef's blade— you wanted a *little* bend, but had to hold firm when it counted.

"Be interesting to see if it's a skill that has a civilian application," Jake said. He pressed a finger into a chocolate shaving on the counter and sucked it off the tip.

She sat very hard on the lid of that behave yourself box.

62

TRUST ME

"So." A level gaze. "I hear you like shy, geeky guys."

"Chase cannot keep his mouth shut for a second, can he?" she said, aggravated.

"Depends on the subject."

Yeah. He'd been freaking close-mouthed about her terrorist cousin, for example, and if he'd *warned* her, maybe she could have confronted Abed one last time and somehow changed events. It made her want to hit Chase every time she thought of him laughing in Vi's apartment even as he pursued a threat of terrorism they knew nothing about and which put their lives on the line.

Unfortunately, she couldn't hit him, because he was lying in a hospital bed, like Vi, having helped save their lives. Lina had helped save their lives, too, but she hadn't gotten hurt, and given that the assailant was her cousin, the fact that her friend had paid the price instead of her...yeah.

It cramped in her stomach all night, every night, twisting her and turning her, not letting her sleep.

"So why shy geeks, do you think?" Jake said. "Easier to control?"

"They don't try to control *me*." Or lie about things that were vital to her life and choices, like Chase had done with Vi. At least, the shy geek in her imagination didn't. She hadn't actually found the one she wanted in real life.

"Why does that matter? You don't know how to fight for your own space? Stand up for yourself when someone tries to take you over?"

Okay, you know what...? She put her hands on her hips. "Do you have any idea what it takes to make it to executive pastry chef in a two Michelin star establishment by the age of twenty-six?"

He shook his head. "Why don't you tell me?"

"I can fight for my own space just fine, thank you."

"Then that shy, geeky thing is just a vague preference. Not like a hard rule."

63

"Célie and Vi and I do have one hard rule. It's a good one: Just because a woman *can* handle bullshit doesn't mean she *should*."

Jake looked bemused. "Hell, and Vi still ended up with Chase? So what you're saying is that your rules are really more like cat posters. Cute quotes, but not anything you actually live by."

"You can't blame me for the fact that Vi is an idiot." It was a tribute to their friendship that Lina felt comfortable saying that even while Vi was in a hospital bed.

"No, I'm pretty sure I can blame Chase for that one," Jake allowed. "He probably broke her brain."

That did seem to be what had happened to Vi. Lina thumped her rolling pin against almonds in lieu of her best friend's head. Which needed some sense knocked into it, where a certain man was concerned.

"Persistent guy, Chase," Jake said in Vi's defense, amused.

Yeah, persistent was one word for it. "Not like you," she said, watching him.

Jake's expression could best be described as complexly unreadable.

Right.

She'd been reading about U.S. special ops, because a little knowledge might come in handy given that she had drawn U.S. special ops' attention. She might not really understand in her bones and flesh the kind of things he persisted through, but she'd read some descriptions.

"Or you," he said.

She scrunched her eyebrows at him.

He gestured. "Twenty-six. Top pastry chef. Back in here only a few days after surviving a major attack. And half a dozen of those sugar shells you were working with yesterday broke while I was watching you and you never even thought about stopping, just made more as if it was automatic. Seems as if there might be a few mild signs of persistence there."

"What else am I supposed to do?" she said blankly. "Quit?"

His smile warmed his whole face. Warmed his eyes, the hazel more golden. "Hard to imagine, isn't it?"

It wasn't so much the quitting itself that was hard to imagine. It was what you did after. How you let go of the need to somehow make it right. How did you teach yourself to just sit on the couch watching television instead of *trying*?

Watching her expression, Jake's warmed more and more. Letting her in. "Your brain just clogged, didn't it? Trying to imagine quitting?"

She gave herself a shake. "Trust me. By midnight, I'm usually *dreaming* of quitting." And she loved her television by that hour, too.

"Yeah, but only for a night to get some sleep or maybe a week's vacation," he said. "Not the same thing at all. We all hit tough spots."

A subtle tone in his words caught her. Her eyes lifted to his steady gaze.

"All of us," he said quietly, and touched the back of her hand.

Her eyes wanted to sting. She took a deep breath and lifted her hand in a tiny rejecting vibration of *no, no, we can't talk about this, stop.*

He drew back and nodded. Gave her that slight smile and started prowling again.

That had been a close one. She focused on her desserts again, panic easing as she sank into the scents and tastes and textures. Making things beautiful. No matter what happened in the world, she could always do that.

It was the one thing she still had from the person before, the person who seemed so bright and beautiful and innocent to her now—Lina Farah, only a week ago.

The thread that held her together, her past self and the self she was now. The proof that terrorists couldn't win.

She was a top pastry chef and THAT WAS THAT. Fuck them. *I'm the chef. I change things. You cannot change* me.

Jake had been shot at, hadn't he? And he'd done more than throw liquid nitrogen in defense. He'd killed people.

"When you look at pictures of you as a child, do you recognize yourself?" she asked suddenly.

"Does anybody?" he said, surprised.

Well, that answered that question. "I used to."

"Strong family?" he guessed. "Parents who took lots of photos and like to bring them out?"

Didn't all moms do that? "The photos play on their TV, whenever no one's watching anything else."

He nodded, smiling faintly. He didn't ask when she had stopped being able to recognize herself. So she was right. He knew.

"You get through it, then?" she said. "You figure out who you are again? You start being able to imagine, say, an hour from now, or even tomorrow?"

"Well, I got through it," he said, which wasn't very reassuring. He was some black ops super ninja. He was made for this kind of thing. He held her gaze from across the kitchen. "You'll get through it, too. What you're doing right now is probably the best thing you could possibly do." He gestured to the counter. "Something beautiful. What makes you you."

Good to know.

She took a deep breath and let it sigh out, and looked at the small fresh scars on her hand, the only physical sign she had from that night.

"What shows your courage," he said very quietly. "Your determination. Your sense of wonder, in a tough world."

Her eyes prickled. She gave him a desperate look.

"Sorry," he said, low, and prowled again, releasing her.

Thank you, she thought, in the safety of that quiet. *Thank you for the respect. The understanding.*

She watched that smooth, powerful movement of his. That showed his courage. His determination. And sometimes, in the careful way he touched his finger to a plate and sucked chocolate off it, his sense of wonder, in a tough world.

And thank you for being so damn sexy that I can focus on you, instead of everything else.

"Why are you hanging out here again?" she said. "I've got the police guards. Do you guys suspect me of something? Why don't you go home and relax?"

"A bit of a long flight, to go home," he said, amused. "Plus, the military is funny about us doing that when we're in the middle of a deployment."

"I thought you guys were civilians," Lina said very dryly.

Those hazel eyes laughed at her as if she delighted his sense of humor. "Right."

His secret humor was annoying but in such a weird way, like being tickled. Making her laugh despite herself, making her feel as if she could still play like a child.

"I'll tell you what," he said. "Why don't I just catch up with my book club and keep out of your way?"

He went to her office and pulled out the comfortable office chair from it, setting it in a far corner where he could keep an eye on her and both doors, and pulled a book out of the lower pocket of his cargo pants, slouching back.

Lina stared at him. "You have a book club?"

A *book club*? Wasn't that something that nerdy intellectuals did, or else bourgeois women with too much time on their hands and a very unfortunate predilection for boring, expensive clothing?

Those creases in Jake's cheeks as he opened the battered book. "You did say you liked shy, geeky guys."

"Reading a book does not qualify you for shy and geeky!"

"Damn. This is harder than I thought, then." He slouched lower in her chair, those creases of humor very visible.

"What are you reading?" she asked suspiciously.

He showed her the title. "*Le Mythe de Sisyphe.*"

"*Camus?*" That was...okay, that was pretty geeky actually.

Jake shrugged. "Mark thought we should focus on French writers while we were here. Chase says *he* wants to pick the next book, so we can read something fun for once."

Lina hesitated. "I'm not sure there are any fun French writers." Her experience with literature in school had been a turn off, that was for sure. Probably one of the many reasons she had ended up apprenticed in a manual career by fifteen.

"I think Chase was thinking more along the lines of *Harry Potter.*"

Lina laughed involuntarily. That did sound like a book Chase was capable of arguing for, all right.

Jake smiled that secret smile of his at her laugh and focused on his book.

A sense of peace and security brushed over her, like a silk scarf, and she concentrated on her work again, her clutch on that work feeling less desperate somehow. More like her.

His presence pulled on her even as she worked. Strong. Hot. Damn, there was something sexy about a man of action relaxed and focused on a book.

Although, Camus, *merde.* How relaxing did that get?

She came up to him, his presence drawing her so strongly that it felt not so much as if she chose to approach him but as if he lassoed her with that silk scarf and pulled her to him.

He paused in his book and looked up at her. All she could read in his expression was polite attention.

"Would you like a taste?" She offered him a small spoon of the *crèmeux chocolat noir.*

"Yes," Jake said simply and tilted his head back a little. He didn't reach for the spoon.

Lina slipped it into his mouth, a touch of heat running through her body. His eyes stayed on her face as he sucked the chocolate cream off the spoon she drew slowly from his mouth. The heat in her grew.

"Mmm." Now *that* sounded sincere. Deep, as if that spoon had been a kiss and he wanted to keep kissing. The heat flared more insistently in her breasts. Her toes curled against the warmth.

"If you want funny French writers, we should go to the theater," she said. "A Feydeau production, maybe. Or—well, it's not literature, but there are some great stand-up comics."

His expression grew, if possible, even more unreadable. "You want to go to the theater?"

Lina had been the focus of the attack on Au-dessus. Abed had chosen her restaurant because he hated her and Vi.

And what if she was a focus again, in a crowded theater, in…

"No." She turned away.

She didn't want to go anywhere there were people, really. She missed her colleagues intensely. But she wanted to be all by herself, where she was the only person who could get hurt. And yet she was utterly grateful to Jake and the police officers that she didn't have to be alone all by herself and unprotected.

Yeah, she was messed up. But nobody had to *know* that, right? "It's August," she threw over her shoulder briskly. "Theater's dead right now."

She didn't turn around to see if Jake nodded at that or just watched her. Instead she focused on her desserts. Setting the chocolate cream aside to chill. Pistachios and sugar in a pan, stirring them with a wooden spoon until the sugar caramelized, spreading those out to set. Melting chocolate and mixing it with crumbled shortbread and pistachios for the *croustillant*, packing this into the bottom of six centimeter rings to make the individual desserts.

Next a *crème chantilly pistache*, cream, mascarpone, pistachio paste, fleur de sel. Jake, his body calm and easy as if he could sit there with his legs stretched out forever, kept reading. He didn't sink into the book the way she would have, though. His eyes lifted regularly, assessing her and everything around him in one quick flick before he looked back at the text.

Without doing more than turning a page, Jake pulled her back over to him again, this time with a bowl of pistachio whipped cream in her hand. A longing to just curl up in his lap rose in her. He could keep reading if he wanted. She just wanted to be somewhere warm and strong.

Get a grip, Lina. You are strong. You fought them, didn't you?

Despite her and Vi and the kitchen team's best efforts, though, she was pretty sure they would all have died if Abed's gun hadn't jammed and Chase hadn't been there with a gun of his own. *What could have happened didn't happen. You all fought it and stopped it. Now stop imagining it. Imagine freckles on a penis instead. At least a penis is productive.*

She bit the inside of her lip to stop a smirk. *Inherently so.*

Jake looked up and raised an eyebrow at her expression.

"Good book?" she asked hurriedly.

That little quirk of a smile. Her fingers itched to press those little creases in his cheeks. What would his freckles feel like? She wouldn't be able to feel them, would she? They would just be smooth skin, all visual but no sensation. Elusive to the touch. "I'm tempted to skip to the end," Jake said.

"The end's the best part. That's where he talks about the actual myth in the title."

He raised an eyebrow at her.

"I had to study it in *collège* when I was thirteen."

"So I can skip reading it and get you to explain it to me?"

"It's about the absurd. You know—you keep pushing that rock up the hill, even though you know it's going to roll right back down again. You keep doing it, and it doesn't make you trapped in endless torture. It makes you lucid and courageous, knowing your battle is unending but fighting it anyway, happy."

Like fighting against evil whatever way you knew how. Maybe by going out and hunting terrorists night after night. Maybe by making fragile desserts as if that fragility was in itself what was so beautiful.

Jake looked up at her a long moment. "Mark picked a really good text for us, didn't he?"

She nodded and held up a spoon of chantilly.

His mouth curved again as he tilted his head back. She slipped the spoon between his lips, and his lashes lowered a moment. "Mmm." A secret, almost wistful sound.

She swallowed, in time with him. "You know, there's something really sexy about a man reading."

And saying *mmm* in that voice for something she put in his mouth.

His lashes lifted. "There's something really sexy about a woman making desserts in the aftermath of a horrible event, too. Gallant." Hazel eyes held hers. "Heroic."

She flushed. She'd found *acting* like a hero pretty easy—just fear and rage and adrenaline and good

71

reflexes. She hadn't had time to think. But being one…being one was hard. Because you had to keep being brave, over and over, every second, night and day.

"Plus, you're *very* pretty," he said softly, like an admission, watching her.

She tucked a curl back, her cheeks growing hotter.

She had been wrong about the blushing contest. He was winning hands down.

"Sorry," he said. "Not shy enough for you?"

She cleared her throat, went back to her work space, and set the bowl of chantilly down. She stood there, her hands braced on the marble, staring at nothing for a moment. Well, actually, staring at a lot of things. All the things in her memories, and none of them things she wanted to see.

She turned empty-handed and went back to him.

He looked up politely again from his book.

The heat of him ran through her, from her toes to the tips of her fingers.

If you might live or die in a heartbeat, on someone else's random insane whim, it didn't matter what you said, did it? You could say anything, do anything. Go for what you need.

It didn't have to be curling up in his lap begging him to hold her like a fragile kitten. It could be something braver, stronger, like boxing with him only different—reaching out and seizing life with both hands.

"How do you feel about being used for sex?" she said.

Chapter 7

Jake's eyes flared wide, and then his face went blank. Completely blank. Like a glass surface, absolutely no purchase, nothing to read to give her the slightest idea what he was thinking.

Under that unreadable assessment of her, the flush crawled back up her skin, hot in her breasts and against her palms and in her cheeks. She fought through it. She was alive, wasn't she? Screw embarrassment.

"It wouldn't be the first time," he said finally. A faint clipped quality to his words, as if he was cutting each one carefully out of stone before he pronounced it.

Yeah. That was what she'd figured. A guy like him must have had more casual sexual encounters than he could start to remember. No promises and no expectations. Just a hot use of each other that blocked all other thoughts out, and then each participant in that encounter went on his or her way. He was an elite warrior who didn't even share his real last name or possibly even his real first one. What other kind of relationships could he have with women?

"Would you get in trouble?" she said. "Fraternizing with the enemy?"

"You're not the enemy." His voice sounded rather flat. "You're one of our heroes."

One of *his* heroes? A hero's hero? Her nose crinkled over a sudden stinging. "No, I'm not."

"Yes." That level gaze brooked no argument. "You are."

She blinked rapidly. "Is that why you didn't waterboard me?"

"Oh, for fuck's sake." He sat up in a rough movement—but then calmed himself immediately and took her hand. The calluses teased her fingers. They

73

made her feel, just for a moment, as if the world hadn't changed and she was still safe. "We're not idiots. I did hang around while you were talking to the police just in case there were some idiots in on the questioning, when you were sharing all the information you had, but there weren't. Your RAID guys know what they're doing."

"I thought you were hanging around to play bad cop," she admitted, low. "At first."

He stared at her. "Jesus."

"Because everyone else was being so nice." And, well...he was American. Guantánamo. Abu Ghraib. And she was...well, *she* thought she was a top Parisian pastry chef, but he probably thought she was the Arab cousin of a terrorist. Both those people had the same name, but their identities were very different.

"Jesus Christ," he said. "No."

"Well, I know that *now*. Now I'm assuming you're here to play good cop."

"I'm here to help keep you safe. I practically had to throw Ian and Mark out the hospital window for the privilege."

She was silent a moment while she tried to digest that. Really? She was really one of his heroes? That felt...precarious. She didn't feel heroic. She felt fragile, as if her life and the lives of all her friends could be ended at any moment. And she'd never even know it was coming.

So she made fragile desserts, which survived long enough to fulfill their purpose in existence—making someone relax in delighted pleasure. *See this hair-fine spiral of sugar? It's not broken, so neither am I.*

"Maybe we should talk about sex again," he said. "That was an...unexpected topic of conversation."

Her breath felt shallow in her chest. It wasn't that she was afraid to hit on a man—she'd never really met a man who wasn't at least flattered when she flirted—but she'd never been this brazen, either. "So you wouldn't get in trouble?"

His gaze was direct, a little narrowed, very assessing. "Are you planning to claim later to the media that you were assaulted by a U.S. special forces operator?"

"I thought you were a civilian."

He made a sharp little motion of his hand.

"No," she said. "*Merde.* Of course not. Who would do something like that?"

He shrugged minutely. "When you have sex with a near stranger in a complicated situation, you put a lot on the line."

Well, yeah. She guessed so.

Damn.

All she'd wanted was...something simple. To *forget.* To *be alive.* And looking across at him reading, she'd thought that nothing in this world right that second would make her feel more alive than him.

"Never mind." She made her own dismissive motion of her hand and turned away. The last thing in the world she wanted right now was complications. Maybe she'd be better off going to a bar and picking someone up. "I'll find someone else."

Behind her, a sharp intake of breath.

Or maybe one of the police officers, she thought. They rotated regularly, and she bet she could find one that was kind of hot. Hell, they were putting their lives on the line to keep her safe. That was inherently hot.

She returned to the counter and pressed her forearms to the marble again, her back to him.

Imbécile. It was all very well refusing to be embarrassed because tomorrow you might die. But also, tomorrow you might *live.* And have to deal with the memory of having made an idiot of yourself.

Merde, the way things were going between Chase and Vi, she would probably one day find herself having to dance with Jake at their wedding because she was Vi's *demoiselle d'honneur* and he was Chase's best man. She needed to think about those things. Just because they were in the future didn't mean they wouldn't happen.

The chair creaked slightly. Then she couldn't hear him.

But she could feel him. The shift in the air. The heat of his body. The way he made her nape prickle.

A battered beige book was set on the black marble near her arm. His hand settled beside it. Callused. Sinewy. Gold and brown flecks blurring into tan.

A little wistful breath escaped through her parted lips, as she gazed at that hand.

He said nothing. Behind her, the heat of his body was only a forearm's length from her back. From that distance, she could imagine she felt his breath against the nape of her neck but never be quite sure. The hairs there prickled in longing for him to bend closer. Close enough that she could feel the heat of his breath for certain.

"What do you want?" His voice was ridiculously neutral. No one should be able to speak so neutrally about such a subject. "You want to be able not to think, is that it?"

She gave a tiny little nod, not looking back at him. "And feel alive."

Again he said nothing for a long moment.

"Look, don't worry about it," she said roughly. "It was just a...whim. Are you married or something?"

Only the space of the book lay between their two hands on the counter. Camus. Life was absurd but you kept trying. "I'm not married," he said. "No girlfriend."

Oh, and yet he still didn't...? Well, fine, then. So he'd just been bullshitting her when he said she was pretty. She jerked at the strings of her apron, suddenly frustrated with them beyond belief. *Obviously* she wasn't at her sexiest when she was in a chef's coat and apron. Although *he* was the one who had started flirting.

76

Jerk. She had never in her life offered mindless, instant sex to a man before, and she'd kind of assumed that the man would *leap* at the opportunity, no questions asked.

Idiot. Him and her both. She—

His hand left the counter and pressed over her frustrated ones. Just that one big hand, holding both of hers to her belly, where the roll of the apron rode. Calming them.

She stilled.

Gently, a pressure easy to slide away from if she wanted, he eased her back against his body.

A wall of heat the length of her. *Purée*, that felt so good.

Human warmth. Life. She closed her eyes, shutting out the kitchens, shutting out what had happened in them, shutting out the sight of one of her best friends on a hospital bed hooked up to tubes, shutting out *everything*.

Just that heat. Just that hand on her belly.

"We doing this right here?" he said.

Her breath drew in. She held it a long moment. And then she nodded tightly, closing her eyes. Here. Right where someone had tried to kill her, her best friend, and all their team. *Exactly* here.

His other hand touched the nape of her neck. Then stroked it, petting her.

Oh. The most perfect touch, shivering all through her. It promised not to hurt her, that caress. It touched her most vulnerable spot and touched it gently.

Maybe too gently?

"You—you can be bossy," she said. "I just—don't want to think."

"Bossy." His thumb traced down below the nape of her neck, pushing at the collar of her chef's jacket. She shivered. "Any other instructions?"

77

She started to shake her head and then stopped, keeping her eyes shut hard. Her head bent. "Make me come," she whispered.

Because she didn't know how these things went, exactly, but maybe in a using-someone-for-sex situation, the guy didn't think he needed to pay attention to the woman's pleasure. And she definitely, definitely didn't want to add another traumatic shitty male asshole experience to the other trauma she'd survived in these kitchens.

"Got it." He had a voice that was like his skin, golden and textured, hiding layers and layers of possibility. But right now it was as expressionless as it was possible for a voice to be. He was touching her so intimately. And yet she had no idea what he was feeling.

A brush of his cheek against her hair. His breath against her ear. The command a low murmur: "Take off your chef's jacket, then."

Her heart hammered, her nipples peaking intensely. Oh, thank God, this was going to work. She'd been afraid it might not, once she actually shifted from fantasy to reality, and then she'd get stuck in the encounter anyway, like a very bad cruise trip.

Because when you had sex with a complete stranger who was way the hell stronger than you were, you put a lot on the line.

But arousal pooled eagerly, between her thighs, in her breasts. At the nape of her neck. In the flush down from the ear his lips brushed, across her cheek. Her lips felt soft and hungry.

This was going to work.

She had to get her apron off before she could remove the jacket. She fumbled for the ties.

His hand rubbed hers away, rubbing against her belly, sure and warm even through the layers meant to protect her from heat. "I've got this." The hand at her nape dropped to join his other hand at her waist, and he pulled her back until she rested against his chest and against his arousal at the small of her back.

He was aroused, too, then. That was fast. That was good, though, right? *This is going to work.*

His hands moved deftly on her apron ties. The apron fell away. His hand came back to push up under her chef's whites and rest on her belly, firm now, through only her knit T. "Now you," he ordered softly.

It was almost like entering into a dream—the very best of dreams, shutting out all nightmares—to lift her hands to the top button of her jacket. Thick, sturdy material meant to protect her from all the dangers a kitchen should usually hold—hot oil, liquid nitrogen.

And fragile as a spider web against bullets and bombs.

She unbuttoned the first button. If she was going to be all exposed, then she might as well do it her way on her terms.

His hand rubbed her belly with each button, not edging lower. Just warmth, through her middle, and warmth through her back, and the promise of his own arousal. *Don't worry*, that erection said. *I'll make you oblivious to anything else but me.*

She hoped he could keep it up a long time.

Yes. Just...forever. That long.

Never come down and think again.

She could become a woman in erotica, her entire existence consumed by sex and the need for more of it.

That would be *lovely*.

Her fingers didn't even fumble as she undid the last button and peeled the panels of her chef's jacket apart. She was completely dressed under it, and yet the gesture still felt like stripping.

He pulled the jacket off her shoulders and tossed it on the counter.

Her heart thumped so hard. Her thin knit T and jeans would have felt perfectly fine for street wear. And yet standing in her kitchens without her protective layers, she felt naked.

Warm hands rubbed up her ribs to just beneath her breasts and back down, shifting the knit against her skin. Her eyes closed, all her focus going to the sensation. The possibilities. She could not believe in much right now, but this future, the next five, ten, fifteen minutes here, seemed like it might be within her reach.

"You're gentler than I thought," she whispered, not sure if that was good. She liked it, though. No matter how different it was from what she thought she needed.

So gentle. So warm. *So there.*

"Thanks. I think." His hand moved in her hair. A tug and the sting of a couple of hairs caught wrong, and then her hair fell free from its ponytail. It grazed to just a little below her shoulders. He drew his fingers through it, resetting the curls after their time caught high up on the back of her head.

Stirring the roots of her hair in that faintly achy freedom of a fresh escape from a ponytail.

Both his hands threaded up through her hair and massaged her scalp.

She drew a little scared breath. This was *way* too gentle. It felt so good. "I don't—I don't think—I thought we were just going to—"

One hand left her head to dip a finger into the bowl of cream and then slide the finger full deep and slow into her mouth.

She stopped talking, her eyes widening at the deep invasion of his finger, at the way her mouth automatically started to suck the pistachio-flavored cream from him.

"Let's make a rule," he said. "Since I'm the boss." He drew his finger out and ran it over her lips. "You get to open your mouth if I want to put something in it."

She drew a little gasp as that ran heat all through her body.

"But otherwise, you only get to say yes and please. And *more*. You can say, 'More, please, more.'"

She opened her mouth and closed it.

"There you go," he said, his tone so soothing. His voice in his chest vibrated against her back like its own caress. "You'll relax in a minute."

She was relaxing, yes, the heat of him seeping into her, and her own heat growing inside to meet it. She wanted to close her eyes and let him do *everything*.

His hands rose to cup her breasts. "Like this?" he murmured.

"Yes," she whispered.

He squeezed. "Like it harder?"

"Anything," she whispered. Just as long as she could feel alive. In power. Sex made futures, too, didn't it? That was the biology of it. He'd wanted something from her, too, though, she remembered, and giving it to him seemed the least she could do: "Please."

"We'll go by the moans," he said, squeezing her breasts more firmly and finding her nipples with his thumbs. They had already tightened into buds for him, and the first touch was almost painfully pleasurable.

She let her head fall back against him. "More," she whispered.

So he brought more pressure, rubbing her nipples between his thumb and forefinger, through shirt and bra.

"More," she whimpered.

He slid a hand up her middle to the center of her bra. But it wasn't a front catch.

So he settled a hand on her nape and pushed her gently but firmly down until her face was against the cold marble. His thumb stroked her nape as he held her there, that one touch all by itself enough to keep her pliant.

With his other hand he released the bra catch, and she gave a little gasp of relief as the band fell apart.

But he didn't let her up. His hand ran up and down her spine that the band no longer blocked, calluses stroking there until she was shivering and arching to that touch, only to have his hand on her nape hold her in place. He played with her back until she couldn't think of anything else but how good his fingers felt there. The cold marble warmed against her cheek, and her whole body melted.

He stroked her back until she was boneless with bliss, until she could have fallen asleep there on the marble like a cat on a lap, just sinking into bliss. She never wanted to wake out of it.

"Like that, do you?" he said.

She made a little sound.

"Like this, too?" His fingers traced her spine all the way to the waistband of her jeans and dipped under. But the jeans were snug. So he rubbed the shape of her butt through the denim, leisurely, taking his time, and then around her body to cup between her legs.

She jumped at the pleasure in the middle of her debauched relaxation. His hand firmed on her nape to hold her down. She didn't fight that hold. The caressing of her back had left her feeling too sleepily, wonderfully his.

This was *completely* different from what she thought using each other for sex would be. But it felt *so good.*

Fingers walked up the seam of her jeans until he found the button. That, too, he managed to undo one-handed. Such clever, clever hands. Loosening the zip, petting down, down, slowly down, into her curls there. Farther. His fingers hovered, and the counter stopped her hips from pressing herself into them.

"How many times did you want to come?" he asked, his tone almost conversational.

Her eyes opened. The long length of the counter lay before her gaze, black, with a steel bowl of chantilly, and beyond, just a glimpse of the door to the street. A door that had burst open.

TRUST ME

"I don't want to stop," she whispered. "Not ever."

"We'll take it one at a time," he decided, and touched his fingers to her clitoris.

She jumped uncontrollably. He held her down, his fingers sliding farther into her wetness and stroking back to that nub, bringing some of that lushness with him. He petted her easily, as if he had all night. Almost absently, as if she were a cat on his lap and he was reading his book.

She *wanted* to be a cat on his lap while he was reading his book. She wanted to be petted and petted and curled up and warm.

No. She wanted to be here.

Right here, in her kitchens, which were becoming in some strange way her own again with every stroke of his hand.

His fingers were so clever and so sure. This intimate invasion of a man into her life so very different from the last one.

The hunger for more growing and growing. Pushing out everything else. Her body tried to twist again—to twist toward him, maybe, to grab him—and again he held her, keeping his rhythm.

Stroke, stroke, stroke, easy and sure.

She tried to reach behind her with her hands and grab at his hips to pull him closer to her, but the reach was too awkward. He did let his pelvis rub against her butt, through her jeans and his cargo pants. Pressure, delicious but elusive. Not enough.

But his fingers kept stroking, the texture of his calluses applied so precisely that it was maddening, her brain was breaking in its efforts to get more of it, this stretching pressure of pleasure that kept pushing and pushing and pushing at her like she was a balloon about to pop. No, she was a bubble, floating on the air. No, she was, she was—

Coming apart. Shattering. This heavy, hot wave of oblivion that was nothing like bubbles or balloons. It surged through her, demolishing all thought, all memories, everything but it—that wave, chased and ridden and ridden until it tossed her at last up limp upon the shore.

"Oh, God," she gasped as he at last withdrew his fingers.

"Good?" His voice was maybe a fraction tighter than it had been before, but still calm.

"No!" She covered her face with her hands. "Damn you. You were supposed to come *with me*! *Do it*. Rough, wild, I don't care! *Alive*."

"Shh." His hand eased its firm hold on her nape and stroked there, gentling her. As if he was soothing someone very traumatized. Which, okay, maybe he was. "Shh."

She took deep, shuddering breaths, but the stroking on her nape got through to her, easing her down almost to a place where she could be bent over a counter, debauched by a near stranger, whom she had asked to do this to her.

"It's my body, too." His voice was very even as he petted from her nape down her back in sweet, soothing pleasure. "And maybe this is as much as I chose to have it used today."

Her eyes opened. Her eyebrows crinkled together.

"Plus, I don't have anything." His voice was still so neutral. This whole time. "Do you?"

Her eyes widened. Then closed tight. She shook her head against the counter and pressed her hand over her face.

She didn't know why it mattered so much. She was on the pill, and diseases could only happen to people who believed in the future.

And it still didn't uncurl before her, that future, not farther than this counter.

But he must have a future. Didn't he? Even though a man like him lived on the edge of death all the time?

How embarrassing to have this role in his future. Oh, hell, he wouldn't—"Please don't tell Chase."

And then Vi would know, and the guys when she brought them desserts, and—

Embarrassment had a future, too, interestingly enough. Embarrassment was another way of being *alive.*

"You sure as hell don't think much of me, do you?" A faint edge slipped into his neutral voice. He stepped back from her.

She kept her face covered.

She could feel him watching her, but *he* hadn't come and that meant she was the only one exposed here. It wasn't *fair.*

Behind her, he took a deep breath and let it audibly out. "I've got to go now," he said finally.

She pressed her hand down harder on her face.

Callused fingers touched, just lightly, the nape of her neck. A stroke like tenderness.

And then he left.

She peeled her hand from her face to watch his back as the door closed on it. Straight shoulders, that prowling, lean grace of his movements gone stiff.

And just for a moment, she wondered if she should have gone with her first instinct—the one to curl up on his lap and beg him to hold her tight.

Chapter 8

"I still say she's just using him for sex." Ian's voice. Jake checked just short of the door. Their team had been pulled from covert ops after Jake and Chase had had their covers blown the week before. Now they had been assigned to pursue a goal of greater cooperation between nations and their team had been set up in the barracks in the RAID garrison in Bièvres. Which meant they were living in an actual castle. On nearly forty hectares of graceful grounds like you saw in fairy tales, in a pretty little town of more of the same, forty minutes from the heart of Paris. One of these days, Jake hoped this deployment got unclassified and he could show his mom the photos. It was one hell of a long way from their little failed mining town in West Virginia.

"Don't break his heart by telling him that." Mark's voice.

"He shouldn't be getting in so far over his head in the first place," Ian said. "I mean, come on. They've barely met. Why is his heart on the line?"

Fuck you, Ian.

"Because she's a hot blonde in leather who threw knives at him? You know Chase."

Oh. Jake drew a slow breath and stepped into the doorway.

"He's acting like an idiot," Ian said summarily. "Hot sex does not a relationship make."

Yeah. No kidding.

"It's not like there's anything else," Jake said, rather flatly. Ian and Mark were working on their gear, and Jake moved to his bunk to pull out his. They were going out tonight. In the wake of the latest terrorist attack attempt, RAID and GIGN and BRI, France's internal counter-terrorist units, were conducting sweeping raids. Their team was accompanying RAID on tonight's raid, a symbolic gesture with real world consequences. It was an opportunity to cooperate and to better understand French operations and the challenges the French faced conducting raids like this among their own citizens. But the three of them were symbols who carried guns and wore their plates.

Mark said nothing in answer to that, checking his weapons. Not much to say to such a depressing statement, really. He started to slide on the dust cap automatically, then stopped. In verdant France, dust wasn't nearly the same problem.

"Who would *want* anything else?" Ian said. "Come on. Our choice of hot women, all the time, just like that?" He snapped his fingers. "Who wants to settle down?"

Mark lifted his gaze from his Sig and looked at Ian a moment. Jake focused on checking over his H&K. Neither called Ian on it. Bravado was bravado. An inexcusable sign of weakness in a combat situation, but in emotional situations...well, a man handled the emotional shithole this job made of their lives the best he could.

It was easy enough to find sex. Hell, it was just like that afternoon. Hot sex just dropped into their laps. Women couldn't even *look* at them without thinking how fun they would be for a quick encounter, no strings and no tomorrow.

Jake gazed with grim intensity at his rifle, determined not to show anything on his face.

Trust and a relationship on the other hand...that was a whole other question.

A relationship you could *count* on, he meant, because even marriage, another thing guys on the teams managed to talk women into with amazing frequency, usually turned out to be a betrayal of trust within a few years. The divorce rate was phenomenal. Also the death rate, but at least in that case you were *dead* when the woman you loved moved on without you.

The worst was when you lost your career and your body and your wife at the same time. As a twenty-year-old newbie, Jake, like many newbies on the teams, had been assigned to escort wounded SEAL warriors at Bethesda. He'd seen the wives who took one look at their hot hero, now that he had lost a limb or had his face half blown off or been burned all over his body, and dropped the divorce papers on the bandages wrapping his belly and fled. Sometimes wives met their husbands with those papers. Like, before they even *tried* to deal with the wounds; it was the *very first thing they did* when they saw him. Some wives started getting the papers drawn up as soon as they got the call from Iraq or Afghanistan or Germany that the man they had promised to love forever was badly wounded.

It had been a cold, hard dose of reality, that time as a wounded warrior escort. Just before his own first tour.

"Speaking of hot sex," Ian said as he finished slipping his side plates in. "This shy, geeky guy thing."

Jake tightened his belly hard, putting his instinct to stiffen down in his abs, where no one could see it.

Ian, oblivious, sent him a glance full of mirth, deliberately poking a lion to make life more interesting. "I figured I'd wear these." He reached into his gear and pulled out a pair of black-framed glasses, settling them on his nose.

"You keep a pair of fake glasses in your gear just in case you want to flirt with women who like nerds?" Jake said, irritated. Damn it, why hadn't he thought of that? He slid his knife into place at his back.

"I figured I'd sit in a corner wearing them and catch up on our book club book. Camus. Can't get much more nerdy than that." Ian rolled his eyes at Mark.

Mark sighed and didn't bother to respond.

"It's actually pretty interesting," Jake said, trying to turn this subject of conversation to the safe one their book club was supposed to provide them. "I got most of it done earlier this afternoon."

Ian gave a slow, indignant whistle. "You *dog*. You already pulled the reading trick?"

"Some of us read for other reasons than to trick women, Ian."

"Not Camus, they don't." Ian prodded Mark. "Right, Mark? That was the whole reason you picked Camus this month, so we could impress French women?"

"Next month it's Sartre," Mark said blandly, well aware that sometimes it was better not to even fight it, when the team started talking shit at each other.

"Damn it," Jake said. "Chase is in a hospital bed, you know. You could at least let him pick this one."

"Yeah, I bet she'd find it cute as anything if I were reading *Harry Potter*." A dreamy look grew in Ian's eyes as he considered this image. "Oh, yeah, that could work."

Jake elbowed him extra hard. "We're up."

Infill here was in black SUVs. They rode with Elias and more of his RAID team, their gear black like the RAID team but without the black panther patch on the left shoulder. After the series of attacks in France, SOCEUR (U.S. Special Operations Europe) had ramped up training sessions with RAID. The rise of terrorist cells in France, a major ally, had been a chief concern for some time, and the order from the top was for greater cooperation between allies in intelligence and operations.

Working together here, not in training but in actual raids, was a chance to consolidate—to better understand each force's methods and issues. Their element was small—at least the part of it the French president knew about—but that didn't mean it was politically advisable for photos of U.S. forces to show up in the media as participating in raids in Paris suburbs. So, not for the first time in his career, Jake was sheep-dipped and out of uniform. At least the raid was in an allied nation this time and not an enemy one where he'd be totally screwed if he was caught.

"And you can put those damn glasses away," Jake said. Or loan them to him. "I'm the one keeping an eye on her. She's been through a lot of shit. It's better for her to relax with a familiar face."

"I can relax women." Ian grinned.

A vision of a back under his hand, that heart face against black marble, her lashes falling, her body lost in dreamy bliss, and Jake lost all possibility of dealing with Ian with a sense of humor. His head lifted. His eyes locked. "Stay the fuck away." The words fell sharp and dangerous, like weapons.

Ian stared at him. His eyebrows shot up.

Fuck.

"Like *that,* is it?" Ian said softly. "You think you have first dibs?"

I'll find someone else, she had said. Jake knew what that was like. He'd done it himself, sought oblivion in sex, and he sure as hell hadn't limited himself to one encounter with one woman when he was doing it.

Meanwhile, even among the teams, Ian's success with women was legendary.

"She's off limits," Jake said flatly. "Mine."

"*Putain,* it's like working with fucking cavemen," Elias muttered, dropping his head to the wall of the van behind him.

"Yeah, let's not be Neanderthal, Jake," Ian said. "What does she say about who she belongs to?"

"It has nothing to do with her." Jake locked eyes with him and ignored the very ironic noise Elias made at that comment. Did the French just drink a gift for irony in the water, or what? "It has to do with me and you and whether I will fucking kill you."

"Well, now that we've got that settled," Mark said dryly. "Can we save this fight for later and focus on the mission? Try to impress these gentlemen with our professionalism, perhaps?"

The other members of Elias's team were regarding them with an irony not quite as obvious as Elias's but present, just the same. "Oh, it's not your ability to fight we're worried about," Elias said. "It's how the hell you manage to keep reproducing over in your country. Is it just that there are only idiots available and your women learn to settle, or what?"

"Okay, you know what—?" Ian turned toward Elias, taking that aspersion on his gift for women personally.

But then they were arriving. A raid in one of those suburbs full of fourteen-story concrete and broken glass buildings, where the police never came to save you from your neighbors, they only came to get you if you attacked outside your zone. Not so different, really, Jake thought grimly, from their raids in Syria.

They even had a couple of drones up in the air. For surveillance, this time.

He didn't have any sympathy for people who turned terrorist and tried to shoot someone like Lina or Vi, none at all. But he'd grown up in a place he thought had no opportunity himself, where religious fanaticism had sometimes been a refuge for a certain type of mindset. And that failing coal town in the mountains had still been better than this. At least he'd had the mountains. The rhododendrons in the spring, the granite outcrop where he watched the sun set over foggy peaks, and hiking and hunting for hours, even days at a time, alone through the steep forest.

But Lina and Vi and most of their staff had grown up in places like this, too, right? He'd read all the information they had on Lina and on the Au-dessus restaurant staff. They'd made opportunities where other teenagers saw none. So he didn't have sympathy for the shits that chose to destroy other people instead.

And yet...at one point, every military age male he might shoot and kill had once been a cute little toddler, fascinated by balls and bright colors and puppies.

A cute lion cub still grew up to be a lethal predator, and you'd best not let the way it chased butterflies

91

persuade you to turn your back on it as an adult lion. Jake should know. He'd been cute himself once, his mom said.

Humans were even more successful predators than lions were. In a world where pretty much everyone was a predator, Jake would kill to protect his people before he would let his people be killed. He didn't have a soft heart. He just thought too much sometimes.

Mark and his damn books.

He jumped out of the SUV. One of the French guys was on point. Black ski masks were up. Jake shut his emotions off and stacked for the raid.

***

The trouble with not believing in a future, Lina thought, hefting her case of desserts as she left Vi's room, *was that when the future went ahead and showed up anyway, a woman still had to deal with it.*

It wasn't like she could leave poor Chase sad-faced because he hadn't gotten his special dessert today, right? She could imagine exactly how woebegone he would play it. You couldn't abandon a guy wounded on your behalf and now stuck in a hospital bed, just because you couldn't face the consequences of your own actions.

It was just hot sex, come on. Wouldn't be the first or last time in the world that a woman had to face a guy the day after, wondering what the hell he'd meant by the way he'd left.

She slowed as she neared the room, where male voices were busy accusing Chase of malingering so he could stay close to his girlfriend. When they were among themselves, Chase and his "buddies" spoke in an English so full of unfamiliar words—military jargon? acronyms?—that she couldn't follow them. She wasn't entirely sure native English speakers could have followed them. It was like they spoke their own special language, and the only way to learn it was through blood and fire, shoulder to shoulder.

Kitchens were a little bit like that. Not quite as high a mortality rate from the blood and fire, though. Not usually.

She tightened her stomach muscles, let her shoulders settle back and down, into easy confidence, and stepped into the doorway.

Oh. A sinking of disappointment and relief. Jake wasn't there.

She took a slow breath as Ian, Mark, and Chase turned toward her with delight. No Jake. She was both safer and, curiously, without him, felt much less safe. Alone.

"Hello, Lina." The deep, even voice came from behind her, accompanied by a sense of warmth just short of her back.

She jumped and whirled, her plastic case striking him.

"Jake, *fuck!*" Chase yelled.

Jake grabbed the case as it fell and went all the way down onto one knee with it. "Sorry." He stayed down there. Keeping smaller than she was. Not a threat.

"Jesus, Jake," Ian said. "What the hell?"

Jake shook his head. His eyes held Lina's. "That was careless," he said. "I was...thinking of something else."

"It's okay." She took a deep breath and held it two counts before she let it out, embarrassed in so many ways she wished she could just run away from the world and become someone else. Like the witness protection proponents wanted her to. "I just...startled."

"No kidding," Chase said from his bed.

Oh. Right. Because any man in this room, if a voice sounded unexpectedly immediately behind him, would have reacted with similar intensity. And they were reproaching Jake, and Jake was apologizing because...he would have known better than to sneak up on his team brothers, so he should have thought about it with her, too.

They respected what she'd been through? She didn't seem weak and fragile to them? Was all that weakness and fragility deep in her tummy something no one else could see?

Well, *good*. She'd made her entire career out of being tough enough to handle whatever a high-octane kitchen threw at her. Her stupid cousin was *nothing*. Or at least he should be—worth absolutely nothing.

"If you've finished proposing to her down there," Ian said dryly.

Jake looked down at the big box in his hands and came to his feet with that economic grace of his. He gave Ian a dirty look that stiffened Lina's spine.

Oh, the suggestion he might propose marriage to her made him *that* annoyed?

Fine, then.

Ian came up to her to kiss her cheeks and squeeze her shoulder. Then he shot Jake an undecipherable look, took a chair in the corner, slouched back in it, slipped on a pair of black-framed reading glasses, and pulled out a copy of *Harry Potter* from a pocket in his cargo pants. The first *Harry Potter*, the one that was small enough to fit in a big cargo pants pocket. "Now where was I?" he asked Chase.

Aww. That was kind of cute. This hotter than hell guy, with his brown T-shirt clinging to big biceps and a flat stomach, reading to his friend in a hospital bed. "You guys are reading *Harry Potter* now?" she said, charmed.

Elias made a noise like a strangled sneeze, and Jake gave Ian a look like a rattlesnake about to strike.

"Cute glasses," Chase said, blue eyes vivid with mirth.

"We're still on Camus, sadly, thanks to this dork," Ian told her, jerking his head at Mark. "But we're pushing for *Harry Potter* for the next one."

"Sartre," Mark said.

94

"Damn it, Mark, you can't read Sartre to a man in a hospital bed. You might kill him."

That did seem kind of cruel and unusual, actually. "There's always Kafka," Lina said, her lips quirking.

Mark looked intrigued. By Kafka, *ouïlle*. No wonder they wanted someone else to start choosing their book club books.

"Lina," Chase protested, pained. "I thought you liked me."

"In a weird way." She smiled at him, setting her case on his table and bending down to kiss his cheeks.

An unfortunate thought crossed her mind of the last time she had bent over at just about this angle with Jake behind her.

She straightened and focused on opening her case, hoping she wasn't flushing.

She wasn't supposed to flush that easily, damn it. It was supposed to be an advantage of having gold skin. Freckles over there was the one supposed to be flushing all the damn time.

"Or how about Simone de Beauvoir?" she suggested, in revenge for the blush.

All the men stared at her. "Who's Simone de Beauvoir?" Ian asked warily.

"You went to Harvard?" she said. "Really? What, they only teach you what males think there?"

Ian blinked and sealed his mouth tightly shut. He held up his *Harry Potter* book weakly and pointed to the name J.K. Rowling on the cover. As if everybody in the world hadn't noticed Rowling had had to use initials that disguised her sex to help that book start selling.

To her credit, J.K. was also single-handedly responsible for making sure that most male readers had read at least one book by a female author in their lives. Talk about breaking a barrier.

"Simone de Beauvoir is only one of the most famous and influential thinkers of the twentieth century," Lina said. "A vanguard feminist writer."

The men exchanged glances.

"Sartre's wife," Mark explained.

Lina pivoted and put her hands on her hips.

Elias whistled softly. "You guys never cease to amaze me." Wry green eyes met Lina's. "Please ignore these cavemen as best you can."

"Remind me how many women are in RAID again?" Lina said.

Elias looked studiously at his feet. After a second he held up two guilty fingers.

"Yeah, but that makes sense," Chase said cheerfully from the safety of his hospital bed. "Men are stronger."

Lina spun on him.

He grinned at her and, despite being badly wounded, pale, and washed out, flexed his right arm to make his biceps pop.

"I'm telling Vi you said that."

"Aww. Don't tell her until she has recovered more. I don't want her dragging herself out of her hospital bed to come kick my ass." He looked wistful. Like he missed her trying to kick his ass very badly.

Lina missed Vi, too. More than this guy could possibly imagine, surely, since he'd barely known her for a couple of weeks, and Lina and Vi had worked together for years and been friends since they were teenagers.

But of course, being an arrogant man, he was probably convinced he was now the center of Vi's life.

"You're lucky you're in a hospital bed so *I* don't kick your ass," Lina told Chase.

His grin came back. "I just had to help out my brothers. Solidarity, you know."

"Yeah, half the sexism in the world is due to that. Men standing up for men."

96

"Like you and Célie and Vi don't stand up for each other?"

"That's different! We have to, in this world."

Chase just smiled at her.

Lina frowned at him suspiciously, wondering if that smile meant some point was supposed to be sinking into her brain. Chase could be really annoying that way. "I notice you needed a gun, while I took out a terrorist with liquid nitrogen. Explain to me again how much stronger you are?"

A warm, low laugh from Jake behind her, and Ian licked his finger and made a sizzling noise as he scored a point in the air. Chase sighed, dramatically enough to hide the flicker of darkness in his eyes.

"Not wife," Jake said, probably to save Chase from her. "Didn't Sartre and Beauvoir have one of those open relationship things? Used each other for sex?"

Elias pressed his forehead into the palm of his hand.

Lina slanted a glance at Jake, who had settled into the doorway, his back to the frame, his angle such that he could look down the hall toward Vi's room and the elevator and the police there. Lina's escort and Vi's were chatting, relaxed a bit in their vigilance because of the safety of the hospital and the sheer number of top warriors currently present. She focused on opening the case of pastries.

"Some very sophisticated kind of relationship anyway," Jake said. "Parisian."

Lina hesitated with her hand under the first pastry. She had used six-centimeter rings to shape the desserts, the *croustillant* of chocolate and shortbread on the bottom, the dark chocolate cream next, the pistachio cream in a beautiful raindrop shape on top, scattered with caramelized pistachios and a drizzle of dark chocolate.

Simple, crowd-pleasing flavors that someone's palate could love even if that palate's primary education was from military rations. The familiarity and comfort of chocolate and pistachio, combined with a grace and elegance that made her feel she was bringing something rare and precious into their lives.

A gift of beauty. In a form that didn't impose that beauty uncomfortably on them but let them savor it.

And only twenty-four hours before, Jake's finger had slipped a first version of that pistachio cream into her mouth.

You get to open your mouth if I want to put something in it.

Maybe she should read Simone de Beauvoir herself.

But, boy, she hadn't thought of a single other thing but him and her body, the whole time he was holding her down by her nape on a counter.

He'd done what she had asked him to.

The very bare minimum of what she had asked him to, and not a thing more.

She gave one of the chocolate-pistachio pastries to Chase, who was suitably delighted. She gave one to Mark and Ian and Elias, who all told her she was the best thing to ever happen to them and asked Chase if he would mind getting shot by terrorists more often. And then she had to give one to Jake.

He looked down at it in her hands as she held it up to him, trying both to catch a glimpse of his expression and not meet his eyes. His expression was so unreadable and he gazed at the dessert held up in her hands so long without reaching for it that she lost her precaution and studied his face fully, and when his lashes lifted suddenly, he caught her gaze.

Heat climbed up her cheeks but she couldn't look away from that hazel.

His hands lifted and curved over hers around the dessert. Brushes of warmth and strength and texture. She eased her hands free so that he held it by himself.

He touched a finger to the pistachio cream and, watching her, slipped his finger into his mouth and sucked the cream clean.

Oh, boy.

She looked away. He lowered his lashes.

"I can't stay long today," she said.

"Don't tell me you have a hot date." Ian pulled down his black-framed glasses and looking at her over them like a librarian who generally carried a sniper rifle to pick off chatter in the stacks. "I don't want to have to kill anybody."

"Do you want to have to die?" Jake asked behind her conversationally.

Ian grinned as if the possibility of facing death at Jake's hands just filled him with joy. "Besides," he said, "this Harry kid is living in a closet. There are spiders. You don't want to hear how he escapes and grows to be the hero of the world?"

"I saw the movies," Lina said.

Ian clapped his hands to the sides of his head and hissed, "Mark! Cover your ears!"

Lina relented. "I read the books, too. When I was a kid."

"They're suitable for adults," Ian told her severely. "Multiple re-reads. I mean, Myth of Sisyphus. What's more Sisyphean than this kid's battle with Voldemort? Seven freaking books evil kept taking another shape and rising again."

"More," Lina said.

Ian frowned. "No, I'm pretty sure there were only seven. Wait. There wasn't some release we missed because we were stuck in some hellhole, was there? Because if you guys didn't tell me—"

"No. *Mort.* Vol de mort. You don't say the T. He steals from *death.*"

"Like Sisyphus!" Ian said triumphantly. "That's how that Sisyphus guy ends up with his rock up a hill

99

punishment. See, Mark? It will allow us thematic continuity. Comparative studies. If they both cheated death, why is only one an existentialist hero? Because Voldemort's battle is pretty Sisyphean, too, if you think about it. That Harry is one damn big boulder crashing down on him over and over."

"Oh, for fuck's sake," Mark said. "Fine. That can be our next book."

All the guys grinned. Even Elias looked as if the choice filled him with some delight, and Jake looked torn between throwing Ian off a tall building and laughing.

"But don't blame me when some sophisticated, beautiful Parisian quotes Sartre and you don't even know who she's talking about," Mark said.

"Or Simone de Beauvoir," Elias mentioned idly.

All the other men gave him *et tu Brute* looks at that one.

Busy fastening her case, it took Lina a moment to realize she was the sophisticated, beautiful Parisian being referenced by that exchange of looks.

She smiled at Elias, relieved to have someone she understood in the room. At least he knew how to flirt. With these Americans, she could never be one hundred percent certain if they knew flirting was a fun game or if they might have clumsy intentions behind it. Chase's idea of flirting with Vi had been to ask her to marry him in the first two minutes of their acquaintance and *mean it*.

Jake didn't mean anything serious by his flirtation, did he? *Ouf*, surely not. Even Americans could grasp the concept of mindless, hot sex. Especially black ops people. They were kind of like James Bond toward women, right?

Although Bond was British. Hmm. The only American black ops equivalent she could think of off the bat was Jason Bourne, and in the movies he'd been stuck on that one woman for pretty much the whole series.

But surely Jake wouldn't get serious...would he? Not in the circumstances?

"I've got to go," Lina said. "I can't stay long today." She didn't look at Jake.

She kissed everyone on both cheeks again, to say good-bye. Even, not meeting his eyes as he bent his head, Jake.

You can't feel the freckles at all. His jaw is faint prickle and his cheeks smooth skin.

She'd known that would be the case, of course. But it was different to actually feel it. And kind of surreally erotic to only now be discovering this when he'd already made her come once.

She shifted away from him quickly, still not meeting his eyes, and hurried down the hall to her police escort.

***

In the hospital room, all the men looked at Jake.

"*That's* the woman you said was yours?" Mark checked, that familiar grilled note of impatience coming into his voice.

"You know she's not into you, right?" Chase said, with the no-holds-barred frankness of a brother-in-arms trying to save another brother from heartbreak. "She barely even looked at you."

"Yeah," Jake said grimly. "I noticed that."

"She likes *me*," Ian said. "You saw how we were bonding over literature, right? I think it should be my turn to help keep an eye on her now."

"No," Jake said flatly. "Ian—*fuck off.*"

Chapter 9

Think about sex. Lina looked away from her bathroom mirror and the pinch at the corners of her eyes, the way her lips kept parting in a look of panic, no matter how many times she pressed them firmly closed. She turned on the shower. *Think about sex right here.* Not on a counter, where she couldn't do what she wanted to him.

But here. In this shower. Where she pressed that hot body up against the wall of her shower and he got that panicked look he got for her desserts, as if she was about to bite him, and she ran her fingers down those packed abs of his, pressed his wet body back against the wall, and *did.*

And he moaned and...

Yes! She turned her face up into the shower in victory as the vision grew vivid enough to take over her mind.

Thank God for sex.

She could think about *that* instead of the fact that even the late summer light was fading, dark was settling in. And that normally, she would still be out in the city on a night like this, either working or enjoying her night off amid the lights and activity. And if she was tired, well, then, normally, she would be enjoying the chance to watch a movie or curl up with a book. She loved leafing through picture books, for example. She got the coolest ideas from them. She had *Tell Me a Dragon* by her bed right now.

Normally, back two weeks ago, when she was still herself. Lina Farah. Not someone who would never, ever feel secure in her world again. Who never *would* be as secure in her world again, who would always be more likely to draw the attention of the crazies—the ones who wanted vengeance on her for defeating her cousin and

102

the racist conspiracy theory crazies convinced she had really been on his side.

She yanked her mind back to the shower, focusing on that broad chest and those hard abs that would probably be covered with freckles—he'd rudely worn a T-shirt at the gym, so she didn't know for sure.

But definitely, definitely, he would shudder as she—

Why oh why hadn't she gotten his phone number?

Let that be a lesson to you, woman. If you don't believe in the future, when it comes around, there you are stuck in it and you can't even text a guy an eggplant.

Not that she'd ever done that before but hey...if other women could do it, she could, too, right?

She could understand why her dad hadn't thought to suggest this particular distraction method to her when she was eight, but these days, it was *way* more effective to fill her closet and her bed with images of hot sex than fall asleep gripping a bat.

She let the warm water stream over her face, her eyes closed, and—

Was that knocking?

Oh, hell.

Somebody must be really pounding on her door for the noise to reach her in here, and her stomach cramped in sudden fear. Oh, fuck, what if the police had changed their mind? What if they had decided all family members were suspects, even those who fought Abed, or all Muslims, or all Arabs, and they were going to round everyone up and deport them all like the far right assholes kept talking about? The ghosts of the Jewish family that had once lived in the apartment directly across from hers and been swept away in the Rafle de Vel d'Hiv seemed to gather like a family photo in her mind, two adults and two children, and stare at her in accusation and warning. *You're not safe. No one is ever safe.*

She found her heavy bathrobe, trying to dry her hair before someone broke in and dragged her somewhere.

"Lina!" A sharp call through the door. "I'm going to have to break down the door if you don't answer. Are you in there? Are you okay?"

Her face scrunched. That was Jake.

But she hadn't texted him an eggplant.

Oh, shit, had something happened? To her family, to Vi at the hospital? Oh, please, dear God, don't tell her anything had happened. Please tell her that Jake hadn't been playing some good cop-bad cop mind trick on her all this time. He was friends with Chase, wasn't he? They were arrogant, but they all seemed like such *good* guys.

"I'm coming!" she yelled. "I just—" She yanked her robe as tightly closed over her dripping nakedness as she could, so vulnerable her stomach wanted to eat its way out of her body. That was one of the problems—she could fight the bad guys with a chainsaw, but she couldn't fight the good guys with anything at all, and *neither* of them were on her side, so she was stuck in the middle between them, struggling to build a world out of sugar that neither could break. She pulled the door open.

Jake stood there with two police officers behind him.

Oh, *fuck*.

"Shit." Jake took a long breath, staring down at her. "You were in the shower?" He made a *stand down* gesture to the policemen and stepped inside, nudging her back with his body and closing the door between her and the other two men. Who, to their credit, had been scanning her and the apartment beyond her in an *everything okay* way, not ogling her at all.

"Sorry," Jake said. "You're all right? Sorry."

So...he wasn't arresting her? They weren't—"Is everything *okay*?" she snapped frantically.

"Yes," he said immediately, closing his hands around her shoulder. "I'm sorry, Lina. I was worried when you didn't answer the door."

Oh, right, the officers behind him were her guards. To keep her safe.

Paranoia. She'd been caught in another wave of paranoia. That shit. It kept coming back and taking her over, no matter how many ways she fought it.

Immediately, she started telling again through the faces of those she could trust, like her grandmother's prayer beads, the only method she knew besides work, hot showers, hot sex, and deep breaths to fight that paranoia: her grandmother. Her parents. Vi. Célie. Her sous-chef. Her staff...

Jake squeezed her shoulders. "I'm sorry," he said again. His voice deepened, going into that soothing tone he had used with her...when...*you'll relax in a minute.* "You're perfectly safe." Gentle, firm, absolutely bedrock trustworthy. *A lie.* "It was my overreaction. When you didn't answer the door—"

"If I were perfectly safe, you wouldn't have worried," Lina said and turned away. "Don't lie to me. More. Don't lie to me more."

The panic was releasing in a painful slump. She hated, hated, hated having to be *so damn relieved the police weren't going to haul her off half-naked* just because she was Arab.

French. Her family had been French for nearly two centuries. Algeria had been annexed as a department of France in 1848 and still been fighting for its independence when her pacifist grandfather moved to the outskirts of Paris to find work, and with the eager encouragement of the French government at the time, by the way. Hell, Camus was born in Algeria, and nobody ever said *he* wasn't French.

And her grandfather's arrival near Paris had been thirty years before she was born. Lina wasn't an activist like her mother. To be honest, as a teenager, she'd mostly found her mother's activism freaking embarrassing, and she'd strode away from it into the big city lights to live her very own life. She rarely ever even thought about politics or religion at all, although she'd definitely absorbed her mother's girl power message. Deeply immersed in her career and surrounded by a raucous, high-energy team that just took people for who they were as long as they could stand the heat in a kitchen, she had grown used to being herself. Not *not* Arab, but not that as The Main Thing. The First thing, the Only Thing that people saw when they looked at her. The first thing was top pastry chef, and the second thing was accomplished career woman, and the fact that her grandparents came from Algeria had just faded into a taken-for-granted element of who she was rather than her *identity*. Her *otherness*.

And yet, and yet...

The attack and all the media attention on her as the Muslim Woman Who Fought Terrorists and Why Aren't You Wearing a Hijab had made her feel alien.

Fuck you, she thought to terrorists. To her stupid cousin. *I hate you so damn bad.*

And fuck everyone who grouped the victims of terrorism and its perpetrators together just because it was easier than seeing individual people.

"I haven't lied to you at all," Jake said evenly.

She turned back and just looked at him.

"I haven't," he repeated, holding her eyes.

"I'm *safe*?"

He was silent a long moment. His expression grew serious, a little grim. Even talking about this made him look more lethal, and he prowled to the windows, checking the street and rooftops. "You're as safe as we can make you, barring relocation and a change of identity."

"No." She held up her hand. "I'm one of the top pastry chefs in France, and heading higher, and I'm not turning into something else." A victim. The cousin of a terrorist. The media symbol of Arab Woman Who *Wasn't* a Terrorist, as if that was some freaking fluke. Or even just, what, some relocated anonymous baker in a friendly little village. She was Lina Farah, top pastry chef. Her place was the one she had earned, and she was not giving that up. "I worked my butt off to be who I am."

And if she needed to work harder to stay who she was...well, then, she would just work harder.

Be braver.

Jake turned from the window. The late summer light fell on his freckles as he gazed at her, and she could almost imagine that light kissing his skin, the first little romantic overture in the conception of another freckle. She could imagine that light kissing him all over, obsessively in love with his skin and his body and goo-goo-ga-ga over all their freckle children.

"Trust me," he said. "I understand that your reputation and your career are more important to you than your life."

"Because yours are, too," she realized slowly. A heavy sinking sensation in her middle. Wow. It felt a lot...harder to swallow, on this side. The fact that he would sacrifice his life to his reputation.

What does your reputation matter? she wanted to yell at him suddenly. *Next to your life?*

But she of all people should understand. Even to be safe, even to live, she could not give up what made her alive. The heart and purpose of who she was.

"Oh." She stared at him.

He gazed back, hazel eyes level.

She flushed up to her forehead suddenly and remembered that she was only wearing a bathrobe, her hair a tangled, sopping mess.

"I need to get dressed." She took a step back.

"Yeah." His tone flattened subtly. He turned to study the street again. "If you want to."

The way he looked at a street was different from the way she looked at it, even when she was struggling under a wave of paranoia. He knew where to look, for one. Up, down, high, low, at every window. Scanning them all, automatically, as if he didn't even know anymore how to just glance at a view. He had to check for the flicker on a rifle, the suspicious movement, the person with bulky clothing or a backpack that might hide a bomb.

She bit the inside of her lip.

He didn't look back at her as she hurried into her room. She knew because she did look back. At the straight, strong shoulders, the quiet, the sense of danger.

She locked her bedroom door, which she'd started doing ever since the attack. She locked every door she could lock between her and someone bursting in.

Then she stood there for a second, wondering if he had heard the click and if so, how it had made him feel.

Like she trusted him to use him for sex, but didn't trust him not to force his way into her bedroom?

What if he did come into her bedroom...

She picked up her comb and ran it through her hair.

What if she hadn't locked the door? What if he came behind her now and took the bottom of the bathrobe and lifted it up to squeeze the dripping ends of her hair gently dry? What if that exposed her bare butt to him and he nestled his body up against her back and gently began to rub the terry bathrobe against her body, drying the moisture that still clung to her skin.

Her nipples peaked against the terry.

What if he pulled the panels of the bathrobe apart, to expose those nipples, right here, standing behind her so he could watch her in the mirror, so she could watch *herself*, still so perfectly alive and human, and he...

She closed her eyes.

Her hands snuck up to rub the terry against her breasts.

No one caught her at it. And it felt so much better than fear.

Silently, carefully, as if someone might hear a brush of cloth and guess what she was doing, she slid her fingers under the panels of terry and touched her bare nipples. Beaded tight. She savored the shape of herself

TRUST ME

there a moment, the sensations that shot through her body, that made her hungry and sleepily wistful, tighter there and softer and lusher other places.

What if he rubbed his big hand down over her belly, rubbing terry against her, until he cupped between her thighs. What if he stirred that terry cloth against her over and over, his hand so much bigger and warmer than hers was, it would make that life-center of her body feel so much more encompassed and secure and eager...

What if he parted the folds of the bathrobe, gentle and firm, and—

She caught what she was doing—it was the dissatisfying smallness and tentativeness of her own hand, compared to the one she was imagining. Her eyes flew open as she yanked her hand away to grip her comb again. She stared at her dilated eyes in the mirror.

Now she was aroused, though. She wanted more. She didn't want to stop halfway.

She swallowed, glancing at the locked door. Would he start to wonder what she was doing in here that was taking her so long? Would she be able to face him immediately after, as if nothing had happened?

Look at that. You imagined a bit of a future again.

She gripped the panels of her bathrobe closed with one hand and went to the bedroom door.

In her small apartment, she only had to open it to see him. He still stood at the window, back to her. A strong silhouette. Tall. Straight shoulders. Lean hips. Darkness against light, a stranger. At this angle, she couldn't even see his freckles.

"Jake," she said, very low.

He turned. She loved how quiet he was. How smoothly and silently he moved, as if he had no need to make noise to impact the world. He didn't have any of that cocky, show-offiness to him that Chase and Ian both radiated. And he felt more powerful for it.

And, God, she loved his freckles.

109

She smoothed her hands over her bathrobe nervously, and her nipples ached against the rub of the terry cloth.

"Do you, ah—would you, ah—" She gestured to indicate her body.

He stood still in the window. All dark silhouette, impossible to read his face.

Frustrated at her lack of courage—how could it be *harder* to say this out loud the second time?—she loosed the sash of her bathrobe.

The panels fell slightly open, what must be a line of exposure right up the center of her pelvis to the hollow of her throat.

He said nothing. Still in silhouette. Still impossible to read.

Embarrassment caught up with her, sweeping up her in a wave, and she clutched the panels closed again, stepping back into her bedroom.

He moved away from the window.

And with one long, prowling step came after her.

Chapter 10

When he clicked the door shut behind him, Lina stood still in front of him, her breath shortening until her whole body felt too tight. Now she could see him as more than a male shape. Now he was a person again, kissed all over in freckles, the sun a nymphomaniac and he her obsession of choice.

The sun had kissed him right up to his lower row of eyelashes, and over his eyelids, and down the hard curve of his biceps and the sinews of his forearms. The sun had clearly been completely invasive and inappropriate with him and done things she shouldn't have done.

Lina was pretty sure people with freckles were supposed to be cute and snub-nosed or something, but in Jake's case that would be like thinking a hunting lion was cute because it had a fluffy mane. He wasn't cute at all. He was sexy as hell. And he held her eyes as he reached behind him and locked the door.

She couldn't swallow. Her whole body felt tight with anticipation. *Future. The next second, when he touches me. The moment when he lowers me back on that bed.*

Guards outside. Nothing can touch us here. Except each other.

She closed her eyes, her head tilting back and her lips parting.

But he didn't touch her.

She peeked between her lashes, long, black lashes, better for hiding her gaze than his. But then, he hid everything he was thinking and feeling behind a very difficult to read face.

"You, too, this time," she whispered suddenly. "Not just...me. You, too."

"Just because you choose to let me have your body doesn't mean you get to say what I do with mine," he said evenly.

Oh. That sounded...oddly like something she might have to say to a man. Her eyebrows pleated a little, although she couldn't quite figure out why his words made her uncomfortable. What man did not leap at the fantasy of a strange woman opening her bathrobe to him and stepping back into her bedroom to invite him to follow?

Weren't all men supposed to leap at that?

"If you don't want to—" She tightened her hold on her bathrobe.

"Yeah, I know." That faint, clipped edge to his voice. "You'll find someone else."

Well...yeah. She might. Someone big and strong, who wouldn't ask questions and who would just let her focus on sex.

She'd find somebody. Maybe not as strong and sexy as *him*, but it was just for mindless, oblivion sex. It wasn't like she was looking for a guy she could spend her life with. She might not even *have* a life to spend. She'd nearly run out of all life a week ago.

It was a big city. She could probably find somebody she could make do with.

Her mouth drooped as she tried to imagine it, though. All the imaginings made her skin crawl a little, left a bad taste in her mouth. "Not as sexy as you," she said honestly.

His eyebrows went up a little, and one corner of his lips quirked, just slightly. "Well, that's something."

She raised a hand and placed it carefully, fingers spread, on his chest. Wow. Hot and strong and resilient. "You know that, don't you? How sexy you are?"

"Feel free to tell me more about it," he said and reached behind him to—

112

Oh. That was a gun. That he was setting on her dresser. It sat dully there, cold and real.

He set something else there.

That was a knife. Sheathed.

He glanced at her, then pulled off the loose, open shirt he had been wearing that helped conceal that gun and tossed it over both weapons, so they were hidden in a fall of cloth.

She felt very cold again, and she didn't think she wanted to do this after all.

Maybe she just wanted to go back in the shower and see if there was any more hot water left.

Don't let the gun get to you. When she brought desserts to Chase and all the macho buddies who were hanging out with him and giving each other shit to keep him entertained, they were certainly wearing weapons somewhere on their bodies. That was how Chase had had a gun on him when they were attacked. It made sense that Jake would want to strip his weapons off him before she touched him, to keep them both safe.

It was just that they reminded her. Of guns going off, of the existence of things she hadn't properly believed in, a week ago—death, given on purpose, by one human being to another. And the proof of it not in her kitchens this time but right here in her bedroom, inside her apartment, the only illusion of safety she had left.

Her lips drooped lower, her feet chilling.

"Lost the moment?" Jake asked conversationally.

Her eyes flew back to his.

He stepped back, resting his shoulders against the door and folding his arms casually. "Want to call a halt?"

She frowned at his relaxed pose. "You don't even care, do you?"

"It's not my first time at this rodeo, honey. Being used for sex."

Her frown deepened. Of course it wasn't. She knew that. At least, she'd assumed it, when she first asked him the day before—that he had had plenty of experiences of sex for sex's sake. But...well, it was *her* first time. Having sex without at least hoping that hearts were also involved.

"Well, you might show a *little* more gumption about it," she said, somewhat indignant. "As if you actually want it."

"I'm on the fence. About what I want."

Oh, fine then. Lina jerked her robe back in place and stomped over to her mirror, picking up her comb again. If he didn't think he'd just gotten about as lucky as a man could get, *tough luck for him.* He didn't deserve to touch her in the first place.

So there.

She nodded at herself in the mirror and yanked the comb too hard through a snarl.

Aïe.

She threw the comb across the room, a violence that came out of nowhere, caught herself too late to stop it, and clapped both her hands to her face, taking slow, deep breaths. *Not* losing it.

People. People she loved. She told the beads of them in her head. Her mother's hugs. Her father squeezing her shoulder at the door to the bakery, the day she started her first job. Her grandmother, smiling at her. That moment when she and Vi and Célie won their junior competition, the first all-female team to win the internationals.

Places. Beautiful places. The Seine in the evening, when they were dancing on the quays. The illumination of the Louvre and Notre-Dame and the lights of the bridges on the waters.

Hands settled on her shoulders, big and strong, massaging them.

She lowered her hands slowly from her face, under that firm, deep rub, and met his eyes in the mirror.

114

He gazed at her a straight, almost brooding moment. "Shh." His voice dropped deep and gentle. "Shh, Lina. It's okay."

Her body relaxed under the words, the tension releasing first where his hands held her and an ease seeping down from there through the rest of her.

He pulled her back against him. His hands rubbed the terry cloth of her bathrobe against her ribs slowly, slowly, until her weight sank against his chest and her breathing slowed under the gentle pleasure. Only then did he stroke up her body to cup her breasts.

She closed her eyes. But then she had to peek.

His gaze had lowered in the mirror, no longer on her face but watching the reflection of his hands against her breasts. The multiple shadings of gold and brown of his hands, against the white of her robe. Big, lean, tough, capable hands. Rubbing that cloth.

She drew her lower lip under her teeth as pleasure sighed from his hands all through her body, and the world fell away.

He rubbed there until her hips were twisting against the arousal of his body behind her. Until she was biting her lip and arching back against him. Only then did he rub his fingers under those panels, to touch her nipples with a callused, sure touch.

Exactly like her fantasy. But his fingers felt so much better than hers. Stranger, hotter, harder, the demand for her body from someone else, not just herself.

She made a little mewling sound and gripped his hips behind her, her head back against his chest.

His fingers trailed down over her breastbone, down the center line of her belly. Her breath stopped. Her head pressed back hard into him.

He pulled the bathrobe tie loose, so that the panels fell apart and one long strip of her nakedness was revealed in the mirror. The subtle golden tones of her skin not much paler there than anywhere else, she spent

115

so much time indoors. Dark, intimate curls, framed by bulky white terry cloth.

Lean fingers, variegated gold and speckles of brown, eased just to the start of her curls and stirred the first few.

"You, too, this time," she whispered fiercely. "You, too."

His eyes met hers in the mirror. His fingers stirred a little more deeply into her black curls. "You don't get to choose that, Lina."

Oh, yeah? Really? Because in her experience, men had zero resistance to the potential of sex. Surely she could crack him. She settled her butt more firmly back into his erection and twisted her hips, stretching her arms behind her to try to curve around his butt and pull him in harder.

He slid one arm through the crook of her elbows, tightened, and lifted—locking her arms up behind her. So that she couldn't move them, and she couldn't now properly bridge the distance that hold forced between their pelvises, and she couldn't get away.

She stared at him in the mirror. Stared at *herself*, held prisoner by him with that strip of nakedness from her cleavage down to her toes.

Heat flooded her. She had to bite her lip against a hungry sound that wanted to escape. *Yes. Do what you want to me. Make me come. Please, please, please.*

"You chose what you wanted," he said, and gave a petting push to the panel caught on one nipple, so that it fell free, her breasts thrust up by the way he held her. His fingers trailed over her nipple a moment, enjoying the way it beaded, before he petted down the curve of the underside of her breast and, in drifting, slow, wandering motions, back to the curls between her thighs. "You didn't ask what I wanted."

Lower. She tilted her hips, trying to trick those gold and speckled fingers deeper into her curls. *Lower.* "I asked you how you felt about being used for sex!"

"And how do I feel?" His fingers stroked down to the lips of her sex.

They parted for him at the first kiss of his fingertips.

"You don't know, do you?" His fingers slipped a little deeper, stroking up and down the length of her. "You asked, but you didn't really notice you never got the answer."

Her body felt so hot and heavy. Plump and full, like a peach ripening in a blazing July sun until it was ready to split its skin.

His fingers celebrated lushness. Squeezed all her folds together and ground his hand against her until she made begging sounds.

"I fucking hate it," he said into her ear, holding her eyes, and slid one finger deep inside her.

"Oh, God." She needed to wrap around his body. To hold on. To pull him in. Bigger, harder than his finger. She needed purchase. She needed thrusts.

And she could only hang out there, utterly precarious, caught between him and a mirror that showed them both everything he did. She could see her own moisture, gleaming against his fingers and her thighs. She could see how taut her breasts were, her lips red not from his kisses but from her own teeth.

"And you don't care, do you?" He added a second finger to the first, thrusting them into her deep.

She writhed and tightened her body on his fingers, trying to hold them. "I do," she panted. "I *do*."

"Really? Enough to stop?" His thumb found her clitoris.

"*Oh*." The sensation whiplashed through her. Oh, God, she was so sensitive to his hand. "I—oh, please don't stop. Not yet. Please—"

Please let me come. Everything in the world was all right, while she came.

"Don't worry," he said, rather flatly. "You don't choose a career like mine without a strong streak of masochism."

"But—if—you—hate—it—" She writhed against his thumb with each word. He was merciless with it. He wouldn't let her think.

"Yeah," he said, watching her in the mirror, watching what his thumb did to her, making her take more of it. "I hate it. But I'll tell you something. You're fucking beautiful when you come."

And he pressed his thumb down hard and *made* her. Made her come. Even while he was telling her he didn't want to. He made her come and come, made her see herself there in the mirror, as she lost herself. Made her see the way her hips arched and her sex clung, made her see the way the orgasm tightened all the muscles in her stomach and released them again, in wave after wave, made her see the expressions that twisted across her face, like bliss and agony all blurred together.

Made her see *him*. His eyes glittering, his face taut, merciless. But whether that lack of mercy was for himself or her or both of them she didn't know.

What gorgeous, wonderful visuals. They overwhelmed *everything*, more powerful than blood and bodies, more compulsive, more insistent, more embarrassing, more vivid, wrangling, brawling, demanding *life*.

He made her come until she couldn't anymore. Until she begged him to stop.

And then he picked her up and carried her to her bed. He peeled her bathrobe all away, leaving her completely naked, and came down onto the bed beside her.

Now, she thought. *Now he's going to crack.*

She lifted a knee, parted her legs, turned toward him. *Yes. Use me. Do it. Hard. Make me forget everything again except how that hard body feels in mine.*

He propped himself on one elbow, still fully clothed.

Then he brushed his fingers over that parted invitation between her legs.

Her over-sensitized body jerked at just the touch. She tried to cover her clitoris in self-protection.

He caught her hands. And brushing, brushing, brushing, made her come again.

But he never even unzipped his pants.

Chapter 11

Fuck.

Jake stared down at himself. How had it come to this? Standing in a woman's shower, with his penis in his own hand? It wasn't any effort to make himself come after that mirror episode. He did it almost like a punishment. *That will teach you, you fucking idiot.*

While Lina slept on her bed, a sprawl of naked gold and black curls and the glowing trace of his fingers trailing over her breasts, down her stomach, into her body. That was what he saw, anyway, as if his eyes were blacklight and he was the only one who could see the fluorescent trace of his touch.

A small body, tough. A tight core, strong shoulders and arms and forearms and hands, from her work. He'd bet the grip of those hands would be—

There. Done.

Yeah, he'd known it would only take him thirty damn seconds to come.

Was there anything more fucking lonely and futile?

Take her up on her offer. What are you, an affronted virgin?

So she wants to use you for sex. Like every other woman out there. She said you could use her, too.

It's not like it would be the first time.

He sank his head against her shower wall, deflated both physically and emotionally in this literal anticlimax.

She was so fucking beautiful, inside and out. He didn't believe in whining, but, Jesus—*it wasn't fair.*

He dried himself and wrapped a towel around his waist and went back to her bedroom door.

She slept. Black curls touseled around her face. Innocent.

Peaceful.

Young.

Twenty-six. Eleven years working her butt off, which made her "adult" life the same length as his. He'd joined the Navy at nineteen. She'd apprenticed when she was fifteen.

But she looked younger by the deaths of too many men at his hands, by the deaths of team brothers, by a thousand encounters with explosives and rocket launchers and bullets, by being crouched down under scarce cover as the men who had them pinned down in the dark strafed the earth closer and closer to their location and one of his brothers in arms lay trying not to moan and give their location away beside him, two limbs blown off.

Lina was younger than he was by a million years.

And yet...

She was older by a century than what she had been just two weeks before. Older and younger both. This new person—the person she was now after someone had tried to kill the person she was before—was only a few days old.

Yeah.

Grief squeezed him, that she hadn't stayed innocent. That no matter how many deaths stained him, he hadn't been posted as a sniper that day on the rooftop across from her restaurant, to add two more lives to the weight on his soul before they burst through the restaurant's back door to burden hers instead.

It was his job, to keep people like her safe. It had been his job to keep this whole battle entirely out of her country, and his own, but even though all the teams were being stretched to their absolute limit, somehow they were still failing at that.

He should go, shouldn't he? Or at least get dressed. Go do his job. No rest for the weary.

He leaned a shoulder in the doorway and sighed. *Don't be an idiot.*

But she was so damn pretty. Too small for war, and yet she'd gone to war anyway, when her people were threatened. Used the weapons she had to hand—that damn liquid nitrogen and her own body, throwing herself at her fucking asshole cousin's legs, to try to take him down.

And now—God, the way she sought life. Making her desserts. As he'd sat there pretending to concentrate on a book discussing suicide—*thanks a lot, Mark*—she'd about wrung his heart out of his body, with those beautiful, fragile things she kept making over and over. Every time one broke, because it was *impossible* for something that fragile and beautiful to exist, she had just gone right on to the next one, adjusting her technique in ways he couldn't tell.

Until eventually they had stopped breaking. They had shone perfectly.

And once she had them perfect, she'd fed one to him.

Making life. Making something beautiful. Giving it to others.

He'd never done that. He fought for her life, and for her right to make beautiful things, but he'd never made anything beautiful himself. Hell, the last time he had *made* anything to give someone pleasure was probably some flower pot for his mom in grade school.

Of course Lina was going to seize on sex as another way to seize on life. Talk about the two most potent biological drives to life right there—food and sex. He sure as hell had done it, back from missions. Hell, he'd done it as a nineteen- and twenty-year-old before he ever even got sent into combat, just from the pure, cocky joy of the feast of women that had opened up before him as his body and the way he carried himself changed in the first two years of intense training.

He lov—he *admired* that about her, that instinct to life. The way she chased those demons back down into the hellhole where they belonged. And he fucking hated those demons for having opened up that hellhole inside her, one that she might try to cap with a heavy lid, but which she would always, forever after, have in her.

Okay, so go now already. Don't just stand here watching her sleep. That's not helping you out.

But he straightened from the door and his feet took him the opposite way of what he told them, right up to her bed. He picked up her bathrobe and spread it over her like a blanket, then sat down on the edge of the bed.

She lay on her stomach, one knee drawn up, black hair and golden skin against the warm, rich pattern of her comforter. And his heart just kept swelling up bigger and bigger until he was surprised it didn't settle down on the bed like an enormous blimp and crush them both.

His hand stretched out of its own volition to trace her shoulder.

She startled awake, hand jerking up to strike, body flinching back.

Idiot. A sleep without nightmares was going to be very hard to come by for her, for a long time. It was one of the things she was using him for, right? To sink into oblivion.

He kept his voice deep and easy. "It's just me."

Her eyes focused on him in the low light of the late summer evening.

She drew a breath, and the tension eased out of her.

That was nice. That he eased the tension out of her.

Given that his entire life had been devoted to keeping people safe, it was nice to see it work in person. Mostly in person he only got to see the people his presence terrorized. Break into a compound in the middle of the night, covered in weapons and night goggles, to arrest all the men in the place, and you tended to terrorize. Somehow, at nineteen when he'd signed up, he'd thought he would only scare bad guys. And that bad guys weren't really human.

Lina's gaze settled on his bare torso. He tightened his muscles subtly to try to leave a lasting impression.

She managed to get that last bit of panic stuffed down into the tight spot in her middle where she must keep it—he knew it well—and her mouth eased. "I love your skin," she said, stretching out her hand to rest on his belly.

A little twitch ran through his body at the touch—the first one he had allowed—but otherwise he managed to keep himself pretty steady. "I like yours, too." He traced her shoulder again, the smooth gold. Resilient skin. Skin that could handle a beating from the sun.

His own skin kept mentioning to him, *You know I was designed for a rainy, northern island, right? Why the hell do you keep taking me to the Middle East?*

"Has anybody ever tried to kiss every single one of your freckles?" she asked, spreading her fingers against him, her eyes tracing him in fascination.

The shock of that thought tightened his whole body. Oh, shit, this was not going to end well for him. "There must be a million." He tried to make his voice dismissive. Casual. *We're just hooking up for sex.* That kind of casual.

A sparkle of sensual mischief in her eyes that just slipped right between the folds of his towel and grabbed him down there like he'd never taken the edge off in the shower. "I bet I've placed a million sea salt flakes precisely in my life. I'm pretty patient and thorough."

Hell. The helplessly hungry vision of that lithe, strong body and that pretty heart face curling up close to him, slowly, thoroughly pressing kisses to every millimeter of his body. She carved her demons out of ice and fought them with a chainsaw. She turned them into sugar and made them do what she wanted. How was he supposed to withstand her?

Her fingers shifted over his skin, and he looked down at them against his flat belly as she gently pressed one of his darker freckles and then another and another.

Oh, hell. *This is why you should have gone. Before she started messing you up even worse.*

124

"They're so intangible," she murmured, fascinated. "I love how they don't have any texture at all beyond smooth skin. It's like I'm trying to catch moonlight."

Whereas he'd always expected her skin to be smooth. Gold and warm under his hands. And it had been.

"Knowing me, I probably could freckle just from moonlight," he said ruefully.

She laughed, curling closer to him on the bed, the bathrobe slipping a little on her body. "I think the sun is obsessed with you. She's got some pathological need to keep touching you." Her eyes met his, wry and self-deprecating. "Kind of like me."

Another shock through his whole body. He found it hard to breathe again. Damn it, his initial instincts to tighten his ab muscles against a sucker punch whenever she approached had been spot on. "Obsessed with me?"

"Surely you noticed?" Still self-deprecating.

"I thought you said anybody would do."

She winced, and her body tightened a little in on itself, her hand falling back to the comforter.

Idiot. But—"Well," he challenged, overriding his own brain telling him to shut up, "wouldn't they?"

She rolled away from him, pulling her knees up, her face growing stubborn. And a little desperate.

Oh, shit, shut up, Jake. It's not her fault. You of all people should understand.

You could understand someone's actions and still suffer from them, though. Especially if you were an idiot.

Her eyebrows started to crinkle together. She rolled suddenly back in his direction to search his face. "You hate it?"

He probably should have a rule that when he was hurt and desperately sexually frustrated he just kept his damn mouth shut. He looked down at the comforter, running his thumb over it, planning on keeping his damn mouth shut. "Yes," he heard himself say.

Her eyebrows knit more deeply. "But...why didn't you say no?"

He gave a minute shrug of one shoulder. "I might have a tiny case of hero-worship." Tiny, yeah, right.

She pulled back, her face crumpling in utter bafflement. "On *me*?"

That pissed him off. He met her eyes. "Yeah, on you. What, did you even look at yourself in the mirror just now?"

Her lips parted. She flushed and gripped the bathrobe to make sure it was covering her. "That's not *heroism*."

"Yeah," he said, increasingly pissed. "It is." He grabbed her hand, where the spots of healing skin showed from the cold burns she had received punching a terrorist after her nitrogen soaked his sweatshirt. "Someone—a *family member*—tried to kill you and the people you love. And in response, you're seizing life with both hands. Driving death away. That's heroism."

Not to mention fighting terrorists with a damn bucket of liquid nitrogen and her own body. No body armor, nothing but flesh and bone.

She wrapped her arms around her knees under the bathrobe, looking vulnerable and confused.

"What did you think it was?"

"Escape," she said. "It makes me feel really alive. And I stop thinking."

Yeah. Tenderness softened him. Jesus, the emotional place this whole thing left him in. Fascinated by her, just starting in on the flirting that he'd hoped would lead to more, and—bam. Used for sexual release. As if all those women from when he was a stupid-ass twenty-year-old had finally brought their karma back on him with a vengeance.

He smoothed one of her curls off her face, despite himself. "They're not mutually exclusive."

"Heroism and escaping?" she said wryly.

126

TRUST ME

His palm opened to curve against her cheek. "You live to fight another day," he reminded her.

Her eyes flickered.

"Not literally fight," he said quickly. *Idiot!* "That's why you've got these guards on you."

Her expression schooled itself to neutrality. He had a very bad feeling that she was imagining the waste a suicide bomb could make of him, her guards, possibly her friends or innocent civilians in the area, and her all together. He tugged one curl of hair sharply to shatter the thought. *Don't go there.* At least she couldn't see what that would actually look like.

He could.

"But what you do every day when you go back in those kitchens and make something ridiculously beautiful again. That kind of fighting," he said. It made him want to kiss her just thinking about it.

Yeah, but if he started kissing her on the mouth, he'd get too emotionally involved and...Jesus, now he felt like he should star in *Pretty Woman.*

She gazed at him a long moment. Her face crumpled again. "You should *not* be having sex with me if you hate it. That's screwed up, for one thing. And it makes me feel yucky."

"*Hate* is maybe too simple a word for a very complex feeling."

Her nose crinkled in a way that was so kissable it was killing him. "You mean, like you want it, but you hate yourself for it? Like something kinky?"

One of his eyebrows went up involuntarily. He tilted his head, scanning her from curly black head to the tip of her toes—chipped polish, like someone who had last kept her toenails all pretty a couple of weeks ago and now could barely remember them. Yep, he'd definitely gone insane, because it kind of made him wish he knew how to paint toenails, so he could set her feet on his thigh and do them for her. "Is there something kinky you find intriguing?"

Her face crinkled more in confusion. "Isn't this kinky?"

He laughed out loud. His hand pressed his belly as it burst out of him, the laughter out of nowhere almost a painful pleasure. He shook his head, trying not to laugh so long he offended her. "You might have a narrower range of kinky than I do."

She looked a little worried.

He found himself stretching out on the bed beside her, as he got lured into greater and greater intimacy, despite every instinct for self-preservation. Granted, he didn't have many such instincts, but *emotionally* he usually did. "Don't worry," he said, amused and possessive and gentle and all those crazy, dangerous things at once. He rested his hand on her hip. "I won't do anything you don't want."

"Well, no, I know *that*," she said.

He smiled a little, relieved by her growing trust in him. When she'd said that thing about waterboarding, it had hurt like hell. He was used to women and children being scared of him, especially when their team didn't have a female MP or interpreter along to help reassure them, but he'd never learned to like it.

"That's why I showed you that rose," she said, a little glint in her eye. "So you'd understand the possible consequences of trying to do anything I don't want."

He started to laugh again, which was quite a feat on her part, given that the image she was evoking was of his cock shattered in small frozen pieces like those rose petals. "I'm fairly warned."

She grinned at him.

Shit, this was getting too cute. This was hellishly unfair behavior by a woman who was just using him for sex.

But he found himself curving his hand around hers anyway, playing with her fingers. *Because you're an idiot*, he reminded himself.

Fools rush in...

128

She sure would make a nice angel, though. One of those naughty, fallen angels who hadn't quite lost all her memories of innocence but who had developed a taste for black feathers and messing with poor mortals.

Her gaze drifted over his body in a way that made him feel glad he was only wearing a towel. Nice to show off. "You are quite honestly the hottest man I have ever seen," she said and shook her head wonderingly.

Well, now, *that* was nice to know.

"How do you get such a great body?"

"They don't feed me enough in the Navy." He tried for pitiful. Hell, it worked for Chase.

She smiled at him. "Want me to make you something?"

Actually, he'd been thinking he might want to get over his affronted virgin issues and curve his hand over her hip and pull her in a little closer. But his mouth opened and closed as the idea ran through him. He'd loved the way she had fed him tastes in her kitchen, as if she just couldn't stand to leave his mouth bored while hers was having so much fun. It made him feel vulnerable, like he could get too used to having someone beautiful in his life, but he'd loved it just the same.

His thumb ran over her knuckles. "Really?"

She laughed at him. "Of course *really*. What do you think I love to do most in the world?"

See, the problem with giving a woman multiple orgasms and then starting to regret he hadn't taken advantage of the opportunity himself was that she had a bit of a head start on him. Shower or not, he wasn't sure that *food* was his priority yet. He loved to eat and all, but it wasn't what he loved to do *most* in the world. Still, her food was special. Nearly as pretty and defiantly gallant as she was.

"Hey, will you meet my eyes now, when you see me at the hospital?" he asked, tightening his hold on her fingers.

Color climbed up her cheeks, burnishing the gold. "It feels different, out in the open."

Yeah, because he was her kinky sex. Did she hate herself for it afterward?

The idea hurt, but he still had to smother another chuckle at her belief that anything they'd done could possibly be classified as kinky. That remained hilarious. He wondered if he would still be teasing her about it on their tenth ann—

What the fuck?!

He rolled out of bed abruptly. Grabbed his towel before it could fall and expose him even further. "I'd better go."

She blinked, startled. And then stiffened a little. "Oh, right, sorry. Getting too intimate?"

Yeah, but...she made it sound as if *he* was the one using her for sex. Not as if he was a war weary soldier just trying to keep himself from ending up one miserable, heartbroken bastard.

She sat up, drawing up her knees, the bathrobe slipping enough to give him a quick glimpse of her naked body before she caught it.

A whooshing slide of that view through him. And then of the corrected view, her covered up with that bulky white bathrobe but all naked behind it, brown eyes on him. Trusting and wary both at once.

You know, there's an easy way to break the cycle of meaningless sex. Walk away.

Leave her struggling alone to deal with this horrible thing that happened to her, when she asked you for help the only way she knew how.

"Why did you come by?" she asked.

Because I couldn't keep away? "To check on you."

"Were there more death threats?"

Both the women who had been on the scene got far more death threats than any of the male chefs. Part of that was because Vi was head chef and Lina was head

130

pastry chef, the positions of greatest power, but most of it was because they were women.

And Lina's Muslim heritage had made her a particular magnet for the crazies. The kind of fanatic who could throw acid in a little girl's face for going to school considered Lina's courage and strength and successful resistance to fanaticism a denial of their very right to exist. Which it was. And on the other side, the kind of crazy who thought all Muslims should be burned alive and their countries carpet bombed—oblivious to the fact that their country might be, say, France—had gone hysterical over her and their conviction she must have been in on it all along.

"Nothing credible," he said. They sure were following a lot of rats back to their IP addresses, though. RAID and GIGN were conducting sweeping raids, and his own government had covert ops throughout Europe doing all kinds of things they couldn't legally do. He was glad at the chance to be here by her side, but it still made him restless that his team had been sidelined and couldn't take much more than a symbolic part in some of those. The curse of why a guy like him couldn't retire so easily— it was that damn hard to leave the fighting in someone else's hands.

She tried to keep covered by the bathrobe as she stood, and he tried to look politely away, but as she got her arms back into the bathrobe and belted it around her, glimpses of her body showed. And his gaze kept being drawn back to them, even as he kept his head turned.

You said no to that? What the hell is wrong with you?

He was an emotional coward was what he was. He saw clearly that she was going to batter his heart bloody and leave it for roadkill, and he kept trying to find a safe way around the ambush. Effective weapons. Body armor. *Something.*

Meanwhile, the only safe way out of this was to turn around and not take the road through the ambush in the first place. The damn road was doubtless mined to hell.

She got her robe belted and looked at him again, directly, holding his eyes. "So you didn't have a real reason for coming by."

Well...he bit back on the urge to tell her she needed to take a closer look at herself in the mirror, if she thought a man didn't have a *real reason* to come to her apartment. *Not productive. Try something else.* He pinched his eyebrows, trying to think of something else.

She watched him. That kind of steady *go ahead and admit it* gaze that reminded him that in her own field, she was a commander, used to leading and controlling men—people—in high stress situations. Not as stressful normally as bullets, but those French culinary *artistes* she had to lead might not be as good at going calm under pressure as his own teams were, either, who knew? Maybe they were all emotional and Gallic all the time, and she was the calm under pressure.

Under that gaze, heat started to climb his cheeks. Fuck. The trick to keeping his redhead blushing tendencies under control, he'd learned by eighteen, was to turn off the emotions behind it, but somehow under that brown gaze, those emotions just kept boiling up.

"Ah," she said very softly. A faint and somehow very *womanly* smile curved her lips. "I see." She played with the tie of her bathrobe.

His face felt on fire. Hell, if this was as bad as his blushing used to be in high school, it might even be spreading down his neck to his chest. "Look, I've really got to go."

She performed a fragile pout. "And leave me all alone and defenseless?"

He gave her a dirty look. That was a fucking low blow. She had her guards, but he still hated to leave her, every time.

"I was kidding." She turned away. "I'm fine."

Yeah, right. That was why she was asking a stranger for sex. She was so fucking fine.

He gazed at her back in some temper. Straight, slim, strong shoulders. He wanted to walk forward and start massaging them again.

It would hardly be helpful for her if he told her, *You are clearly not fine.* He shoved his hand through his short hair. A lot of men in special ops turned themselves into shaggy bearded creatures, but he had had no desire to start looking like some male version of Orphan Annie. So his look now, in Europe, wasn't that different from his look for most of his military career. Close-cut. Contained.

"You're amazing," he said honestly. There, that was true. It was even constructive.

She stilled with her back to him and bent her head a little. Then angled it enough to glance at him over her shoulder, her face crinkling in that doubtful, searching way.

He shrugged. "I'm not the first to tell you that, sweetheart. I won't be the last either. I can guarantee you'll be getting some kind of medal."

"Oh, I know," she said dryly. "The chance to prove they don't think all Muslims are terrorists will be too good to pass up."

He frowned at her. "Okay, try your best to snap out of the paranoia. Vi will get a medal, too. Possibly several others on your team."

She turned around. "It's rather difficult not to be paranoid just at this second."

He softened. "I know, sweetheart. But one moment you're thinking we're going to waterboard you and the next that you'll only get a medal as some diversity symbol, and neither one of those are a remotely true perspective on who you are and who intelligent people think you are. Or how we operate. Lina...we've been fighting terrorists a long time. We're not airport security, and we're not idiot political pundits. We know we can't just profile our way to a solution because that *doesn't fucking work.*"

133

"Abed was my cousin," she said tensely.

"That's why we say people like you are on the front line of this battle," Jake said quietly. Before, he'd always wanted to ask journalists who used that term, or who claimed that the war was being fought over women's bodies, if they'd like to experience what an actual front line in a battle was like and an actual war being fought over your body. Your buddies' bodies. But...here she was. The front line had quite literally been her.

She studied him, reluctant, unpersuaded.

Was he going to have to start sharing personal details of his life now? Grow more intimate with and more exposed to a woman who had performed the most unique cock-block ever—interrupting his attempts to flirt with her by asking him if she could just use him for sex?

"One of my cousins is in jail for life for getting in a shoot out with cops who tried to break up his meth lab and severely wounding one of them." He spoke as evenly as he could about this subject. "I had an uncle who was a preacher who played with poisonous snakes, went into public raptures where he claimed God was speaking through him, and told his followers women should keep their heads covered and be submissive and they should refuse all modern medicine for themselves and their children. He killed kids with that shit. Trust me, my country has plenty of religious fanatics who self-identify as normal all while thinking things like if a woman has a position of authority she has weakened her womanhood and weakened the manhood of the men who 'let her' have that position of authority. I'd hear that shit on television or in churches all the time where I lived. But of course we have plenty of Americans who think that stuff is batshit crazy, too. See how that works?"

Lina's expression was ironic, as if she'd seen how that worked all her life.

"So I'd profile if it was helpful, but mostly we've found it very difficult to use skin color or religion to tell us the difference between a radical and a normal human being. You can either go for the carpet bomb approach, the one where you treat an entire group of people as if they're of no more value than a bowl of candy you can throw out to protect yourself, and I can tell you flat out that you'll make a hell of a lot more enemies with that one. You kill an innocent person's kids with your careless bomb, and he will devote every breath he takes for the rest of his life to destroying you."

Jake would, certainly.

She watched him unblinkingly, her eyebrows drawn slightly together.

It made him impatient, frustrated, as if he was facing some damn soldier-turned-politician who hadn't seen action in two decades but was going to still force his idea of what war was like in the Vietnam era down the chain of command onto them. "Or you can do what we've found to be the most effective—hunt for terrorists through individual patterns of behavior and contacts rather than tarring everyone with one brush. But I've only devoted my entire career to this business, why the hell listen to me?"

Lina gazed at him a long moment. He gazed back, because he didn't in the least feel like looking away and therefore yielding to her insulting opinion of his intelligence and prejudices. Well, maybe it wasn't his intelligence and level of prejudice personally, but he did get the sense sometimes that she was...tarring him with one brush.

Because she was paranoid now. Yeah. Of course. And that wave of tenderness washed back over him, and he just wanted to pull her into his arms and make her feel as if everything would be okay.

What would it have been like if he'd done that, when she first asked him for sex? If, instead of taking her up on it, he'd just held her and petted her and given her strength and reassurance in a more intimate and more dangerous way?

One corner of her lips finally crooked up. Her eyes crinkled just a little. "Do you really have that weird a family?"

"Oh, hell, yeah." It had been part of his motivation to get away. The determination not to be them had carried him through the brutal trials by cold and exhaustion of BUD/S. He let his lips crook back at her. "And you can't talk."

She almost had to laugh at that.

Which he felt pretty damn proud of, as he went back to the bathroom to reclaim the feeble armor of actual clothes.

Chapter 12

Jake Adams sure did run fast when things started to get intimate, didn't he? Lina thought the next day as she spread a pastry cream infused with orange blossom water on a crust of ground walnuts and almond flour that had been lightly sweetened with date sugar, combined with a faint hint of cinnamon.

She should have been offended, and possibly she was, but what was a hot affair without a dose of angst?

It might be terribly French of her, but she'd take being the woman in a screwed up love affair over being the woman in a screwed up terrorist plot *any* day.

She made the pastry cream as erotic as she could. As lush and full of sensual promise as was humanly possible. Her hands were starting to warm after her latest bout with a recalcitrant dragon. She'd finally gotten the damn thing to fly upright, but when she tried to make it roar it looked as if it was sticking its tongue out at her. Either that or trying to "French" kiss her, which probably just about figured for a French dragon.

(Meanwhile, maybe her dragon could give a certain American a few lessons in kissing. Because he hadn't kissed her once. That would teach her to get involved with someone from a country so hung up about kissing they had to blame even that on the French.)

She sliced barhi dates so fine each slice was translucent. They were in the rutab stage at this time of year, only partially yellow, crisp like an apple. Later they would get softer, sweeter, more mellow, earning their honeycream nickname. But she wanted to try them now. Be the first pastry chef in Paris to truly exploit all that dates could be, in all their stages.

She placed each translucent slice carefully at an angle to the riverlike curving base of cream and gazed at that, dissatisfied. Maybe more fanciful? The slices

137

arranged like a flower here at the edge, just so, a blossom of difference, of the unexpected. For the vast majority of her clients, the first time they ever bit into a date at this stage of maturity would be at her tables.

If she got the chance. The restaurant was going to stay closed through August, the traditional vacation month for non-tourist restaurants anyway, which would leave only a very short window for barhi dates in this stage to still be available.

She gazed at her dessert, frustrated by how sweet it looked. How smooth. It looked like a damn lie.

She poured a sheet of caramelized sugar, let it harden, and then smashed it, picking the shards of it and sticking them at dangerous angles into the base of custard cream where they glowed with amber in the light.

Better. Now she needed to do something completely different with the original flowing river form of the base and with the barhi date flower, though.

Her cell phone rang. She glanced at the screen, didn't recognize the number, and ignored it. Her publicist was supposed to field media requests, but sometimes they got hold of her private number. Or some crazy did. But it was amazing how fast the media moved on to the next thing. From fifty people outside her apartment the first two days, to thirty, to a dozen. This morning, she hadn't spotted *anybody*.

She was still getting requests for interviews, of course, especially from the bigger and more serious outlets that wanted to do something in-depth, and she was still torn about whether she should eventually accept one. She didn't *want* to be some kind of representative of all Muslim women—hell, since she didn't really practice, there were plenty of people who claimed she shouldn't be calling herself Muslim in the first place, this eternal damned-if-you-do damned-if-you-don't that having an ethnic identity left a woman in. But at the same time, she felt some obligation to use the role thrust on her to make the world see a little more of the vast range of individuality that a *"beurette"* could have. Maybe she could give her opinion on the damn burkini question.

But mostly, right now, she just couldn't handle it. Couldn't handle talking about what had happened on television or even for print, couldn't handle facing probing give-us-the-gory-details questions from people dying to imagine how horrible it had been. So she ignored the call.

A knock on the back door of the restaurant. She froze for a long moment before she remembered she didn't just have to open it blindly and called the number of her police guards. "It's Jake Adams," the policeman who answered said. "Do you want to let him in, or...?"

Oh, hell, yeah. Sexy, complicated feelings for a guy who walked out as soon as the mood started to grow too sweet and trusting?

Bring it on.

She yanked open the door, giving him a huge smile of delight.

He paused just a second, framed by the light, looking down at her. "You are so fucking unfair to me," he muttered, and moved in, pushing her in front of him— "Excuse me, ma'am"—and to the side as he shut the door.

Had he just been rudely shoving, or was he using his body automatically to block her from any line of fire as he moved her out of it?

Fuck, she was so paranoid. But...hard to imagine Jake pushing her around gratuitously.

"Ma'am?" She raised an eyebrow at him.

One corner of his mouth curled as he realized what he'd said. "I apologize for being polite."

She took a deep breath of lusciously dirty pleasure as she imagined him saying *excuse me, ma'am* with that same polite firmness as he took over her body some other way. *Excuse me, ma'am,* as his thumb settled right over her—

aSummon

"Oh, no need to apologize." She tried to make her voice a sexy purr, as she moved back to her counter, untying her apron as she went, but she was afraid her voice sounded more like a brook burbling with delight.

Oh, yeah, she liked how fast her body had set up a certain pattern of expectations. He showed up, and that meant hot sex.

Mmm.

Instead of, say, guns and death and violence.

She folded her apron and set it on the counter, but going straight to unbuttoning her chef's jacket seemed a little brazen. Rude even, like she wasn't even going to bother to talk to him first.

Like she was using him just for sex.

Which he hated.

In a masochistic way.

She frowned and turned back around to consider him. He sure did know how to complicate a simple situation, didn't he?

She broke into a grin. Good for him. She might have wanted to keep things simple the first time, but today...well, life *was* complicated.

That was the great thing about life.

"Will you quit looking at me like you're happy to see me?" Jake said irritably. "It's messing with my head."

She held up a chiding finger. "You have a problem with intimacy."

He stopped dead, staring at her as his lips parted and closed. "*I* have a problem with intimacy?"

"It's okay," she said reassuringly.

"I should hope so," he said dryly. "Since the accusation is coming from a woman who is *just using me for sex.*"

"Oh, *as if* that's not every man's fantasy," she scoffed, to cover uneasiness.

"That's a self-fulfilling prophecy if I ever heard one. If you typically use men for sex, I'm willing to bet you don't have many relationships with men who want more than just sex, do you?"

She frowned at him, folding her arms over her chest. "You're an exception."

"Hoo-rah," he said, deadpan.

"I mean—" She waved her hand. "This is an exceptional situation." She frowned more deeply at him. *And you know why.*

"Yes, I think you've made clear what's exceptional here, and it's not me." He prowled around the room, but then came back to her counter as if she held him on a leash and he couldn't get away.

The idea fascinated her. He pulled *her* as if he had her lassoed in silk, and she pulled him, too?

Maybe she was yanking him too hard, then, or something, because he acted far more restless on his leash than she felt on hers. She *liked* being pulled in sure and strong to him. He promised all kinds of yumminess if she yielded to his temptation.

He glowered down at her, but the glower slowly faded into something more serious, that straight, steady gaze of his. His callused thumb touched lightly under her eye. "Not sleeping?"

Damn that stupid concealer. She lifted her chin. "Like a baby."

"Waking up every fifteen minutes screaming?"

Pretty much. She frowned at him very hard. "I was up all night watching a *Lord of the Rings* marathon."

Fantastical violence that came from evil orcs not other human beings. Honor, courage, hope against sadness, and good won out. Also Viggo Mortenson.

Plus, anything was better than falling asleep. And having nightmares in which her body moved slow, slow, slow, while the muzzle of a gun lifted, pointing at Vi. The person lifting the gun was never a stranger—it was

141

LAURA FLORAND

always someone she trusted, turned into horror. Her father. A favorite teacher from childhood. The pastry chef who had first taken her on as apprentice. Jake, this last time.

She never knew who the attack would come from in the nightmare, but the rest stayed the same. Her body never could move fast enough, no matter how desperately she tried, and then there was Vi, blood all over her, on the floor, and—

Warm hands slid over her shoulders, squeezing them.

She blinked back into focus on that hard face, on the brown speckles scattered amid the layering of shades on his skin. As if Van Gogh had decided to do his impressions of gold that day and used Jake's skin as a canvas.

She reached up to trace his cheekbone on a wave of that whimsy his skin always evoked in her, as if she would feel the dots of paint. But no. All smooth, even his jaw fresh-shaven.

"Did you just shave?" *For me?* The idea utterly charmed her. Him shaving at three in the afternoon, maybe to impress her?

"I just got up."

She blinked. She'd slept until noon herself, but she hadn't fallen asleep until somewhere in Mordor after dawn broke outside. Middle Earth had been growing darker and darker, and the light had shown through her window, and she'd finally drifted off, dreaming for a little that she was the fallen head of a statue with flowers curling across her brow. Then Sam in her dream got possessed by the Ring and started firing an AK-47 at her and Frodo. "*Lord of the Rings* marathon, too?"

"Something like that," he said mildly, inscrutable.

She frowned a little, her hand still curved against his cheek, thinking about what he did for a living. Well, he never actually said what he did for a living, but his team's cover had been blown ten days ago, at least as far

142

as the Au-dessus staff was concerned. She knew. And he knew she knew.

He just couldn't break his country's need for deniability and say it out loud.

"Is everything okay?" she asked.

"Routine."

Also, she was herself related to a terrorist, meaning he could have particular concerns about information she might let slip if he told her anything. "You know, I would *never* say anything that would put you more at risk," she said suddenly. Her palm pressed against his cheek.

His expression changed. Searching. Easing open. "Why, thank you, sweetheart," he said very quietly, his hands rubbing her shoulders.

She felt that delicate heat touch her cheeks. "I don't blame you for not trusting me, but I wouldn't."

He kept rubbing her shoulders. "It's not a question of trust. Men aren't even allowed to tell their wives what's going on. Because it's the silly slips that betray a mission. Maybe you call your mom and say you're coming over for dinner after all because you got stood up last minute. Maybe she mentions to someone else that she's worried about this guy you're seeing, and how he just stood you up without explanation again. Maybe someone else overhears that conversation and puts two and two together."

"My mom doesn't know about you," Lina said, horrified. Her mom might have taught her about contraceptives long ago and how to make up her own mind and not let the pressure of some man make it up for her, but that didn't mean she needed to know Lina was having a just-for-sex affair. That was *way* too much information.

Jake's expression closed. His hands fell from her shoulders as he drew back. "Understood."

Lina gazed at him, a little at a loss. Did he *want* to know her family?

Jake shifted a step down the length of the counter to study her current dessert experiments instead of look at her. The smooth, golden, riveresque S-curve of the first one, with its flower of date slices. A second version, the same curve pierced with shards of amber sugar-glass. The third one, the river cut at the middle and the two sides separated by three centimeters, each with only one shard of sugar-glass, there at the point of separation, like two guillotine blades that had cut one half of the river from the other.

His lips twisted. He looked back at her.

"Would you like to taste the cream?" Lina tried again to make her voice seductive, promising. *Would you like to taste this erotic, lush promise of deliciousness?*

His breath released from him in a sigh of surrender. "Sure." He sounded like a man who had given up hope of rescue.

Seriously, he had the most offensive reactions to her desserts sometimes. "Don't let me force you," she said coolly.

"No. You're not forcing me. I can say no."

O...kay. Seriously, what was she? Crack or something?

She dipped a clean spoon in the leftover cream, trying to figure out if that was a good or bad thing to be.

Crack was bad. But being so addictive he couldn't say no to her felt pretty damn hot, too.

Of course, crack ruined people's lives.

Nope. That's melodrama. From here on out, on a one to ten scale of ruining someone's life, if ten is bursting into a woman's kitchens with suicide bombs and machine guns, then luring a single guy into an affair is a...minus one thousand.

"Have some cream," she said firmly and offered it to his lips.

Hazel eyes glinted just a little as he looked down at her over the spoon, but he parted his lips and let her slip

144

TRUST ME

the cream between them. His hand rose and closed around her wrist. "That's beautiful. Fresh and lightly sweet and with this taste to it that's almost like a scent in the air. It's what you must have been like just two weeks ago."

She met his eyes.

He winced a little, as if just realizing he shouldn't have said that last part out loud. "I mean—what you still are like, of course," he said, but the words sounded lame to both of them.

She took pity on them both and held a date slice up to his lips. "I bet you'll never guess what this is."

"It's not dates?"

Oh. "You've had them like this before?" she said, disappointed.

"I've spent a fair amount of time in Iraq and Syria."

Oh. Oh, right. At war.

She'd never been to Syria at all, even though her mother's mother came from there. She had visited Algeria and neighboring countries as a tourist with a deep culinary curiosity, and she had met up with some second cousins one trip, but that was really the extent of her knowledge of the Maghreb and the Middle East. From his own troubling perspective—an enemy on foreign soil—he probably knew a great deal more about the regions some of her ancestors came from than she did.

"Plus, there's a branch of them right there." He nodded to the branch behind her on the other side of the counter's L, thickly clustered with yellowing dates.

She was pretty sure most people in Paris wouldn't recognize fresh, half-ripe dates on the branch, but oh, well. She handed him the slice anyway, still disappointed.

"Thank you," he said quietly and bit into it. "You shouldn't be so sweet to me, you know."

145

What? "Why not?" She held up a hand. "You weren't serious about that masochism thing, were you? Because I'm not into that."

He let out his breath. "I know. You're just a human being caught in something you should never have been caught in and dealing with it the best way you can." He proffered the other half of his date slice to her lips. Hers parted in surprise—only another chef usually tried to tempt *her* with flavors—and he slipped the sweet, fresh crunchiness into her mouth. "Don't worry about me." He dropped his hand to cover hers. "I can handle myself."

Well, *that* was obvious. It was probably his life mantra. *I handle myself. And anything else the world comes up with, too.*

"I can handle myself, too," she said, just as quietly, just as firmly. Violence might have been a shock to her world, but she was the head pastry chef of a two-star kitchen. She'd climbed her way to this point from a fifteen-year-old girl in *banlieue* who needed to work for a living. She could and did handle everything and ran her crew as tightly as any elite Navy team. She'd handle this violence, too. It might just take her a few days.

"I know," Jake said. "I can see you doing it."

Did handling herself mean she had to stay strong and not yield to that desire to just press her body into his and ask him to hold her until she could sleep again?

Probably. Sex sounded more...proactive than just asking for a big hug. More taking charge. Less helpless.

Although the way he did it, she was pretty helpless.

She looked down at the counter, at his hand on hers, and flicked a glance up through her lashes at him. "I wish..."

That I hadn't been so panicked and grabby, when you started flirting with me. That I'd let things develop naturally. That she hadn't gone straight past appetite and hunger to gorging herself on some cheap snack because she didn't trust food—or anything—to be there later.

146

His fingers curled around her hand, turning it sideways so he could rub his thumb against her palm. "I'm granting wishes today. What do you wish?"

She wished they were back on her bed, that moment when he had started playing with her hand. She wished they were right here, with him stroking her palm, asking her what she wished.

"What do *you* want?" she asked softly. Why did he keep coming back if he hated it?

He shook his head, his expression impossibly neutral again.

Her head tilted. She searched his face. "You can't say it?"

He wouldn't have made as good a poker player as he thought. There was a flicker in his eyes, despite his neutral expression. Some kind of tell, but she wasn't sure of what.

"There's something you're afraid of reaching for?" she said slowly, her fingers curling into his palm, holding on.

He tried to pull his hand away. But she'd been grabbing strong male wrists and directing them to *get the damn technique right* so that her desserts went out perfect since she'd first made second pastry chef at a three-star restaurant, at the age of twenty. The strength of her grip clearly surprised him. His eyebrows went up a little, and he looked down at their hands, with that subtly bemused expression he got sometimes, as if he had no idea what to think of her. Or of them.

"What would you be afra—" She stopped. One single act of insane violence had made her afraid to believe in a future.

He must have seen a lot more death than she had. Lives cut short. And no river that continued flowing on the other side after the jolt of it either. He must know lives that were *ended.*

"Do people get hurt a lot in your job?" she asked, which was a ridiculous question. She knew they must.

147

But it was just a mishmash in her head of her own experience and Hollywood films. What was it like *really?*

His expression changed, a tangled attempt to cover incredulity and confusion with neutrality.

She lifted her hand to her lips. "They do, don't they?" And he couldn't understand how she, a civilian, could be so incredibly ignorant of what his normality was.

"Don't worry," he said. And, "Shit." A quick, puzzled search of her eyes. "*Are* you worried about me?"

She was *now.* "Don't do that," she blurted absurdly. "Don't get hurt." Oh, what a *stupid* thing to say.

His expression softened at it, though. His hand rose and very gently tugged one of her curls and then stroked it back behind her ear. "Yes, ma'am."

Tears stung her eyes for no good reason. This *stupid,* fucking world. And up until a week ago, it had been a glorious world, a magical playground of the senses, and all she had to do to embrace it was be willing to work hard.

A big hand stroked her curl around to the back of her head and settled over her nape, massaging gently.

"Sometimes," he said very slowly, gazing at her as if he wasn't sure why these words were coming out of his mouth. "When a guy survives, but he's messed up—he's lost a limb or two, or he's lost his handsome face and he has years of plastic surgery ahead of him—sometimes he comes home from war on a stretcher, and his wife comes in to his hospital room, *their first meeting* since he was wounded, and she drops the divorce papers on his table and runs out."

Lina's lips parted on the shock of that, viscerally nauseating, the image punching her right in the stomach. "*Merde,*" she said. Her mind couldn't process it. "People *do* that kind of thing?"

Quit. Just like that. Not even *trying.*

"Yeah," he said. "It's tough because—" He touched his chest. "We're not made to be quitters."

No. She tried to think what a quitter's personality must be like, but quitters usually, well, quit, after their first few days in a top kitchen, and so she didn't really know any personally.

"If you're on the teams," he said, "it's because you don't quit. Not in any situation. Not for anything. If your arm's blown off, you have a tourniquet on your gear"— he touched the left side of his chest, where that tourniquet must be attached when he was in uniform— "so that you can tie the wound off yourself and not distract your buddies from the firefight. And keep on fighting yourself, if you possibly can."

The shock of that image was almost too great. She had much better visuals of violence now than she had ever had up until ten days ago, and she took a step back under the pressure of what she was imagining, both hands on her cheeks. In kitchens, they worked with badly burned hands and sliced-open fingers and didn't stop for them, so they had the same concept in essence, but the degree of difference was so great it was mind-blowing.

Jake closed his expression tight. "Sorry. Why the hell am I telling you this?" He pivoted away, prowling the kitchen again, a restless predator checking his perimeter in compulsive habit.

Lina took off her chef's jacket and came around the counter.

On his next pass, she reached out and grabbed him. Strong sinews of his forearm under her hand. He stopped for her.

She gazed up at him, not even sure what she was going to say. And then heard herself say, "I got condoms."

A flush immediately hit her cheeks. Okay, that was *not* smooth. But a wave of heat hit her, to have said it, and all that erotic heat was a lovely lure away from thoughts of death and violence. *His* death and violence.

Jake stood still, half-turned away from her, head angled to gaze down at her hand on his arm. He had *fantastic* forearm muscles, her hand couldn't help noticing. And it sent that message of how fantastic they were right up her arm and tickling down into all her erogenous zones.

"Did you?" Jake said evenly. His eyes glinted. He turned them both suddenly, so that his lean, hard body framed hers against the counter, and the hollow of his throat was only a slight lift onto her toes away from her lips. "That was pretty nervy, Lina. Considering what I told you."

"Oh, *come on*," Lina said indignantly. "What man says no to easy sex?"

"How many have you asked?"

She pressed her lips together, narrowing her eyes at him. "That is *not* your business."

The frustrated heat in his eyes suggested he knew that.

"Unless you want to detail all *your* sexual past," she said. Which she very definitely did *not* want to hear.

"Hell, no." He pushed away from her.

She sighed as his body gave her too much space. "Mostly I date a long time first."

At the bottom edge of her peripheral vision, she saw his fist clench by his thigh. "You don't know how flattered I am that you skipped that step with me."

He half turned, but at least he didn't pace away. She watched the way his clenched fist made the muscles of his forearm more pronounced. Her hand started to reach involuntarily in her need to stroke those muscles.

"I don't," he said suddenly, clipped. "Usually date a long time. I usually pick women up in under half an hour."

Oh. "Well, what are you complaining about, then?" she asked indignantly.

He looked down at her without turning. "You I wanted to date."

Chapter 13

Of course Lina lit like a Christmas tree for that one. Instead of looking repelled or something that would at least stonewall him consistently, that heart face brightened up so much, like he was her Christmas mornin—well, maybe not Christmas, in her case, but whatever. Special. "Really?" she said.

She was messing with him *so damn bad.* "Give me a break, Lina. You knew that. As soon as I started flirting with you, you shut me down by asking for sex instead."

"Well, excuse me for being just a little fragile and screwed up right now!" She flung out her hands.

Oh, fuck. "I *do* excuse you." Damn it. Otherwise, he could just run like hell. "And you're not as screwed up as you think," he added. "You're impressing the hell out of me."

She looked incredulous.

"You just don't have a frame of reference, that's all," he said more gently. "You've never dealt with something like this before, or known anyone else dealing with it."

She smiled wryly. "We're going to be our own support group. The kitchen teams."

"That's not a bad idea."

She nodded ruefully, but then she folded her arms and scowled at him. And she would probably be pissed at him for finding that an utterly kissable look on her. "Anyway, it's not so much that I *shut you down.* Maybe it's more like I got greedy. Couldn't wait."

Well, *that* was a very nice thought. He toyed with it, not sure he trusted it.

Still, if that was what she believed now, it kind of reflected well on him, didn't it?

"Also was afraid," she admitted, low and rough.

Bingo.

"But not for any good reason. I'm kind of scared all the time now. But I'm trying."

He sighed in surrender, and just picked her up and set her on the counter, nudging her desserts out of the way. He kept his arms loosely around her, his hands resting on the small of her back, and settled between her spread legs.

Her pupils dilated instantly. Jesus, he'd become her opiate of choice.

A painkiller, Christ.

Which made his current actions that of an enabler, but...shit.

"What kind of condoms?" He kept his voice deep and easy, sneaking his thumb under the edge of her knit shirt and rubbing the small of her back.

Her head arched back a little, and a long breath moved through her body. And, as he watched her, through his, too. "Just, like...basic."

"Yeah?" His thumb climbed higher. "I can do basic."

Her eyes opened. "Not too basic," she said quickly. "You have to be involved this time. That's the point of having a *condom*."

"I already told you that you don't get to make that choice, sweetheart."

She bit into her lower lip. He ran his fingers farther up her spine.

She shivered, her eyes closing again.

"You okay with that?" he murmured. "Giving up your right to choose?"

Her eyelids were growing heavy already as they flicked to let her look at him. Her lips parted, that pretty bow almost impossible not to just lean down and lick. Her eyes fell closed again, and she let her head tilt forward in a drugged nod.

He knew it was just sex for her and she didn't care who was providing it, but erotic pleasure captured him anyway. That, in her battle with paranoia, she had chosen to trust herself to *him*.

She *hadn't* "found someone else."

Okay, now you're just being pathetic, he told himself.

But damn, her back felt smooth under his hand. Slim but strong, with that definition of her trap muscles and delts that came from a very physical job that involved a lot of heavy lifting and kneading and thumping. He traced the shape of those muscles, her shoulder blades, found her nape and after one circle there that made her shiver and sigh, let his hand stroke all the way down her spine again.

He loved her sighs. The peace and bliss that took over her body at his stroking. His world still held—his peripheral vision still active against all possible dangers, so that he still saw counters and burners and all kinds of steel, and her, human and small in the midst of it. But her own world was shrinking down to pure sensation. Soon she would see nothing at all. Only feel.

He wanted to kiss her, and again he thought: *You are fucking lost if you do that. Don't do it.*

God, her mouth tempted, though. Just to take it and kiss it, kiss her and kiss her until he lost himself in—

No. Don't lose yourself.

You can't be the drug and the drug-taker. Talk about a trap.

But he could make *her* lose herself. His hand rubbed around under her shirt, cupping her breast. Not huge but full. Perfect. The right to touch those breasts could have been the most perfect gift to him. If only it had been offered a slightly different way.

She made a sleepy, hungry sound, her eyes still closed.

Probably no point in making her open her eyes to prove she actually knew it was him, was there? His teeth pressed together in temper.

154

And he shouldn't agree to do this if he was going to get angry at her while doing it. As she'd pointed out, *You can say no.*

And let her seek out someone else? Yeah, right.

Handling his desire was like bracing with his back to the ocean. The surges kept coming in at him, hard, no warning, and he had to hold firm against them. Only they were hot surges, not the icy Pacific. No team counted on him, and no team linked arms with him as they all braced against the battering waves together, either. He was on his own.

He pressed his knee against the counter wall to keep that surge from bearing him in against her body and rubbed his hands down over her ribs to her hips and back up to her breasts again.

She set both hands on his chest and spread her fingers, stroking up over his shoulders as if the exploration fascinated her.

Shit. See, this was why he'd held her with her back to him the other two times. Keeping himself out of harm's way.

Away from that little smile on her face, as if she thought his body was this amazing treasure he'd offered her. Away from the feel of her hands on him, small and strong and curious. Those hands loved textures. Loved sensation.

Loved him.

No, they don't. Okay, not *loved* loved him, but...loved the feel of him. But it was that whole blurred line thing that was going to screw him the fuck up.

He tried to lift his hands to peel hers off him, but he couldn't bring himself to.

She was pressing her fingers into him. Squeezing and testing, so fascinated by...his muscles, he guessed. Hell, it was good to have muscles right now.

She stroked and squeezed up his chest to the edge of his T-shirt and then pressed one finger lightly in the hollow of his throat. Shifted it. Pressed lightly again.

Shit, was she touching all his freckles again? She was going to kill him with that.

She leaned forward suddenly, straight up into him, and touched the tip of her tongue to where her finger had pressed.

He made a rough, wounded sound and sank his fingers into her butt.

She sat back a little. "They *do* almost taste golden," she murmured, her voice sleepy and sexy. "Or like Hawaiian sea salt."

"Lina," he said helplessly. *Don't do this to me.*

"You are so *yummy.*" She stroked and squeezed down his arms to his biceps. "I could taste you all over."

"For *fuck's sake.*" He pulled her into him hard, so that his erection pressed against the seam of her jeans. His gaze went to her mouth. He wanted to devour that mouth so damn bad. Just kiss her and kiss her until she forgot her mouth had ever been fucked by any other guy but him.

Oh, just give up and do it. You're not Julia Roberts and she sure as hell isn't some asshole millionaire.

He sank his hand into her hair, pulling her head back—

And the back door pushed open.

Jake shoved her backward straight off the counter, throwing himself the other direction, past a perpendicular counter that blocked him from an immediate line of fire, pulling his gun out and up and—

"It's me!" someone yelled, panicked. "It's only me!"

The man stood backlit in the door, only a silhouette with frizzy curly hair wisping around his head.

"Me, Amar!"

A hand caught him and yanked him out of the doorway. From out of Jake's firing line, a voice called in French: "Sir, it's the restaurant chef de partie, one of the initial victims. He has the new code, but we should have warned you."

"Shit, yes, you should have." Jake stood and put the safety back on his gun, tucking it at the small of his back and pulling the tail of his shirt over it.

"Is it okay for him to come in now?"

"Yes, damn it." Jake vaulted over the counter on which Lina had been sitting when he shoved her off it.

She had scrambled to her knees, a rolling pin in one hand.

Jesus, was she going to take on terrorists with rolling pins now? "You okay?"

"Yes," she lied. Her whole body was vibrating with tension. So much for that erotic bliss he'd been giving her.

"I mean, not hurt. By me."

"Nothing broken." She drew a deep breath and held it a second before she let it out, then another, clearly calming herself down.

Jake nodded and vaulted back over the counter to go to the door. In passing, he nodded apology to Amar, who looked as tense now as Lina did. He, too, must have flashbacked to the last violence in this restaurant kitchen.

Jake went past him to the police officers. "What the fuck, guys?"

"*Pardon*," one of them said. There were four of them in the street, Amar's two and two of Lina's. "We knew he wasn't a threat. We forgot you didn't."

"That was *fucking* careless," Jake said. "Jesus, I could have broken Lina's tailbone."

The senior officer nodded, his face rather grim. They were professionals, and they knew they had screwed up. Like any man worth his salt, they apologized and accepted his right to be pissed.

Jake dropped his voice. "And what if she had been by herself? How do you think she would have felt? Just give her a head's up, okay?"

The officers nodded.

157

Jake turned back to Lina. He paused long enough to shake Amar's hand, giving him a firm grip, steadying. Amar squeezed tight a minute and then took a deep breath and released his hand, pulling himself up straight.

Jake went to Lina, who had come around to the other side of the counter, still holding her rolling pin, although lowered now. "I'm sorry," he said low.

She held up a hand. "Yeah, no, it's fine." Her tone was brisk, tough. She did meet his eyes for a second. "Thanks."

Thanks for shoving her off a counter unnecessarily? Damn it, he wanted to just pull her in and hold her. Hold her until her heartbeat calmed. Until the world seemed like a safe place again. He tugged a fallen curl, then squeezed her shoulder.

"I'm *fine*," she said firmly. She looked past him, and her face brightened. "Amar!"

"Adrien and Mikhail are coming, too," Amar said as they kissed cheeks. "We thought we'd just...cook for a while." A long, lean physical guy, he shrugged restlessly.

"Yeah." Lina squeezed his shoulder just as Jake had squeezed hers, in a move that reminded Jake that though Lina looked smaller, she was one of the commanders here. It was up to her to lead her men through a tough time.

And they started cooking. After a while, she called the members of the pastry team, and most of them came in, and they all got raucous. Cooking. Pretending the restaurant was in full swing. Yelling jokes about their non-existent fussy clients at the empty tables. Offering Jake and the police officers outside something to eat in lieu of anyone else to tempt.

They finally Tweeted out that anyone who wanted to come by and get food could donate twenty euros to Syrian refugee relief—Lina's call—and that went around the Internet like a wildfire on dry grass. The Tweet was sent so quickly and so casually—Jake didn't even find out about it until after Lina hit send—and it quickly grew into one of the most powerful and influential political gestures made after the attacks.

The Au-dessus staff, Paris's current favorite heroes, the very people who had nearly been victims and had fought terrorists and won, feeding everyone who came—as long as those people were willing to support refugees rather than villainize them

Parisians freaking *loved it.*

The world loved it.

Jake himself nearly went ballistic. If he did that kind of thing—lost his temper explosively—this would have been the moment. He, and the police guards, and the rest of the police who had to be called in quickly to control the crowds and try desperately to make sure they were safe from insane people, and Elias on the phone telling him, "What the fuck, Jake? Have you and they lost your fucking minds?"

"Jesus, I hate the internet," Jake said. "It goes freaking everywhere. Do you have people on the roofs?"

"Yes, much the fuck good that is going to do us with crowds like this. We should get the riot police to shut the street and shut this down. But..."

Yeah.

"Just let them have it, okay?" Jake said. He didn't want Lina hurt. But he'd lived all his adult life on the edge of death, and he'd done some pretty crazy shit as a teenager, too. Living life well carried risks. Every single person in this crowd was accepting that by coming here. "They need this. Hell, Paris needs this. You have no idea how alive and happy everyone looks down here."

For the crowds themselves, it seemed liberating. Like they could pour into the streets, show they weren't afraid, *do something* to take back their city.

And for the kitchen team, of course...they were feeding people. Going all out to handle a crazy crowd. Doing what they did best.

And as they distributed the food, every single person who took a plate from their hands heaped praise on them, and stuffed animals and flowers piled up to be taken to Vi later, and people tried to kiss the chefs and begged to take photos with them and...it was a fucking security *nightmare*.

But for Lina and Adrien and Mikhail and Amar and everyone else on the teams, it was obviously cathartic. Cleansing their world of ugliness and making it whole again. Themselves, and the people they fed, and maybe even a little healing and help for those other war victims in whose honor they fed the crowds. *We're all in this together, people.*

Jake wasn't religious anymore. He'd gotten the hell away from that crazy stuff when he left the mountains. But still, his main ancient story references were all Christian. And to him there was something almost Biblical about it, like Jesus and the five loaves and two fishes.

Lina might not appreciate that reference, but then again, she might just laugh. She was too busy and too happy for him to stop her and ask her.

Doing what she did best. Making food. And leading her people. Being brave even when inside she didn't feel brave.

She was so small, and that delicate heart face and those lashes and those curls were all so very feminine, that it was hard for him, used to a world of über-macho men, to keep wrapping his mind around the fact that she was the commander here. Adrien had stepped up in his role as Vi's second, and was serving in that role honorably, but Lina was the ranking officer.

And she was a damn good officer.

Jake watched the way the confidence of the line cooks expanded as they worked, back into what must be their normal raucous, outrageous calls and insults and their always focused perfection. The senior chefs were pretty strong already. They probably would have found their feet one way or the other.

160

But there were the younger ones. The newbies. Like that girl who looked about seventeen, an apprentice maybe. Straightening her shoulders. Watching Lina. Learning how to be a strong woman, how to take what life dealt you and serve it back as something beautiful.

So Jake didn't try to stop the madness. He believed in madness.

Instead, he focused on doing what he did best—watch the crowds, stay close to her, and stay prepared to kill anyone if he had to, to keep the people here safe.

For a while there, it was a beautiful synthesis—all of them doing exactly what they were born to do.

Chapter 14

As a gesture of defiant courage, it had worked out far better than Lina had ever imagined. People were just people again. Hungry, kind-hearted, wanting to help, wanting to be part of something greater than their ordinary lives. The Tweet had swelled far beyond her first impulsive imagining, and they'd cooked the kitchens entirely empty, and then neighboring restaurants had started bringing them supplies and pitching in. They'd cooked until dark, when the police had finally drawn the line.

And not a single one of those people had tried to kill her. That had felt so damn good. To meet all those people and not be hurt by a single one.

She felt as if she'd been part of something transformative. And this time, not transformative toward bad, the burst of violence that had twisted Paris darker. No, this time, the twist was toward the light.

We are still Paris.

And we, us, here, at Au-dessus—we're still just cooks.

Okay, "just". They were still just some of the top chefs in the world.

There. That sounded more accurate.

Lina smiled under the hot water of her shower, humming to herself as she scrubbed all the sweat and food smells off.

Vi had been so thrilled at all the photos and videos. She'd been reTweeting everything from her hospital bed with things like "I love my team."

When Lina came out of the shower, squeezing a little product into her towel-dried curls, Jake was slouched on her couch with his feet on her coffee table reading a book. She angled to see the title. It was her original British copy of *Harry Potter*.

She grinned. "Are you seeing the Sisyphean themes?"

"Well, every time this family burns a letter another one shows up. Is that Sisyphean?"

"I'm starting to think all life might be Sisyphean. I just took a shower, and I can guarantee you I'll have to do that all over again tomorrow."

He laughed, his eyes lingering on her face. "You're sparkling," he murmured. "Is that how you usually look?"

"I'll tell you a secret," she said confidentially. "It's hard to look like yourself in a mirror. You just look like someone worried about what other people think of you instead. So I don't really know."

He laughed again, a low, subtle sound that made her feel fluttery and eager. "It's a good look on you, whatever." He stood, so much easy grace in his movements that the fluttering kicked up. "Makes me happy."

"Yeah?" She watched him as he moved past her to take his turn in the shower. It brought him so close to her she thought he would touch her, and her heartbeat kicked up higher. She felt like a girl with a crush and a hope and a maybe.

All centered on this one really cool guy.

He didn't touch her. Just an elusive hint of heat as he turned sideways. Straight, strong shoulders a breath away. Hard face. Gentled for her. "Yeah."

He went into the bathroom. A second later there was the little click of the lock turning.

Her mouth dropped open. That was just—a real slap in the face, that was what that was.

What, did he imagine her sneaking in on him in the shower?

And *not like that vision?*

163

She stared at the door, frowning a little. But for the first time since the attack, she felt strong and she felt happy. She felt that having started down the wrong path didn't mean you had to stay on it. It was exactly like a dessert. If it went wrong, you weren't doomed. You could start over. Try again. Change techniques. *Zut*, you could even, if you wanted, change what the whole dessert was trying to say.

***

Lina had a little bar-height table instead of a regular dining table tucked near one of the casement windows of her one-bedroom apartment, and she was sitting at it when Jake came out of the bathroom. Fully dressed herself now—not huddled in pajamas or in a bathrobe, but dressed in jeans and a stylish amber-colored top, red lipstick on, ready to go out.

Outside that window was a summer night. And she was a person who hadn't been able to go to bed before midnight for a solid decade. She'd worked hard today, but she'd been working that hard almost every day all her life. And she'd always had a couple of hours worth of adrenaline to come down off, after she finished up a busy night in the kitchens.

She curled her toes into her boots and cleared her throat. "So, ah…do you have a friend to show you around Paris?"

He paused. His expression did that inscrutable thing again, the one that meant he just didn't trust her enough to show his emotions.

Couldn't really blame him for that.

"I've got an app," he said.

She rolled her eyes. "Seriously? Some tourist guide app over a real person?"

He leaned his shoulder against the wall of her bathroom and studied her a moment. "But I don't have a real person," he pointed out gently.

She dusted her hands briskly and hopped off the tall chair, making sure her boots hit the floor with an affirmative sound. "*Voilà.*"

He rested his head against the wall, too, the faintest degree of bemusement mixing in with his carefully neutral expression. "Are you asking me out on a date?"

"I'm *offering* to be your local guide. Show you the real Paris." She gave him the brightest, most *so-let's-get-moving* look she could.

He gazed at her a long moment.

She tried to look cute and enticing. A cute little thing, ha.

Like someone who might make him get all fluttery and eager, too.

He scrubbed a hand over his face. "Let me check in." He stepped into her bedroom and shut the door between them for a moment while he spoke on his phone, then came back out. "We're good."

Relief brightened her whole spirit.

Jake made a soft sound.

"What?"

"Nothing." He was watching her face. "You look even prettier when you're happy."

A faint heat touched her cheeks.

He leaned his shoulder against the outer door, studying her with a subtle warmth in his eyes. "So do I get flowers on this date? I'm partial to tulips."

"It's almost August. No tulips. You haven't given a woman flowers in a while, have you?"

He declined to comment.

So he wasn't romantic, or he didn't say it with flowers, or he hadn't dated in a while? Or just spent most of his life deployed?

She frowned at him a little, wondering what a life without flowers was like.

He straightened from the door. "Ready to go?"

She stared at the door to the outside world beyond him. And, as she had to now every single time she braced herself to step through it, took a slow breath, held it for two seconds, and then let it slowly go as she stepped forward.

The world was still hers. No one could take that from her.

***

She took him to the beach.

Sprawled all the length of the Seine, soft sand and potted palms and night-furled blue parasols. It was the craziest fantasy to uncurl below a thousand years of grandiose buildings and five hundred years of bridges, all glowing beautifully above this Côte d'Azur whimsy.

The soft sand seemed like an insanely easy place to bury a bomb, she couldn't help thinking, but Parisians flocked to the area anyway. Tourists were scarce, after this most recent attack, but Parisians had clearly decided to make lemonade and just enjoy the space and having the city to themselves. They sat in the sand or on picnic blankets or on the loungers the city had set out. They drank wine, or played drums, or some groups of men called to passing women.

Jake turned his head and just looked at a group of young men when they called out to her. The men shut up.

On the bridges, because of the heightened alert status in a city under a state of emergency, men patrolled with assault rifles, a couple of men per bridge. On the lower quays, more policemen strolled than normal, so maybe no one would notice the two strolling ten meters ahead of her and Jake and the other two ten meters or so behind them.

Jake had suggested she wear a baseball cap to deflect attention, which had made her look at him incredulously. Then she'd pulled out a jaunty little black hat with a brim, normally something she'd wear in the fall, but they'd been having a cold summer, cold enough

166

she also had her leather jacket on, the zips running up the tight sleeves making her feel stylish and tough.

Jake had gone for the baggy tourist look instead, easy-fitting cargo pants and a long, loose shirt over his T-shirt that hid a shoulder holster.

She wondered what it was like to know how to shoot. She'd started the boxing and muay thai with Vi and Célie, because they'd all been on their own in male-dominated kitchens, coming home alone very late at night, since they were young teens. Boxing was both a good stress reliever and a good way to develop confidence in your ability to deal with whatever crap some asshole threw at you. But it had never even occurred to her to think about guns. Guns were for movies. They didn't belong in real life.

Damn it. They *shouldn't*.

"People have a misconception about tulips," Jake said suddenly, confusing her for a second. Oh, right, his favorite flower. "People pamper them and cultivate them and take them to Europe to grow them in fields around Amsterdam, where they're easy to cut down. But they're native to some of the most remote, barren places of the earth, and sometimes we'd be humping it over some godforsaken barren steppe in full gear and come on a cluster of them, just this splash of red against gray rock. In Afghanistan, they're almost a national flower. Fields of them grow with the mountains for a backdrop. Children sell them by the roadside, and there's a whole forty-day festival dedicated to them. It was banned under the Taliban, but it's come back. Kind of an act of courage, you know. Like girls going to school."

She looked at that hard, lean profile, the short, sandy lashes, the weather-worn freckled skin, strength. He'd helped those girls get back to school, hadn't he? Those were the kinds of things he fought for.

He gestured to her and the people sitting on the sand. "Living is always an act of courage. Some people just get to be more oblivious to that fact than others. But eventually the veil always gets ripped aside, so that you know that living is inherently an act of *survival*, and then you have to make a choice. It's funny, but the choice is almost always to go on living."

She tilted back her hat to glance up at him, mostly because she really liked looking at his face, but she was wearing a cute hat, so she went ahead and took advantage of it, using the brim for flirtation, to emphasize an up and under glance. Jake gave her a dark look.

She touched her fingertips to his forearm. Walked those fingers like a secret around to the inside of his wrist. Slid her hand down and tucked it into his.

Jake took a deep breath and pressed his lips together, gazing straight ahead. Then he slanted that gaze down on her, challenging and just dangerous enough to be erotic. "Oh, are we holding hands now?"

"I think I have a crush on you," Lina confided.

His hand squeezed once too hard on hers. He stared at her.

"A big one," Lina said, spreading her free arm and, more limitedly, the one that held on to him. "That keeps getting bigger."

His lips pressed harder, in such a gorgeous stymied temper, like she'd caught a great cat and was tormenting it.

"It makes me prickle all over," she confessed, tucking herself up against his arm, her head against the side of his shoulder.

"For *fuck's* sake." Jake pulled his hand free and stepped away from her.

He turned to face her, making a brisk pedestrian veer around them, muttering *touristes*.

"Were you an incorrigible flirt in your previous life?" he demanded.

Previous life. That was a good word for it. "Well, I certainly knew how to go after what I wanted," she said, a little amused he could think otherwise. What did he think it took to be head pastry chef at twenty-six in a two Michelin star restaurant? Also, frankly, what did he think it took to handle Vi as head chef and still control her own side of the kitchens?

"So do *I*," he said through his teeth. "Which was what I had started doing, when you freaking *cock-blocked* me by saying you wanted to go straight to sex."

Her eyebrows crinkled. "Does cock block mean something different in your country?"

He glared at her. "Do you just like to keep control or something? You had to take the reins before I could? Is that it?"

"Not all the time," she purred, just to see what it did to him.

He narrowed his eyes at her as if he was going to strangle her.

"As you should know," she added for good measure.

He held up a finger at her. "Stop *giggling*."

Hey. "I was trying for low and sultry," she said, offended.

"Oh, trust me," he muttered viciously. "A woman laughing with delight in herself is way the hell more erotic than low and sultry."

She grinned up at him. "You know, I like that about you."

"Please don't tell me what you like about me," he said desperately, but his expression belied the words.

"What you find sexy in a woman." She winked at him. "I mean, it's *one* of the things I like about you. Do you want me to start a list?"

Yes, his eyes said, catching on hers even as he shook his head no. "It's the post-trauma thing, isn't it? You've decided you can still seize life with both hands, and now you're effervescent with it. What did I do to deserve this?"

Lina stepped back into him and slipped her arm around his waist. "Maybe you were a really good boy," she tried to purr. But even she could hear that her purr came out more like a ripple of pleasure.

Jake cursed low and heartfelt. Then he pulled her arm from around his waist and stepped backward, up into the sand behind him for lack of anywhere else to go.

"*Allez, miss!*" called one of the men in a group they had passed a moment before. "You can come here and kiss *me.*"

Jake turned and gave the man and his entire group a cold look.

This time, that cold look failed in its effect. The young men just elbowed each other and laughed. Their police guards watched them from their ten-meter distance, bemused.

"You know what else I like about you?" Lina said. "You're really hot."

"God damn it." Jake stepped back onto the cobblestones and strode on.

Lina didn't follow.

He stopped in two strides, turned back, and gave her an exasperated look.

She smiled, ridiculously delighted in her own power, and ran up to him, falling into step beside him again. "I'm just happy to be alive," she said. Instead of guilty or scared or determined. She was *alive.*

"That's exactly what I just said," Jake said grimly. "And you want to be alive on me."

Lina considered the image those words evoked.

Jake winced. "I mean—"

"You mean, like alive on *top* of you?" Lina said. "*Yeah.*"

"Damn it, Lina, if you don't behave, I'm going to take us both for a swim in this damn river."

The Seine was a filthy river. But hey, she'd survived bullets, she supposed she could survive a night swim in it. It sounded fun. Romantic. A good *memory*, for someone who was going to live a long *life*. "Can I take my boots off first? They were kind of expensive."

"Seriously, don't tempt me."

Lina grinned. "You keep saying that, Jake, but I don't see you walking away from temptation."

He gave her the dirty look of a man who thought she was striking below the belt. Which was kind of true, she thought, her grin growing wider. She hoped she was doing at least *something* below the belt. "And stop saying my name like that!"

That one threw her. "Like what?"

"*Jake.*" He tried to do something tight and silky and sharp with his normally softer, drawling consonants and vowels.

"Jake," Lina repeated, trying to figure out what he was talking about.

Jake closed his eyes.

Lina gave the Seine a sad look. Over the next bridge, the Eiffel Tower winked at her. "He doesn't like my accent," she told the dark water mournfully.

The Eiffel Tower sparkled in amusement.

There had been a hell of a lot of terrorist plots against that Tower. She'd survived every one.

"You are more trouble than any woman I have ever known," Jake groaned.

One of Lina's eyebrows went up a little. "If you meet most women by picking them up in a bar in under half an hour, I'm not sure you can claim to 'know' that many," she said dryly.

Another dirty look, but this one darker, as if her blows were getting lower and starting to actually hurt. Like maybe the lack of real relationship in his life was a wound.

Oh.

And as that sank in further: *Oh.*

What had he said? *It's not my first time at this rodeo, honey. Being used for sex.*

Oh.

Sobered, she slipped her hand into his again, but this time she linked her fingers with his bigger ones and gave them a squeeze, her brow knit.

He frowned down at her. The frown faded as he met her eyes.

His hand relaxed slowly around hers, shifting to enclose hers in warmth. For a while they walked without speaking, Jake gazing around at everything Paris stretched before him—either enjoying it or constantly checking for possible attackers, she wasn't sure—while Lina mostly snuck glances at him.

"I'm having a hard time buying your inability to find a boyfriend," Jake said. "I'm pretty sure most shy guys would be putty in your hands, and they'd sure as hell put up with your career just to get a chance at you."

Wow. Nice golden glow in her middle at *that* compliment. "I'm busy, I guess. Also, I don't think the kind of guy I like has the nerve to ask me out that often. Either that or he's not out in bars at one in the morning, when I get off."

"That shy, geeky guy?" Jake asked neutrally.

She nodded.

"Mmm." He gazed at the river.

"Quiet," she said suddenly. "Kind. I mean, it's not like he has to be so shy and geeky he trips over his own shoelaces or anything."

Jake proved he could do the quiet part by saying nothing in response to that at all.

"What about you?" she said. "You're definitely not a jerk, and not every woman tries to wrap a man around her little finger. Why don't you have a girlfriend?"

"Busy, I guess." He considered. His lips twisted. "Also, I don't think the kind of woman I like hangs out in

TRUST ME

bars around military bases, hoping to pick one of me up in between deployments."

"One of you?"

He shrugged. "A certain vision of a certain type of man, let's say."

"Strong, capable, quiet, patient, steady? Yeah, I can see that." Who wouldn't want that?

He drew a careful breath, as if breathing was worth a man's full focus, and slanted her a glance. "'Patient,' as in patient and kind or as in patient and predatory?"

"Probably depends on who you're being patient with."

"Right now, I'm being patient with you," he pointed out, his tone a little steely.

"Kind," she said immediately. "Very kind."

He let his breath out, staring at her a long moment. "Define 'geeky'. Does knowing all the X-Men count?"

She found herself biting back the happiest smile, as she gazed down the river. "*Intello* is the word here. You know—a guy who reads philosophy. Camus. Likes to discuss it."

"There's a lot of philosophy in the X-Men."

She laughed out loud, a wonderful ripple of happiness.

"There *is*," Jake protested. "And in *Harry Potter*, too. Were you even paying attention when you read them?"

"I've never read any of the X-Men comics," she confessed, pretending to hang her head. She snuck a mischievous glance up at him from that position. "I did watch all the movies where my favorite actor took his shirt off, though. And that one where he took his pants off, too."

He found her knuckle without releasing her hand and pretended to give it a pinch, amused.

"He doesn't have anything on you," she told him.

Jake's eyebrows went up. He slanted her another glance.

She shrugged. "Just calling them like I see them."

He looked fascinated and baffled both, and he kept sneaking glances at her.

"You've got this awesome body, and then it's covered all over with all those beautiful freckles a woman just wants to *lick* and kiss and *touch*," Lina said, her free hand lifting and curling in a craving for texture. "*Miam.*"

Jake's lips parted. His hand tightened on hers like a vise.

Lina smiled up at him. "Just calling them like I see them," she said again.

"Oh, is that what you're doing?" He sounded somewhere between exasperated and frantic, as if he was about to give up and call for the rescue team to haul him out of the water.

But he must *never* have given up. She'd read about those swim tests guys like him had to pass. Hell, there were men who died in those things before they gave up.

She tightened her hand into her own vise on his.

They had passed the Louvre, and the sandy beach had grown less populated, almost like a real beach might after you walked on past a resort hotel. A young couple had taken advantage of the quieter space and was sitting high in the sand, his head in her lap, her hand stroking his loose curls back off his forehead, the expressions on their faces so vulnerable, so trusting, so full of longing for what they were in the act of finding.

Jake looked away. Lina kept sneaking discreet glances at them, wistfully. They looked lovely to her.

"I've decided to believe in the future again," she said out loud, firmly.

He squeezed her hand and ran his thumb up the side of it.

"Do you want to be in it?" she asked.

174

Chapter 15

Jake stopped dead. He turned to face her, in pure disbelief. He had to disbelieve. Otherwise, the dark thing lurking under that incredulity, ready to surge up if it gave way, felt very like fear.

I go after what I want, yeah. But, when it comes to her, I never expected to get it.

Maybe he'd only ever really expected to get sex.

Lina looked serious but...joyful, too. As if optimism was a choice and a gift, both at once.

He stared down at her. It was deeply unfair that he found gallantry under fire so damn gorgeous. Her playfulness tonight wrapped around him, enticed him and aroused him and delighted him, until he was so tangled in it he couldn't figure out how to unravel its hold on him without unraveling himself.

Her gallantry shone through her skin, her eyes, her hair, turning her so radiant it made his palms itch from not touching her. As if her insides were a golden luminescence and her cute little outsides just a trick. He wondered how many men she had dated who had never even realized how goddamn gallant she was, who had just been content to have a pretty girl smile at them and never looked further. Civilians were stupid like that, sometimes. They just didn't realize how important courage was.

Loyalty, perseverance. All those fine things.

"Do I want to be in your future? Did you just ask me to marry you?" he asked, stunned.

Lina blinked and drew back. "*What?* No, I—we barely know each other!"

Oh. Okay. Probably just as well, right? He had been sucked down into a spinning, deep vortex of want at his very first sight of her, and he still felt as if he would never stop falling. Maybe it was a good thing that she could keep her feet on the ground?

"Are *all* of you guys nuts or something?" Lina shoved her hat back. "I thought Chase was an exception."

Jake could feel himself flushing. Again, damn it. At least in the twilight she wouldn't be able to tell. He pulled her onto the sand, although it took a real force of will for him to step on disturbed sand, no matter how firmly he told himself there would be no mines there.

He set her down on a lounger, and then couldn't fit on it himself without pulling her into his lap, so he knelt beside it, facing her.

Jesus, now he probably looked as if *he* was proposing.

And she'd made it clear that she wouldn't say yes.

"*Date*," Lina said. "You said you wanted to date. I—I want to do that, too." She hesitated, searching his face as if he'd scared the crap out of her with that mention of marriage, and then reached out across that barrier of fear and spread her fingers over his shoulders. "Know you," she said quietly. "I want to know you. I like everything about you so far."

The heat grew in his cheeks, but he knew she couldn't see it in the light from the lamps and glowing bridges, so he just knelt there, staring at her. "Yeah?" he finally managed. His voice sounded husky, even to himself.

He covered her hands with his. They were so much smaller than his, cocooned between his palms and his chest. But they were maybe, in some ways, more brave. *I like everything about you, too.*

"It's okay if you meant something temporary," Lina said. "It doesn't have to be a *long* future."

He blinked, set sharply back. And wondering why she would reach out to him and slap him away at the same time. Maybe her fear still struggled to get out, too? "Why not?"

"I don't know." She looked uncomfortable and wistful. "Do you even have a long future?"

That was a blow right to the gut. He stared at her, unable to believe she had said that.

Her eyes widened. "Here," she said, wincing in distress. "I meant a long future *here*. Before you have to leave again."

Oh. Oh, of course she hadn't meant...she had a generous heart. She never would have said what he had first heard. He adjusted her hat, tugging it down a little on her head, and tucked a curl back. "Five more months. Unless something big spins up somewhere and they pull us for it."

And Europe was a cushy deployment. For those five months, he was fairly unlikely to die. Of course, Chase had thought that, too.

So had Lina.

"Five months." Her face lit with relief. Five months pretty obviously seemed like an eternity to her. Was that a comment on how long she expected to want to date him, or just a reflection of her own inability to really think long term right now, despite her decision to believe in the future?

It kind of felt like an eternity to him, too. All his thinking was in terms of six-month deployments. Since he was nineteen years old, the only thing that had ever lasted more than six months were the tight bonds formed with the other men on his team.

And he lived in the constant risk that he would not have a "long future." He'd pressed his trident into far too many coffins, and the thought of claiming a future with someone so damn beautiful made his neck crawl, like calling down a jinx on them both.

He wanted it. Shit, yeah, he did. But that didn't mean he could have it.

Or rather, he couldn't have both. He couldn't both be there for his kids at every milestone, protect them and his wife, have a home *and also* have a career as an elite special warfare operator called to fast-rope into compounds in every hot spot on the globe.

But he wanted her so damn bad. Jesus, he'd known she would make a mess of his insides. It was a wonder he'd even got up the guts to start flirting with her that day.

Guts.

Tulips. That grew and bloomed in some of the harshest conditions on earth.

He stroked the hair at her temple, his hand lingering so that his thumb could trace her cheekbone and touch just the corner of her smile.

"Sometimes," he said slowly, "planning for the future is kind of like insurance. Because you might live, too, and it's better to have a back-up plan if you do."

Her eyes flared in shock.

He closed his eyes tight. "I'm sorry." Why the *hell* had he just said that? To a civilian, for fuck's sake.

"And I would be the back-up plan?" Lina spoke carefully, but he could still hear the distress and wariness in her voice.

"No." He dropped his hand from her cheek to close it around her thigh. That wasn't what he wanted this fantasy of her with him to be. He wanted it to be central. Real. A real thing they both could keep. "That's not what I meant."

Lina gazed at him soberly a long moment. He sure knew how to put a damper on a pretty girl's happy, flirtatious mood, didn't he?

Her hands came back to his shoulders, testing him for solidity. "You don't believe in a future either, but you want to, and you try to," she said.

Well...yeah. That about summed it up. He felt this strange burst of relief inside him, to be so exactly understood.

"Okay," she said, and ran her hand down his arm to find his hand, curling her fingers into his palm. "We can try together."

***

Lina's happiness felt like a great big swell coming in, dangerous but beautiful, and she wanted to be a surfer, to know how to capture it and ride it all the way in to the beach.

Seize it. Every beautiful possibility life could hold.

Never again in her life would she be able to just trust that she had a tomorrow. That had been taken from her.

Or maybe, in some weird way, given to her. That she would always, as long as she lived, know that she and everyone around her were just as ephemeral as her desserts.

And as resilient as human beings.

She pressed her fingers into Jake's palm and ran her callused thumb up the side of it, so happy to be holding his hand she almost didn't know how to hold that much happiness inside her. It was too much happiness for so small a thing, a hand hold, but she wanted to savor all of it. She didn't want to dial that happiness back one iota to something rational and wise.

"So what would you do now, if you were taking me out on a date?" she asked him.

Jake still had that look as if she was holding him upside down by his ankles over a hundred meter drop into a rocky wild ocean and her grip was slipping. He opened one hand in clear denial of any knowledge of this kind of thing. "Weren't you taking *me* out?" he asked, rather desperately.

She didn't exactly date much herself—no time—but at least she had ideas. She tugged him, pulling hard to try to get his big body on the hard plastic lounger. "*I* think you might stretch out with me right here"—she tugged his recalcitrant body as hard as she could—"and be romantic and cuddly."

A little bit of that secret humor of his was starting to show around his mouth and eyes, at her tugging and its inability to budge him. He liked being so much stronger than she was, didn't he? "Yeah?"

"Yeah. And if you're *good* at it, and make me feel all romantic and sexy and soft, you might even get so lucky that later"—she leaned in until her lips brushed his ear— "I get all alive on top of you." She nipped his earlobe delicately and sat back with a grin.

A deep rumble in his chest. He curved his hands over her butt and pulled her back toward him. "You are so dangerous I think you could only be legal in France."

She smiled at him and pulled. And he relented—or perhaps got his courage up—and stretched out on the lounger. There wasn't room enough for both of them to lie side by side, which was perfect, because it meant he had to pull her in snug against him. Her hat fell off onto his stomach, and she got to lie on her side with her head on his shoulder and her thigh over his.

Oh. He did that so very well—be big and warm and strong and make her feel so solidly held. His arm was firm and sure, his body hard and human, and his free hand sank into her tousle of loose curls, stroking them, massaging her nape gently.

A swell of emotion all through her. *I think I've fallen really hard for you.*

She wondered if she should tell him. He might find it unnerving. She found it beautiful. *If I can die in an instant, I guess I can fall in love in a couple of days.*

She smiled into his chest, deciding not to trouble him with it when his heart was already thumping so hard under her hand. She flexed her hand against his pec gently, trying to knead his heart into calm. His heart might be a little feral after so long out in the harsh elements on its own.

Maybe hers had gone a little feral, too, because she could feel it easing the longer they lay there. This great, spreading sense of peace and warmth. Under her hand, his heart beat got slower and slower. She glanced up at him—

And found him completely alert, his eyes flicking from bridge to bridge to a lone man walking with a backpack to a man on the opposite bank to a passing barge.

She sat up a little, affronted. "You're not enjoying this."

"Of course I am." He sounded startled she didn't realize that.

"You're not *relaxing* into this." Even though his heartbeat was steady and slow now, as opposed to its initial hard thump.

"I'm relaxed." Again he sounded mildly surprised she could think otherwise.

"You're not relaxing into *me*." Was he wondering how long before he could escape? He had said he was used to relationships that were just hook-ups. And she'd bet she wasn't the first hook-up to start getting romantic ideas either. He might be biding his time until he could run for cover.

Hazel eyes stopped their flicking from point to point to finally rest on hers. "It's pretty exposed."

Oh.

His arm squeezed her. "Don't worry. There are policeman everywhere. It's just me. I like to keep an eye on things."

"Your heart rate slows *down* when you're alert to danger?"

He shrugged. The hand that had been in her hair slid to cover hers on his chest, possessively. A sweet warmth ran through her at the gesture. "That's what they say," he said after a moment, absently.

"Who says?"

"The people who study us."

"You?"

"Us." A tiny wry twist of one corner of his mouth. "People like me, Chase, Ian, Mark. Elias, too, I'm sure. You know, us *civilians*."

Lina rolled her eyes. "Oh, yeah, right." Special ops guys, then, he meant.

"That when most other human beings' heart rates pick up, ours slows down. We respond to dangerous situations by growing calmer."

Hmm. Lina considered that from all its angles. In familiar stressful situations, she was pretty sure she grew calmer, too. The calm at the center of the storm, when the kitchen was in full swing. It was one of the reasons she was such a good head pastry chef. Even in the attacks, the panic had hit later. After Vi was stabilized and in the hospital. While everything was going to shit, she was surreally sure and firm.

"So what does that mean when your heart rate picks up for me?" she demanded.

Hazel eyes met hers for a long moment. Then he picked up her hand and kissed the inside of her fingers. "That even I can't be prepared for someone like you."

A big smile broke out on her face. "You're getting better at this."

A raised eyebrow.

"Flirting."

That lurking amusement in his eyes, that teased her and lured her in so much. "You think I usually pick up women by not knowing how to flirt?"

She considered. "I think if *I* saw you in a bar, I'd insert myself right beside you to order my drink, strike up a conversation, and do half your flirting for you."

His smile grew, not so much in the way his lips curved but in that deep warmth in his eyes. He'd actually forgotten about his surroundings, all focused on her again. "You would, would you? Sure you wouldn't flirt with Ian or Mark or Chase instead?"

"Ian and Chase are too obvious," she said. "I like you."

So much warmth in his eyes. He brushed her knuckles back and forth across his lips. "Yeah?"

"And Mark reads Kafka." She smiled down at him. "Pretty sure a woman can't trust a man like that. I think I might be more an *X-Men* type of girl, in terms of geekiness."

The arm wrapping around her flexed and pulled her down suddenly, his other hand curving around her head to bring her mouth right to his.

A kiss. Sweet and deep and warm, his hand tightening on her skull. Then easing to let her free if she wanted.

"Oh." She propped on her forearm on his chest, pressing her fingers to her lips. "Oh, and you're a good *kisser.*"

He kissed her again at that, longer and hotter, his fingers strong around her head.

"You've been holding out on me," she breathed when she could come up for air. Even as he broke the kiss, his eyes were flicking past her, double-checking that no danger had presented itself in his surroundings while he was lost in that moment. "Maybe we should go back to my place where you can just focus on kissing. I think it's one of your skills."

"And *I* think it's like flirting," he said, deep and a little husky. "It's not a skill, it's a synergy. With you."

She ran her fingers over his cheekbones, utterly delighted with the shape of them. "Do you have freckles all over your body?" she whispered.

"Pretty much," he said wryly.

She bent her head to his ear. "I mean *all* over?"

He rubbed one finger up and down along her spine, not answering. That little smile lurked around his mouth. "You know, you are terrible at dating. Always rushing the conversation straight to sex."

He didn't look very unhappy about it this time, though.

"I can't help it. It's you. You make me want to grab you all over and *squeeze*."

His hips jerked against hers. *Ooh.* Nice pressure of his arousal there.

She grinned. "With *all* my muscles. Like, squeeze with all my muscles *everywhere*."

His hips surged again. He caught hers and held her hard to him. "You are a witch. You should be more careful with a poor, war-weary soldier."

"I only know civilians," she said promptly.

Good one, that spark of laughter in his eyes said. His fingers shaped her butt. "What about Elias? What if you met him in a bar?"

"Too ironic," Lina said. "What does he do, practice being French in a mirror?" Jake laughed, and she grinned. "He'd raise that sardonic eyebrow at me one too many times, and I'd have to upend a bowl of chantilly over his head."

"So I'm special?" Jake's fingers kneaded into her butt. "Kind of...unique."

"Yeah." Lina's voice quieted. Even her humor quieted, though not her happiness. "Definitely."

Something about him eased, under her body. He met her eyes for a quiet, alert moment. "Just checking," he said, and brought them both to their feet, taking her hand.

***

Lina's guards declared themselves open to a stroll, so they walked the whole way back to her place in the Eleventh, a walk of over an hour. Night fell, that late summer night of Paris, and all the street lamps came on, the evening cool enough for comfort but dry and summery now after all the long, cold rains that had stretched into July this year, as if winter was never going to loosen its grip on the city. They walked the long gracious walk of the promenade that covered the Canal, then cut right into the more winding streets that led up the hill of the Eleventh.

Despite her pride in how well she'd done being out there in the streets, a great sense of safety and relief enveloped her again as soon as she closed her door and locked it. Just her and Jake. Home safe.

She turned to face him, his face once again hard to read in the one low lamp on the table by the couch, left on so she didn't have to come back to the dark. He gazed down at her, from shadow.

"I asked you how you felt about being used for sex," Lina said softly. Jake took a harsh breath, stiffening. She lifted a hand to his chest. "I never asked you how you felt about sex that wasn't using. That asked for more and offered more."

Jake said nothing for a moment, then took her hand and shifted it to the left side of his chest, pressing it down, so that she could feel his heart. Thumping like mad. "Well outside my area of expertise."

"Scared?" she teased very gently. Because she wanted to see if that might be true.

He hesitated a long moment. "You ever been surfing?"

Funny he should think about waves, too. She shook her head.

"When we were in Hawaii for training one time, we took up surfing in our down time and we hung out with this guy, a world champion surfer."

Of course they did. They were exactly the kind of world-class, self-confident athletes who would hit it off with a world champion in another field. "Even though you're not an adrenaline junkie?"

His lips curved, but he didn't lose his focus. "He said he always felt fear when he faced a forty-foot wave. Every time. But you could either push through or pull back. Pushing through was courage—you got to ride the wave.

Pulling back only meant regret for the chance you had lost."

Yeah. She pressed into him, her head tucking into his chest, just holding on for a moment to savor exactly how he felt against her. And then she framed his face in her hands, went up on tiptoe, and kissed him.

No regrets on me.

Not ever. She'd always been one to seize her chances, even before she'd learned how ephemeral a chance could be.

Jake made a hungry sound, his palms running down her arms until he held both her hands, kissing her. For one moment he seemed to hold himself back, like a man on a brink, and then he sank into it, his hands loosing hers to slide over her butt and back, pulling her into him.

The heat of him wrapped all around her. Perfect. To be facing him at last, to be able to wrap her hands around his shoulders and pull her body flush against his, crush her breasts against his chest. How fragile she had been that day she had suggested sex only, when she had been too afraid even to trust in *this*.

And he was there. When I was fragile and could easily have been broken by a harsh stranger, he held me carefully.

Her kiss deepened, her hands running over his shoulders and biceps, up his back, down over his butt, trying to absorb the shape of him. Lean and powerful and perfect.

She didn't know how long they kissed, learning each other, learning kissing. But Jake's shoulder holster kept getting in the way of her stroking hands, as did the knife along his belt line at his lower back, and he pulled away to strip those off.

His grip tightened instinctively on the holster before he could set it down, though. "Just a second," he murmured. "Sorry."

It took him only a minute to efficiently check out every possible corner of her Parisian-size apartment, and a few more minutes standing against the wall by the windows, studying the street. "Sorry," he said again, turning back to her.

Ah, yes. That compulsion to make sure he had everything possible under control and right. She knew it well. Had built her career on it, as he must have.

She came up to him and tucked herself against him, gazing down the street from that shelter. She used to love this view. It made her feel so happy to live in Paris, to be her—sufficiently successful in her field that she could afford a place in Paris with a good view. Now she wondered if she might rather find an apartment whose windows only gave onto the courtyard.

Jake shifted suddenly and scooped her up in his arms. She gave a startled laugh, clutching at his shoulders, distracted from the view.

He gave her that slight and this time rather wicked smile. "It's fun to be the biggest in the room."

Ha. "Don't let it go to your head," she said, but she was laughing now. "Most of the guys in my kitchen are bigger than I am, and I still rule." She grinned up at him.

"I noticed," he said. But he didn't seem to feel in the least threatened by a woman who could rule. With the gun and knife still held in their holster and sheath in one hand, he carried her into the bedroom. Set her down. Set his weapons down on her dresser and turned on the lamp, its golden glow warming the whole room against the dark.

Then he turned back toward her and studied her up and down with a gleam in his eye that made all her nerves dance with excitement. He took a step forward, and then another, backing her up to the bed.

She lost all patience, grabbed his shirt, and pushed it off his shoulders. But of course he had to go and dress in layers. So she grabbed his T-shirt next and pushed it up his body.

Oh, yeah. *Yeah.* Those hard abs tightening under her hands. Those freckles *everywhere.* That taut belly of

187

his had even been protected enough from the sun that the little dots separated into individual brown and reddish points against the paler skin. She spread her fingers over them, trying to catch as many as she could.

Sandy brown chest hair, maybe a hint of the reddish tones in his hair. Not too thick. Just perfect. She ran her fingers through it, tested the strength of his pecs. He grabbed the edge of his T-shirt and ripped it the rest of the way off his shoulders, dropping it.

She whistled softly. That was just a *lovely* view.

All for me. She spread her greedy hands all over him. That leanness and strength. The powerful shoulders. The ridges of his abs. Everything about him radiated capability—a body that had been honed to handle any physical challenge, or threat, that could possibly be thrown at it.

Her body radiated capability, too. She lifted her chin, arching into him to show off her own body and maybe tempt him as much as he tempted her, wondering if he liked her strength and capability as much as he liked her being a *cute little thing.*

If he'd first gotten interested in her when she was fragile, how might he react to her actually being strong? She'd run into some men in the past who handled it badly, including her cousin, but not all of them were as obvious as Abed. Some would use words instead to undermine a woman's strength so they didn't have to feel weak next to her.

Jake took a rough breath and bent and captured her mouth again, hands flexing into her butt as he kissed her. He found the edge of her silky amber top and rubbed it up her ribs, pausing to cup it over her breasts and rub the silk there. Then he broke the kiss to pull it over her head.

He paused then, taking a long moment to study her, his hands closing around her upper arms to hold her far enough back that he could. She breathed in enough to lift her chest a little, glad she'd made the right choice in going with the sexy see-through black lace bra.

He was breathing deeply, and she could almost swear there was a hint of a flush across his chest and shoulders. His eyes traced her body as if it was some extraordinary, hard-won treasure. "All for me?"

She shook her head and touched his chest. "All for *me*," she said smugly, sparkling up at him.

Yes, yes, I'll just take this, thank you. And keep it. Mine, mine, mine.

She was pretty confident of her ability to fight off all other women if she had to. Hell, she'd had to hold her own against Vi half her career. Any other woman better watch out.

That little smile of his, but in his eyes there was so much heat and a vibrant, wicked happiness, as if happiness was running wild in him and the only thing keeping that smile small was a habit of containment.

"I'll toss you for it," he said.

"What?"

He tossed her. Gently, back onto the bed, coming above her on all fours, his eyes so wicked and alive. "Heads, I win," he said smugly.

"Oh, hold on just one damn minute," she said, and wrapped her arms and legs around him, making him take all her weight as she tried to grapple him off his hands and knees onto his side. "I didn't understand the contest."

He gave a growl of delighted arousal—she had to admit that wrestling half-naked with that powerful a body was *delicious* fun—and just crushed her down to the bed by lowering nearly all his weight on her. He braced on his elbows to leave her enough room to breathe. That little smile slipped into an open grin. "Go ahead. Keep wiggling."

So she did. She wiggled her hips against his as they crushed hers to the bed, and he made a sound in his throat as if she had just strangled him. "Sure you don't want to lose this battle?" she teased him.

And he groaned and rolled over onto his back, taking her with him. She sat astride him and pretended to pound her chest in triumph.

He laughed and grabbed her fists and kissed both of them, until they relaxed and spread open on his cheeks. She bent down and kissed him.

He snuck his hands around her back and freed the catch of her bra.

"Oh, hell, Lina." And for a moment, he didn't look amused at all. He looked half-frantic again, in over his head and about to drown.

"Like?" She made her tone teasing, but...well, she really did want to know.

"You are a glutton for compliments, aren't you?" His hands closed so carefully over her breasts, as if he was afraid his calluses would be too rough on her skin. "You know damn well I think you are fucking gorgeous."

Her face split into a huge smile of delight. *Fucking gorgeous.* Yeah. She liked the sound of that. She tightened her thighs on him in reward, pressing her hips down with a little wriggle as she ran her hands down his biceps, squeezing. He gave a little rumble, one of those deep in the throat *yum* sounds, the kind she kept trying to draw out of him when she gave him a taste of one of her desserts.

"What about you?" She stroked her thumbs over the curve of his biceps. "You a glutton for compliments, too?"

He gave a tiny shake of his head even while his eyes held hers. "I'm confident in myself. I don't need compliments."

Oh, really? She was confident, too, and she *loved* his compliments. And when it came to her work, she was practically a black hole, sucking up every compliment offered and always wanting more. "I guess I won't tell you how cute this little freckle is, then," she said, touching her thumb to one that was in the crook of his elbow.

A little jerk of his arm at the touch in that ticklish spot. He controlled it.

190

"Or this one." She touched a freckle just a few millimeters from the small flat aureole of his nipple. "That one's pretty damn cute."

"Lina..."

"Or this one." She touched a freckle that showed just under the waist of his jeans, with his belly sucked in taut like that. "This one, you have to admit, is adorable."

"You are such a witch," he said. As if he loved it. As if he couldn't get enough of it.

"I am," she agreed and smiled down at him as she bent and kissed him again. "You should never have messed with me."

"I like that. *You're* the one who started messing with me."

She shrugged. "I couldn't help myself." She ran her hands over his torso. "You're so fucking gorgeous."

"Lina." He sank both his hands into her hair, holding her still for a moment. "I'm not made of sugar. So if you crack me like one of your sugar globes when you fill it too much, you can't just make another one of me."

"No. You're human and resilient and no man ever died from having a woman tell him he was fucking gorgeous." She smiled down at him.

"I might be the first," he said, in perfect seriousness.

She shook her head. "Tough it up," she said gently and dipped her head to kiss the hollow of his throat. Faintly salty, entirely human, and her lips loved the shape of the bone under his skin, the vulnerable hollow and the stalwart line of his shoulder.

His arms wrapped around her, squeezing her in tight, tight and then loosening into stroking—her hair against her shoulders, the muscles of her back. He seemed to love to trace the delineations of muscle and shoulder blades and spine, all the things that worked together to keep her shoulders straight against all challenges.

It felt *delicious*. She freaking loved it. Sighing into his body, going limp, all while trying to muster enough strength to reward him with caresses he might like just as much. Nuzzling her face in his chest hair. Kissing his nipples.

"Sweetheart." His hands slid down and flexed into her butt muscles. Also strong. Strength met strength.

She slid her face down to smile against his belly. "Oh, look. It's much smoother here." She blew across his belly button and the fine, flat line of hair V-ing into his jeans. Then she grinned, pulled the waist of his jeans to provide more space between it and his sucked-in belly, and blew down into the darkness.

"*Merde*," she said. "I need a flashlight. I can't tell if there are any freckles from here."

His hands flexed into her hair now. "God *damn*, you are trouble."

She sat up, pulling thoughtfully at her lower lip. "Hold on. I think I have one somewhere." She reached into the drawer by her nightstand.

"Li-na." The exasperation and delight in his tone made her feel giddy with pleasure.

"Oh, no, wait. That's not a flashlight," she said, holding up a foil packet and looking at it doubtfully. "I wonder what that's for?"

"I could probably show you."

"Crazy the kind of random, useless junk you accumulate in your drawers if you don't clean them out." She tossed the packet to the side.

Jake snagged it. "I'll just keep track of this. In case it might come in handy."

She laughed low in her throat and twisted her hips over his, settling down more firmly on him.

He gripped her hips, the packet pressed between his palm and her hip bone. "You're giggling again."

She sighed. "Still not low and sultry?"

He gave her that little smile. "Still sexy, though."

Yeah? She grinned down at him, delighted to be sexy.

"Oh, yeah," he said, heartfelt. "Sexy as hell."

"Well, I can't find the flashlight," she said sadly, wiggling downward over his thighs so her pelvis no longer pressed into his. "I guess we're going to have to do this the hard way."

Jake made a little snorting sound. She paused with an eyebrow raised.

"Nothing," he said hastily. "Nothing. I just...can guarantee you we'll end up doing it the hard way." And his own grin broke through that tight containment he kept on his expressions, hazel eyes flashing wicked and happy.

"Just think of me as a researcher." She held up a soothing hand, the other on the button of his jeans. "I have some unanswered questions."

"If they're about where babies come from, it might be easier for me to clarify that with a little demonstration."

Babies took nine months just to get them started, and last she'd checked, he was only here for five, but she bit back that dry remark, which would have spoiled their play. She couldn't imagine a future long enough for a baby to grow, either. "Little?" she said instead, thoughtfully.

He narrowed his eyes at her.

She laughed and unbuttoned his jeans, easing down the zip.

"Oh, look," she said in complete delight, a second later. "You actually do have freckles *everywhere.*"

"Lina—" He tried to grab for her hands and surged up into them at the same time, caught and helpless.

"Some of them are so tiny and faint, though, I have to look really close to see," she said wickedly, bending her head until her hair was brushing against his cock in her hands. Her thumb rubbed over the faint freckles that he had even there.

193

"Oh, fuck," he said wildly.

"In a *minute*," she said reprovingly. "Don't be in such a rush."

And she lowered her head a centimeter further and pressed a little kiss on one of those freckles.

His hands tightened in her hair and pulled it, trying to get her head back up his body, even while his hips surged against her lips.

"I did say I wanted to kiss all your freckles, didn't I?" Lina said.

He hooked his hands under her shoulders and hauled her up his body. "Start up here." He offered her his elbow.

She frowned at him. "Are you into self-denial or into keeping control?"

He rolled them over, pinning her legs with his thigh. "I'm into making sure you have a good time, too."

"I'm having a *great* time." Wasn't that obvious? She felt giddy with life and the pleasure of seizing happiness.

"You're still laughing," he said, his voice deep and dangerous. His hand cupped her breast. His head lowered over hers. "Got to give you something you can't laugh about."

His mouth closed over hers, and this time the kiss was lush and invasive. It didn't test for her consent. It took it for granted and took her over, then invited her to take him over, too. Heat and tongues and lips, and his hand squeezing her breast, his callused thumb teasing her nipple until she scraped her nails gently down his back and started to whimper.

There was nothing in this world sweeter or hungrier than kissing him. Touching and being touched by him.

"That's a little better," he whispered, taking her lower lip between his teeth for a gentle nip before he slid down her body.

His tongue teased her nipple. His hand went farther south, cupping her through her jeans and rubbing gently. Then, as he drew her nipple into his mouth and sucked, his hand squeezed, squeezed, as if she was an orange and he was going to draw out all her juices.

Lina bucked and grabbed his head, holding him to her. Heat flooded through her.

"There you go," Jake whispered, unbuttoning her jeans and sliding his hand down over her panties to rub her own dampness against her. "Let's warm you up."

"I'm warm," Lina said, arching against him involuntarily, dragging on his shoulders.

"Yeah, but you're not begging yet." Jake slid his hand under the elastic of her panties.

Heat and strength and calluses, playing with her. Pressing into her. Squeezing her. Easing back to torment her by the barest of touches. He pinched and he kneaded and he toyed and he thrust one, two fingers in her until she was writhing and incoherent, grabbing at him, pulling. "You," she said again and again. "I want you, you, you. *Jake.*"

"Yeah," he muttered. "I want you, too. *You.*" He rolled away abruptly. His hands were shaking as he ripped open the packet. She sat up on one elbow to follow him, to touch those faint freckles again wistfully before they got covered up.

He grabbed her hand off him and kissed her fingers, then pressed her hand away as he took care of the condom.

"I wonder what freckles will feel like *inside* me," Lina said, happy and hungry.

He kissed her hard on the mouth. "They don't feel like anything. Except possibly latex at this point. Shh."

"In here, they do." She touched her forehead. "They feel like *you.*"

His eyes were dark, intense, as he stared down at her, a hint of color spreading all the way down over those powerful shoulders and that hard chest. The man who liked to be so inscrutable could be read like a recipe from the shade of his skin, once you got his shirt off.

"You're so fucking gorgeous." It was a rough exhalation as he nudged his hips between hers. "Be gentle with me. It's not my first time."

***

He didn't mean to thrust into her as hard as he did, but she was so goddamned pretty and strong and inviting, and she dug her fingers into his butt and pulled with a low sound of pleasure as if her vagina could taste him and he had the best damn flavor.

He'd never known a woman quite so playful, quite so confident, quite so tough and resilient and sensual and determined to forge ahead, quite so warm and...thoughtful. Compassionate, maybe—willing to think about what he said. He'd sure as hell never known a woman so damn pretty.

Oh, God, her body felt good yielding to his. Her thighs wrapping around his hips, her hips pushing up to meet his. He sank, sank into her and pulled back and sank again, just for the all-powerful pleasure of feeling her body yield again to his hardness. Addictive pleasure, a man had to do it over and over once he started, ease out and thrust, ease out and thrust, yes, her lush heat yielded, her muscles wrapped around him every time.

He settled his thumb over her clitoris to make sure he took her with him, rubbed and rubbed in time with each thrust, a careful discipline, but it sure as hell was worth it.

It made her cling tighter when he was deep inside. Made her fingers dig harder into his butt. Made her make more little sounds when he pulled out of her, little begging sounds that spilled all over his skin, tightened around his head and his heart and his cock, squeezing all of him out of his body toward her. An intensity of pressure, as if she had started from his top and just squeezed, squeezed, squeezed him on down, until the whole of him was built up in that one outlet, desperately trying not to explode too soon. Before she...before she...*please, dear God, honey, hurry up so I can let this pressure out.*

She made a sudden, whimpering sound, and her nails, which she'd been careful with up until now, scraped once harsh against his butt, and she arched into him, shattering, those shaking little convulsions of her body as she turned her head away, her eyes closed, her black curls spilling all around her face.

Thank you, Jesus. And he followed right after her, too rough, too hungry, too overwhelmed.

It shattered him. She shattered him.

He had warned her. *You make me feel like I'm fucking blown sugar.*

Oh, shit, what was he going to do to pull himself back together again, later? Five months from now?

Don't think about it. Count on now.

He braced there, breathing as if he'd just finished one of their more masochistic PTs, his muscles slowly easing. She didn't open her eyes, but a little smile curved her mouth.

He touched it, traced the shape of that happiness. *It looks good on you, sweetheart.*

He wished some genius would invent self-disposing condoms so he didn't have to even think about getting up from this bed. But they hadn't, so he eased to the side, circling his thumb and forefinger around himself to make sure he kept her safe as he pulled free.

Her smile deepened as she curved immediately into him, her hand over his hip. She found his other hand without opening her eyes and kissed it, then nestled it down into her own curls so that her cheek was pressed against it as her weight seemed to dissolve more and more into the bed.

She was falling asleep.

He waited for that. Waited for it to deepen enough he wouldn't wake her, then went reluctantly to clean up.

He hesitated by the bed when he came back, still naked and not at all sure what to do. It had been one hell of a long time since he'd slept with a woman after.

There'd been a period—after his stupid twenty-year-old days when women were just his prizes for being a badass and he didn't quite realize really that they were people, too—when he'd started staying the night, wanting something more. But it just didn't work out right. It opened a man up too wide, to spend the night, when that more never really felt possible.

It felt awkward to climb onto the bed beside her. But it would have felt stupider to leave.

She gave a little sigh, when his arm settled over her waist. He pulled the edge of her comforter up over her body.

Nice.

Really, really nice.

It reached up and pulled him under, that niceness, like warmth might to an exhausted man come in at last from the cold. He could feel himself growing fuzzy around the edges, sleep claiming him, little dreams stirring as they lost the confines of the waking world. They could fall in love, they could get married, yeah, he could see the whole team there, all the maleness that would pack around him in support and Lina handling them all with that amused, don't-mess-with-me affection she showed Chase. They had kids, they lived happily ever after. *This is a dream,* some part of his brain mentioned. It was the blithe confidence in the *live* and *ever after* that alerted it. But that bit of sense was too fuzzy from niceness and warmth and blurred silent again.

Yeah, that would work. All kinds of things could work when you were falling asleep.

And he did fall asleep, content and oddly secure.

Chapter 16

"So this is why people date," Jake said. The month of August had been a gentle one in some ways for them, in the aftermath of the harsh July. Jake's schedule had been fairly constant, shifting more toward daytime training with RAID and GIGN, and Lina's had been more or less up to her, since the restaurant was closed until mid-September. Plus, the blasted country seemed to have finally remembered it was summer, and they sat on a picnic blanket on the Champs de Mars on a balmy Sunday afternoon, the great field in front of the Eiffel Tower scattered with other couples and tourist families but not too crowded. Other than her police guards on active duty and the uniformed soldiers toting assault rifles around the base of the tower, he was by far the most alert person on the field, unable to completely relax, but he'd probably be that way all his life. Didn't mean he couldn't enjoy an afternoon in front of the Eiffel Tower with his girl. It made him smile to think of her as his girl.

"So that they can be romantic in front of the Eiffel Tower?" Lina said, amused. "It's true that might be fifty percent of the reason. At least, that's the impression I got from Hollywood films."

"Parisian snob," he said, amused. "You guys are so spoiled."

If anyone had ever told him as a kid growing up in a failing mining town in West Virginia that one day he would be sitting gazing at the Eiffel Tower with a pretty Parisian who thought he was something special...he would have believed it. As a kid, he'd thought that anything was possible.

And given that everything he'd ever aimed for *had* been possible in his life, you'd think he'd find this whole situation a little more credible now.

LAURA FLORAND

She waved her hand. "You guys might run the world, but *we* have the Eiffel Tower. By the way, it's totally offensive cultural appropriation to keep building imitations of it all over the damn United States."

"Last time I checked, you guys were convinced your culture was inherently superior and we all should be trying desperately to imitate your savoir-vivre. Now you're blaming us for cultural appropriation?"

Lina grinned. "First time I've heard Las Vegas described as an attempt to imitate savoir-vivre. I'm not sure you should brag about that."

Jake laughed. That was a thing she did to him. She worked her way inside his heart and then that warmth of hers expanded it, until he laughed with her easily. Until, half-sprawled on a blanket in front of the Eiffel Tower, he felt almost as innocent and easy as that twenty-year-old American-student-in-Paris over there acting sappy with his girlfriend. Even after a month, he couldn't get used to how good being with her was. "So basically, if you're not French, you can't win."

Lina patted him consolingly. "Maybe if you're nice to me I'll bestow honorary Frenchness on you."

Jake's heart gave a weird, hopeful jump. He was pretty sure the Navy would frown on him accepting a second citizenship, but the only way she could bestow legal Frenchness on him was through marriage. And if that idea ever drifted through her visions of possible futures for their relationship...well, that was scary, but talk about a giant wave worth taking.

Although she still hadn't even introduced him to her family. She'd finally talked them into leaving on a short vacation in Brittany last week, mostly on the grounds that she would join them there this coming week for her ice sculpting contest, and all she'd said when he asked about meeting them before they left was, "Don't borrow trouble before you have to."

What did that mean? That she didn't think that they were that serious? Or that she just didn't want family nosiness? He sure as hell wouldn't be the first soldier to

200

start dating a local girl whose family didn't exactly have positive views of the American military. Or any military, possibly, depending on her grandparents' experience of the Algerian war.

"So why do people date?" Lina asked.

"So they can have someone to kiss," Jake said and did that, for the intense happiness it gave him, every time. This part he was very sure about.

It seemed to make Lina happy, too. She laughed a little when he raised his head and rested her own on his shoulder. "I should have known the other fifty percent was about sex."

He shook his head. "No. That was about romance. There you go again, rushing the conversation straight to sex."

Lina smiled, letting her head slide down his chest until it was resting against his thigh as a pillow, while he braced on his hands. "You know, you are very inconsistent in how much you complain about that."

He twined one of her curls around his finger, taking the high road on that one rather than trying to argue. Lina's strength and generosity and laughter, her defiant embrace of life, her sugar and *lots* of spice but fundamentally nice nature, her irony and complete conviction that she could get her own way if she set her mind to it, and layered over that the fact that she was so damn pretty...it made all his insides knot in anticipation every day, as he showered and shaved and headed to her place.

The knot would get tighter and tighter with every action that brought him closer to her, with the opening of her building door, with the couple of minutes speaking to whatever police officers were on duty for her there, with the climbing of her stairs, the knock on her door.

And then...

"You unknot me," he said quietly.

Lina searched his face quickly, a surprised pleasure in her eyes. Then she spread her fingers over his arm, kneading gently. "Me, too."

Yeah? As well as she did him, though?

Because sometimes it only took two seconds for her to unknot him. The touch of her hand on his chest, her kiss, all that tightness in him loosening and smoothing out. Sometimes just the scent from her apartment as she opened the door would do it. The fresh smell of her shower or maybe of mint tea, which she knew he liked because it reminded him of the better human moments in Iraq and a few other countries he wasn't supposed to admit he'd been in, those moments when he felt as if the West and the Middle East didn't have to be at war forever, that they might actually be able to sit down and talk. And she said it reminded her of her grandmother and moments of warmth and comfort, so he liked what it represented, when she curved her hand around a pretty glass of tea and handed it to him.

Sometimes he meant to take her out and what he ended up doing was turning her right back against the wall nearest her door, sinking more and more into that first kiss of greeting, unable to stop, until she was ripping off his clothes, arching up into him, sinking into him, too.

He was pretty sure he would be dead before he ever got tired of being greeted like that.

So a lot of times they didn't make it farther than the bed—or the wall, or the couch. But mostly the roomy bed was his favorite, because Lina *liked* sex. With him. She acted as if he was one of the sexual wonders of the world or something, and she had to get her hands all over him. She liked to sink that strong grip of hers into his muscles—or around one non-muscle—and *feel* him.

And when their greeting was so urgent, she liked it the second time, too, when everything slowed down, when her stroking was slower and sleepier, when his was gentle and lingering, wondering. She liked taking long slip-sliding showers after, she liked to lie on her side facing him on the bed and let her fingertips touch here and there and there on the nearest part of his body, claiming she was working her way slowly through all his freckles.

He thought he might have a lifetime of freckles to touch at that rate, and sometimes he almost said that, but bit it back on the rush of fear that woke at giving himself that much to hope for.

Stroking down her arm at the thought, he took her hand and touched her index finger to one of the freckles revealed by the inch his T-shirt had pulled up. Then to another. It felt like a spell, every freckle she touched, like if she did manage to touch every one, he would be covered in some magic invisible armor and could never really die.

Not in a way that mattered anyway. Not in her heart.

He angled his head enough to gaze at her black curls against his shoulder. Her head had snuggled against him until it rested nearly over his own heart.

Yeah. That seemed about right.

He drew a lock of her hair through his fingers and wondered how sappy he was going to get. If he might cut a lock of her hair to take with him on his next deployment in Syria, for example. That was ridiculous— he'd be much better off with a tablet full of photos, five gigabytes of photos he could set to slideshow in his hooch. He shifted awkwardly to pull his phone out at the thought and stretched out his arm to take a selfie of them. Lina didn't realize what he was doing in time to pose for it, and it turned out just perfect—her nestled peacefully against his shoulder, all right with their world.

I want to keep this. Not just a little. Not just a few months of the year. Not on a tablet. All the time.

A whooshing swirl in his gut. He'd walked the path he'd chosen for eleven years, always laid out before him, always clear. Any woman he met was supposed to handle who *he* was. Change, adapt, tough it up. It had never occurred to him before that maybe he should be the one to adapt.

Maybe for a long time, he'd delayed coming up on this fork in the road because the road he was used to traveling on was so comfortable, even if it wasn't a comfort most people would understand. It was so familiar—a road where he himself was filled with strength, where he had a band of brothers, where orders came down to tell him what to do, orders that meant he never had to make the wrong choice, he was always his country's hero and had the medals to prove it.

But now his own craving for what was missing had left him standing at the biggest fork in the road of them all.

On his left hand, the path was clear: dust and desert and bullets and strength, saving his brothers, killing his enemies. Things he knew how to do.

And on the right, the road he'd never traveled was perplexing, tangled with strange and powerful emotions. He couldn't make that path out, couldn't tell exactly who he would be on it or if he would always make the right choices. He might not have the right skills for that road, he might have to learn new ones, and who knew if he would be as good at living as he was at fighting for others to live? He didn't know who he was on that road.

And yet part of him longed to find out.

Her fingers kneaded down over his belly, as if she liked the texture of him. "So that's why people date?" she said softly. "The unknotting? I never knew that."

Oh, so she'd never felt it before either? That was a...really important thing to know.

"I thought dating was because you had to *try* to make something work, even when you knew it never would," she said.

Jake tensed. Was she talking about the fact that he was here only four more months? The fact that neither of them really knew how to believe in a future?

"You know what I mean?" she said. "When you don't have the right tool, and you try to improvise with whatever you can even though it's scary as hell to have to rely on it in a pinch?"

Ye...e..ss. He knew that feeling. Yes. You hooked up with someone who hit on you in a bar, then sometimes in the morning you felt you couldn't keep living like this, surviving on hook-ups, you had to try to make it work. And so he did try, and it usually felt like trying to cobble together some desperately needed piece of equipment in the field out of chewing gum and scrap metal. You could make it work, but you always felt uncomfortable about having to rely on it in a matter of life or death. It might be better than nothing, though.

Yeah, he knew that feeling. But it wasn't the way he felt about dating her.

Jesus. And she did? He had gotten himself so far in over his head—no, in over his heart—in this relationship.

"It's so different from this," Lina said softly. Her hand slid around his ribs, until she was holding onto him possessively, and his tension relaxed with a little hint of fear, as if he was going under even as they wheeled him to the operating block. Having to trust someone else to do the right thing by him in a situation he had no power to control. "Going out with you is more like...nurturing those tulips of yours. Because if they get a chance to grow, you know they'll be beautiful."

Oh.

Such a tangle of sweetness and hope and all of it painful in its intensity and precariousness. He tried to swallow to clear that tangle, but it didn't really work. "Tulips can survive in very harsh conditions," he reminded her.

"Not the ones they grow up in the Netherlands," she said, and found his hand, linking fingers. "But maybe the kind we're talking about...maybe they do."

His fingers squeezed gently on hers. Yeah. Maybe they did.

"Not that this feels very harsh," he said quietly.

Lina turned his hand over, drawing patterns in his palm. Feeling his calluses. Stroking the more sensitive skin right at the center of his palm, where the tickle of her finger made his own curl over hers. Spreading his fingers back out and tracing up their calluses, too.

Such a profound sense of rightness filled him whenever he was with her. Of security, oddly enough. As if the emotions he'd kept tight-reined all his life had found their safe space.

They'd been dating a month now, all through Paris's warm, relaxed August. Usually Lina would have gone on vacation somewhere in August, she had told him. But this year, Vi had been in the hospital for half of it. And Jake liked to think that he himself had been more important to her than escaping to a real beach, instead of the great sandbox on the edge of the Seine.

"So why do you think people date?" she said. "Really."

So they had someone to kiss, just as he said. But really? "Because it makes them so happy."

Her face lit. Jake thought he would never grow tired of how a few words from him could turn on that radiance of hers. She hugged him hard, her nose pressing into his belly.

"I take it that it makes you happy, too?" he tested, just because he liked the confirmation.

"Yeah," she said, with a curious wonder in her voice. She sat up enough that she could expand her arms to apparently take in the universe. "It's kind of amazing, isn't it? How resilient life is?"

Jake thought it was kind of amazing how resilient *she* was, but he didn't interrupt.

"You can know it's as fragile as an egg you're trying to keep juggling in the air without breaking, and yet still forget that and seize it with both hands."

Jake hesitated. "Not sure that works, because you don't break life by seizing it with both hands. Like you would an egg."

Lina waved her hands. "Exactly. That's what's so cool about it. The more you seize it, the less it matters how fragile it is, because you've got the *now*."

Yes. That was pretty much how he, and most of the men he knew, had lived their entire lives.

The problem was with him. Because the more he seized the now with her, the more he wanted it to last forever.

"I think I need to stop wallowing," Lina said abruptly, and Jake felt the shock right through to his gut. *He* was her wallowing.

"What do you mean?" he asked very carefully.

"I mean, I'm being ridiculous," she said. "Look at those kids in Syria. Talk about *trauma*. I just had to deal with one little incident."

"I'm pretty sure your one little incident would have traumatized most people."

She gave him a haughty look. "Do I look like most people to you?"

He compressed his lips over his urge to grin. "No, ma'am. You look like Lina Farah, one of the best damn pastry chefs in the world."

She nodded approvingly and smacked her thigh. "Exactly. It's about time for me to do something about this mess."

He sure as hell hoped she didn't want to do something about the world's mess the way he had when he was nineteen. He did *not* want her in a war zone. "Are you sure you were fighting that dragon that day in your kitchens? You weren't more carving a self-portrait?"

She grinned in pleasure at the idea, but she said, "I hope not. I cut its head off."

He took her hand and rubbed his thumb over her knuckles for the pure pleasure of enjoying her strength.

"Maybe you're more like a hydra. Someone cuts off your head, and you just grow back two more."

She considered that with visible satisfaction for a moment. "If I ever run into Hercules, I'm going to fucking kick his ass."

Jake laughed out loud, tightening his hand on hers and pulling her close to him again. So the scariest monster down that untraveled road was her, was it? No wonder that road was tempting as hell.

"Who does he think he is, going around slaughtering the last of every marvelous species he finds? Asshole."

Jake could not stop laughing.

"Slaying the Nemean lion, for example. I *like* lions." She slid a glance at Jake that seemed filled with meaning he completely failed to get. "I *like* the way the Nemean lion's golden fur was impervious to all attack and its claws could cut through any enemy's armor."

"I thought you said you didn't like your lit classes," he said, amused. "Where's all this mythology coming from?"

"Well, I went to *collège*," she said, offended. "What do you guys learn in middle school?"

Jake tried to remember. "Math and science? The history of the United States?"

Lina looked taken aback. "How long can that take to learn? You only have a couple hundred years of it. You don't have time for the real history of western civilization?"

Jake was laughing so hard. He hugged her, wondering how to tell her how much fucking delight he got out of being with her, all the time.

"Besides, we learned mythology in my French class," she said, and it took him a second to remember her French class would have been nothing like his own experience of French in school but more like English. "We had a lot of other stuff to cover in history." She gave a tiny sniff and slid him a mirth-filled snooty glance. "Unlike some countries I could mention."

Jake grinned at her. "We just appropriate your history and pretend its ours."

Lina looked indignant.

"Kind of like you do the Greeks'," he teased.

She laughed and hugged him, too, as if she got nearly as much delight out of being with him as he got out of being with her.

"So now that we've taken care of that bastard Hercules," she said, "and I'm a hydra and you're an invulnerable lion—"

He was? He had bad news for her about the ability of his body to resist all weapons turned against it, but he sure as hell didn't want to bring it up. His job always had required that he live in the moment and simultaneously somehow stay convinced he was indomitable. And that same balancing act, that dual belief in the moment and in forever, might be essential to a woman in a relationship with him, too.

"—here's what I think. I think I can help fix things."

Oh, hell. That was what he had thought, when he was nineteen. And he hadn't been wrong, but it sure as hell had been a violent road. And a lot of the ways he fixed things for his country meant someone else was broken.

"I do," Lina said firmly. "These kids who end up in refugee camps here. The ones escaping out of war zones, who've seen people they loved killed before their eyes. They can't just sit there gazing into their past. That's no way to recover. They need something they can do, a goal, a task, and a path into their new society. *Une raison d'être.* And they need training. Don't you think some of them would be like me? That they'd love being able to make something beautiful with their hands, that they could feed to other people and help make their lives beautiful, too?"

Jake felt himself softening, that painful wave of tenderness she provoked in him, over and over. "I bet they would."

209

She nodded firmly. "Plus, if the girls are going to be living in France, it would be helpful to them to have a role model so they know how to handle idiots who ask them things like why they are or aren't wearing a hijab, as if being Muslim makes their private religious convictions anyone else's fucking business. I mean, do I ask *you* why you don't go to church every Sunday?"

Jake bit back a smile. "I hope your recommended way of handling it doesn't involve chainsaws."

Lina brooded. "No, but it might involve strangling some people with the scarf in question. Especially journalists."

Lina had finally done exactly one interview. It had drawn even more death threats her way, but what had really made her give up interviews altogether was how freaking pissed off she'd been at the interview hosts. Between their discreet glee in probing for gory details and their intrusive questions on her religious identity and practice, it was a wonder Lina hadn't punched somebody. Jake had watched it and had had a strong desire to punch some people himself.

He winked at her. "Want me to show you how to more effectively garrote people?"

"Hey, you never know when it might come in handy," Lina said, and he laughed again. "Although I'm getting pretty good with a chainsaw." Her ice sculpture contest was that week. She was heading out to Brittany tomorrow, and Jake had already arranged to be able to trail along with her. Au-dessus re-opened in two weeks.

Garroting and chainsaws aside, he did kind of fundamentally believe that it was better for anyone he cared about to know multiple ways to kill their enemies, just in case. Liquid nitrogen was a lousy self-defense weapon.

Jake frowned at the Eiffel Tower. Those police guards of hers wouldn't last forever. But some crazy person's desire for vengeance might. And she'd never learn to protect herself as well as he could protect her. If he was around.

"Tell me more about this plan to help refugees," he said.

"I guess I thought of refugees because if my own grandparents hadn't been able to immigrate to France back in the fifties and sixties, those refugees could be me. My grandmother on my father's side was born in Syria."

Jake nodded, feeling more and more somber. He had been part of the special forces sent to Syria. He had seen how civilians there suffered. Particularly women. Those civilians were the *reason* he fought. He'd gotten into this job to be a hero. But he wasn't nineteen anymore. He paid attention to politics now and knew how often the decision as to whom he fought wasn't made by someone who wanted to protect the innocent but by someone with strong ties to weapons manufacturers or the oil industry. He had doubts now. "I've thought about doing something along those lines, when I get out," he said. "Maybe next year, if I don't re-up."

Lina slanted him a cautious, hungry glance. "Are you thinking about that?"

Oh, yeah. More and more every day. "I think it might be time," he said. "I've been at war eleven years. Time to find another...*raison d'être.*"

"And you want to work with refugees if you do?"

"With the war-torn, one way or another," he said. "What I'd really like is to rebuild things. I've seen a lot of places destroyed by war, and rebuilding once the war is over requires a certain kind of person."

He'd thought about that a lot, too. His skills and how they might come in handy in recovering war zones—the ability to handle danger and persist, the ability to form and work with a team, the ability to put things together and make something work, no matter how hard.

"Who knows?" Jake said, watching her. "Maybe it might be compatible with what you want to do. Maybe we could work side by side."

She eyed him sidelong, too, looking deeply intrigued by the idea, almost shyly fascinated. She wasn't very shy, so that probably meant the idea was important to her, right?

"I was thinking I could set up a program," she elaborated. "I think at this point in time, I'm a focus of enough international attention that I could draw donors, and probably other chefs who would volunteer to help. I could *definitely* imagine famous chefs all willing to visit the program center to give week-long workshops just like they do for famous cooking schools in Paris. And we'd have the base constant training, of course. I'd select the instructors for that and oversee the structure of it. It wouldn't be too much more complicated, logistically speaking, than opening another restaurant."

It would be a tough job. But then, she was a tough person. Down deep under that sweetheart face of hers, just as tough as him. She had wrapped her arms around her knees as she hugged the idea to her, freeing one arm from her grip of herself to gesture, all that indomitable determination of hers very visible in the set of her chin, in the burn of her brown eyes.

"You are fucking gorgeous," he said. "I don't know if I've mentioned it before."

Lina gave him a lopsided smile. "Are you talking about sex when I'm trying to talk about something important?"

"No," he said quietly. "I was talking about something else entirely."

He wrapped his arm around her and thought that sometimes, against all odds, a man just had to make up his mind and seize life with both hands. Because there was at least one lesson he had learned in the military that he could apply to civilian life: *If you let fear win, you always lose.*

Chapter 17

It was so damn cold, Lina's nipples hurt. Ice sculpting was a ridiculous culinary art, she'd pretty much decided. But she'd be damned if she'd give up now.

"You can do it." Her mother gave her a hug.

"Of course I can do it!" Lina said, exasperated. Inside her gloves, her palms sweat with terror. "Maman, the whole family did *not* have to come." *I'm so glad you're here.*

"We were going to Brittany for our vacation anyway," her mother said loftily.

Oh, yeah, right. Like herself, her parents and her grandmother infinitely preferred warm weather vacations and usually headed south in August.

"Burkinis are hot," her mother said. "Best for cold beach wear." And Lina had to laugh.

"Ready?" Jake stood in front of her, holding her eyes, and beside her, Lina could feel her mother eyeing him very thoughtfully. She could *see* her father eyeing him, from a little over there behind him, assessing and far from trusting, possibly like he might be ready to hand Lina another bat.

Lina lifted her chainsaw in her hands. Her father, beyond Jake, opened his hands in admission that she really could take care of herself now, and shook his head ruefully.

Right. She could handle herself. In all situations. Even walking out where hundreds of eyes could stare at her from the stands.

I have to do this. I can't hide.

"It's just an ice sculpture," her mother murmured suddenly, just for her ears, bending close. "I mean, it's going to melt in a day. If you're not ready, just...skip it."

213

Her mother had been born in a shantytown and never backed down from anything. So she must be absolutely terrified for the heart she had placed out of her own body, her daughter. Lina turned and met her mother's eyes. Brown eyes met brown. *I know you can do this,* her mother's eyes said. *It's just...I'm terrified, too.*

Their eyes held a moment longer. *But I can't back down, Maman.*

But don't back down, her mother's said simultaneously, and Lina felt her lips curve into a smile.

"I'm ready," Lina said firmly.

"Go kick ass," Jake said. She looked at him. He was scanning the crowd, but he met her eyes again immediately. Calm. Steady. Like a rock.

"You don't want to keep me safe, too?" she murmured to him.

"I am keeping you safe," he said. "That's my job. You go do yours."

Right. Lina looked at the crowds.

The sculpting was timed, of course, and the contest public. Normally, ice sculpting did not exactly draw soccer match crowds. But a certain part of the stands was pretty packed already. The part with the best view of her ice block.

Why do you even bother with nerves? You know damn well you're not going to back down.

She just didn't have it in her.

She pulled her hood over her head as her family retired to their reserved seats and Jake climbed up to the very top of the stands where he could keep an eye on the whole crowd. Elias was there, too, in another corner, and multiple police officers. She was pretty sure no one had ever had to go through metal detectors to watch an ice sculpting contest in Brittany before, but this time...she was there.

Her palms kept sweating inside her gloves, despite the cold maintained in the tent. Her shoulders prickled as if she had a target painted on them.

It's just nerves. Nobody can actually get you here or hurt this crowd because you're here. Security is very tight.

Nerves like when she stepped inside her first top kitchen as an intern, and she was the only female there, and a small one to boot. Nerves like when she and Vi and Célie walked into their international competition, the first all-female team to represent France, with every jealous chef they had beat out for the chance claiming France only chose them because they were girls, all those chefs waiting for them to fail and confirm their belief that women just weren't able to take the heat. Nerves like when their maître d' swore up and down that the man in glasses at table four was really a Michelin reviewer and Lina was personally putting the final touches on his table's desserts.

They might be for a different reason, but they're the same nerves. Find your calm, and step through them, in the exact same way.

She took a slow breath, held it for two seconds, let it slowly out. Hefted her chainsaw. And walked out onto the floor toward her ice block.

The crowd started to clap. The announcer said her name. The crowd erupted into a huge cheer.

Huge. Swelling. Everyone clapping, yelling her name.

Lina pushed off her hood and stared at them.

The cheers swelled even higher. People waved signs with her name on them. And Paris's symbol: *Fluctuat nuc mergitur. She is tossed by the waves, but she does not sink.*

Oh, hell. She could feel her eyes getting damp. Talk about *pressure*. If she cried out here...

She revved her chainsaw. *All right, dragon. It's just you and me.*

The contest was timed. She had two back-up ice blocks, but it was better if she got it right the first time. Blade whining into the ice, all the power in her arms holding it steady, as she made the big cuts for the body.

Okay. Good. She hadn't cut off any heads.

She set the chainsaw down and dropped to smaller tools, the crowd buzzing in her ears like the chainsaw had, fading to the background.

She made the dragon flying, mouth open, roaring. It was hard as hell, so much harder than carving it curled up sleeping. She had to make a slim enough base that it looked truly as if it was flying on its own, but not cut away all its support. You should never, ever, try to fly without support, if that support was available to you. She looked into the stands at her family, her father gripping the rail, her mother clasping her hands together, her grandmother running prayer beads through her fingers, almost certainly murmuring *bismillah* since she knew her granddaughter was too much of an eye-roller over religion to do it.

She looked up at Jake, high in the stands. He was checking the crowd, but as if he felt her eyes on him, he looked down at her. Their eyes seemed to hold across that whole distance, and he lifted a fist to her.

She focused back on the dragon, feeling as if her eyes were shining so bright she could melt it into shape with a look.

Wouldn't *that* be nice. But no, she only had her power tools. Refining the wings. The long necks now. Two necks. Her two-headed dragon.

Its sharp teeth.

Even a hint of the curve of its tongues, inside those mouths opened to roar.

Take that, she thought as she finally stepped back, as the buzzer rang to end her time. The dragon gleamed there, beautiful, flying dangerous and free, ready to take on any enemy who tried to stop it, two heads grown from the base where the last enemy had tried to take it down.

I'm Lina Farah.

The crowd was applauding wildly. Cameras flashed. She pushed off her hood again because, hey, it might be cold in here, but if she was going to be famous and in pictures all over the place, this was the way she wanted it, standing proudly beside her accomplishments.

Thank you, she mouthed to her family. And lifted her hand to wave at Jake.

And the dragon soared.

***

"*Second place?!*" Lina could not stop fuming. "*Second place?*" She gesticulated and stomped up and down the beach. The cold blue waves of Brittany crashed against dark cliffs beyond her. "They gave first place to a stupid basket of flowers?!!"

"I think they were oysters," her mother said. Lina's mother looked very like her daughter, even to the messy bun in which she currently had her brown-black hair. Jake assumed she was in her fifties, but she looked barely forty, with maybe two strands of gray in her hair. Hell, if Lina aged like her mother and Jake kept treating his own body the way he did, people were going to think he was twice her age by the time they were in their fifties.

Maybe he should really think about some choices that would...give them a long future together.

"Those were *oysters*?" Lina said, outraged.

"Open. On the half-shell. So he was honoring local specialties. And the sculptor worked in the Brittany flag in at the base. You know how they are over here."

"Why didn't he just carve a flat stack of crêpes," Lina said, very dangerously. "I mean, I could have done that, with a lot less trouble, if they wanted local symbols."

"Also, he was a local sculptor," her father said. "He probably knew everyone on the jury. Probably married to one of their sisters or something."

217

"They probably just wanted to show they couldn't be swayed by the crowd." Her mother sniffed. "With whom you were *clearly* the favorite."

"Second," Lina said grumpily.

"Sure was a beautiful dragon, though," Jake said, and looped his arm around her shoulders, pulled her into him, and kissed the top of her head.

Which was almost fraternal of him, come on, but three sets of brown eyes fixed on him like hounds on a bunny rabbit.

"So," her father said, far too neutrally. "I don't think we've really gotten a chance to get to know each other. Jake...Adams, is that right?"

Jake made a concerted effort to look upright, trustworthy, and like he had been a monk in a previous life and had only been convinced to come out of the monastery because their daughter had made him. But he kept his arm around her shoulders.

"I'm pretty sure Adams is not his real last name," Lina said.

Oh, thanks a lot. "That is not helping, Lina," he muttered.

"Oh, really?" Her father folded his arms.

"It's complicated," Jake said. He gave her mother a hopeful smile.

Her mother cocked her head, considering him thoughtfully. "What's your job in life, Jake?"

Hadn't his LERC teachers insisted you weren't supposed to ask about jobs right off the bat in French culture? Maybe parents got a special dispensation. Jake considered his response a moment. "Keeping your daughter safe."

Lina eyed him. And he stilled, as that answer just kind of unfolded itself inside him and sat there. Like an essential truth.

That was his job, wasn't it? Single men went off to fight for their whole society. But once a man had a family, really, deep down, that was his most fundamental job. To keep his family safe.

"Are you any good at doing that?" her mother asked.

"I'm...pretty good," Jake had to admit. *One of the best.* But a man should never brag about being the best. Just put it into practice.

"How long are you planning on doing it?" her grandmother asked. She had her hair mostly hidden by a hijab the wind kept tugging at, and the flowers on it made her look sweet, but as Jake knew, flowers could be a lot tougher than they looked.

"Djadeti," Lina hissed at her.

"Aren't you curious?" her grandmother asked her inexorably.

Lina clapped her hand to her forehead. "And you wondered why I didn't introduce you to my family."

"Oh, is that why?" Jake said to her. "Because they pressure you into long term when you're not ready?"

Lina lowered her hand and met his eyes. Beautiful brown, a little questioning, searching. "Or...or you," she said. "They could be pressuring you. Before you're ready."

You know what was an absolutely terrible place to pursue this discussion? In front of her fascinated, openly testing parents and grandmother. "I'm hard to pressure," Jake said.

"Me, too," Lina said.

"I get really calm under pressure."

Her eyes held his. "Me, too."

And when under pressure, in that space of calm, he could think, very clearly.

About what it would mean to give up his entire career—his entire life. To leave his team buddies out there in the field, while he withdrew to civilian life. To leave his team buddies, period, not have them around him anymore. Would Chase choose not to re-up soon, too? Or would Jake end up entirely alone?

No. Not alone. Forging a new path. With her.

And he thought about what it would mean *not* to make that choice. To either lose the relationship entirely or maintain it with months and months of separation at a time, while anything could happen to him. And anything could happen to her.

"Now, *pucette*," her mother said soothingly. "It's not really pressure to ask a man about his job plans. Is it?" She checked with her husband.

"It's a little bit of pressure," Lina's father admitted. But he didn't let up on it, continuing to regard Jake with an assessing eye. "So how long do you plan on...keeping my daughter safe, Jake?"

Jake smiled, knowing suddenly exactly how to answer. "You'll have to ask your daughter about that."

Chapter 18

You don't believe in a future either, but you want to, and you try to.

Near them, the ice dragon was starting to melt. The refrigerated tent had been dismantled around the sculptures post-contest, leaving them glistening under the stars on the *place* in front of the little rose stone city hall, overlooking the sea. Once in a while, a handful of people wandered past, studying the sculptures.

"I guess they could be oysters," Lina said, disgruntled.

"It's actually pretty delicate work." Jake examined it.

Lina lanced him with a look.

"Pathetic pandering," Jake said immediately.

"Who picks oysters over a dragon?"

"The mayor of a town dependent on its oyster production?"

"Exactly," Lina said. "This kind of thing would never have happened in Paris. We know quality, in Paris." She looked at her dragon with immense satisfaction.

It shone, the surface slick. It wasn't a warm night, here by the cold northern sea, but it was above freezing.

"I like the teeth," Jake said. "They look as if they could bite someone's head off."

Lina touched one of the sharp points, pleased with herself.

I like the wings, Jake thought. *I like the way it soars.*

"Can't we put it in a freezer? It's melting."

Lina shook her head, smiling as she leaned against its base and looked at the night-darkened sea. "It's ephemera, Jake. It's more beautiful if it doesn't last."

Jake frowned sharply. But Lina was watching the sea, her face calm.

"It's all a metaphor," she said. "Nothing lasts. You seize it with both hands."

Right. Right. He got that. No one better. But...

"So is that one dragon with two heads, or two dragons with one heart?" he said.

She studied him sidelong. "Once the work of art leaves the artist's hands, it's entirely up to the person who partakes of it to make his own interpretation." Bright-eyed and curious, she waited.

Well, if he was going to make his own interpretation...he studied the two glorious roaring heads and the single body. "How do they have sex?"

Lina exploded with a laugh.

"If it's two dragons, I mean."

Lina clasped her hands soulfully. "They're joined at the *heart*. It's a love that transcends the sexual, rising to another plane."

"Fuck that," Jake said, horrified.

Lina laughed and laughed.

Jake grinned. He really never got tired of making her laugh. "I do like the way they're flying in the same direction, fighting the same enemy."

Lina lifted a fist. "Watch out, Hercules."

Jake smiled at her, and for a little bit they just watched the waves together.

"Nice save with my parents about your long-term plans, by the way," she said. "I mean, you dumped it all on me, but nice save for yourself."

"Hey, they're *your* parents."

Lina smiled ruefully and shook her head over her parents. But then her eyebrows slowly knit. "I don't understand what you meant by it, though. You weren't serious, right? When you said it was all up to me?"

Jake paused. That hadn't been a perfect response? "Why wouldn't I be serious?"

She held up her little finger. "You're too big to fit around this."

Oh, yeah. "I'm surprised you didn't slap me, when I said that."

"For your belief that a man had to make himself smaller to be with me? You're lucky I prefer nonviolent solutions."

Jake folded his arms and studied the sea. Once, not so long ago, boat loads of men had crossed this dark Atlantic and died on beaches not far from here. Lina was going with him to visit Omaha and a cemetery tomorrow. They'd been fighting for what was right. And they'd left a lot of women and kids and parents weeping.

"Maybe a man might have to make himself bigger," he said. "Big enough to choose her over him." White crests danced and broke along the dark sea. "If he wants something longer than a few months. If he wants something he can count on."

She straightened away from the base to turn to him, the dragon soaring by her shoulder. "And you think you can't count on me?"

He shook his head slowly, and her eyes flared in shock. "You can't count on me," he tried to explain. "I can't control when I'm called into action or where. I can't control the level of risk I take. I can't *keep you safe*. So how can I expect to count on you?"

Lina folded her arms, eyebrows knit in thought, gazing at the paving stones.

"Unless I get out. It's another year before I can make that choice, but if you can last that long..."

Lina lifted her head suddenly. "How is it your job to keep me safe?"

Jake's mouth opened and shut. *Oh, come on*, he thought. *It's been my job since the species was evolved. That's why I got the big shoulders and the strength.*

LAURA FLORAND

But if he followed that trail of thought down its logical length to something about her job being to make babies, she would get over that reluctance about violence really damn fast, he was pretty sure. *But it is why she got the wider hips and...shut up, shut up, shut up.*

"Jake." Lina spread her hand. "You have to choose what's best for *you.*"

People said that all the time. *Choose what's best for you.* And it was a load of bullshit. No one on the teams would last ten seconds with an attitude like that. All the other guys would kick his ass off it, as fast as they could. "I don't agree. I have to choose what's best for us. If I want there to be an us. And I do."

"*You* have to choose?"

He shoved his hand over his head. "*We* have to choose."

Lina fell silent for a moment. Her expression changed. Softened. She snuck a glance up at him, suddenly so shy she looked ten years younger. "You want there to be an us?"

"Yes," he said, and she took a step toward him. "And I'm willing to give up my career for it."

There. A man couldn't make a bigger declaration than that, could he?

Lina stopped still. Her arms folded. Her eyes narrowed. "The career you worked so hard for?"

"Yes."

"The field in which you are the best of the best?"

Well...a man should never brag. But... "Yes."

"Where the Navy offers a million dollar reward for your recovery if you get shot down, because that's a minimum of how much you're worth to them?"

Had she been reading up on special ops? "Maybe."

"That you love, where you have all your team, those guys you are so inseparable from?"

"Yes." Well, he did love the guys. He'd *loved* catching Al-Mofti, that fucking asshole. But the older he got, the

224

more he thought too much to be someone else's weapon. People didn't always aim him at the right targets. Mark and his damn book club. "I am thirty, Lina."

Lina flung out her hands. "Why would you do that for me?"

He stared at her helplessly. *Because I am crazy about you?* "Lina..."

"Jake. Don't get me wrong. I don't want you on the other side of the world, getting shot at. But I can handle whatever I need to handle. Don't you believe that about me?"

He started to speak and met her eyes. Slowed. Thought. "Of course I believe that," he said quietly. He'd seen it.

"You can't freeze your life for me." She laid her hand on her icy dragon. "You have to keep doing what you believe in. What makes you feel alive. I would *never* give up my career for you."

Jake was silent a moment. "What if you had to?"

She stared at him.

"Because it works both ways, Lina. Ninety percent of military wives don't have jobs, and it's not because they're rolling in riches and happy to live off their husbands. It's because he can't choose where he goes, so she has to give up her career or he does. Or they give up their relationship. And you know who always, always is the one who gives up the career? She is."

Lina's eyes snapped at that.

"But I can see what your career means to you, Lina. Hell, you were back in your kitchens days after a terrorist attack, pouring yourself into it. So I've thought about it. A lot. I'm not sure you have. I'm not sure you're listening to what I'm offering. I think I can be ready to move on. There's a reason you don't see many forty-year-old special ops guys. They either *die—*"

Lina flinched.

225

"—or they change. They *have* to change. We think we're immortal at nineteen, but by thirty, our joints are starting to point out that we're not. But *you* don't have to change your career. There's no age limit on yours. Although, hell, Lina, you might end up having to compromise your ambitions, too. If we—"

He broke off. *Have kids. For example. I hear those take up a lot of time. Who knows? Maybe you'd want to have evenings free, if you had kids. The same way I'd like to be home to make sure they grow up right, and not fighting a war for who knows what reasons.*

He tried again. "I know neither one of us is very good at believing in a future right now, Lina, but I'd like to plan for one anyway. One where we're together."

Living in the moment has its good points. But I'm not that person anymore. I want to build now. Build something that will last.

Lina flexed her fists uneasily. "I just don't want you to make yourself smaller for me," she finally said helplessly. "*I'm not small.*"

He reached out and took her hands. "And I already told you. I don't think I have to make myself smaller for you. I think I have to make myself bigger."

Chapter 19

Terror struck into the heart of the Au-dessus kitchens the day they re-opened. It was a ghost terror, but the shade was a tenacious one, as it was meant to be. It was the goal of a terrorist, to scar a city and warp its people into something terrorized.

They all felt it. They'd changed the security system on the kitchen door—no more easy access for delivery people. Police had set up security at each end of the street and at the restaurant doors.

But still, they all kept glancing toward that kitchen door, then focusing quickly back on their work.

Lina's nerves stayed tight, even as she kept her brigade at an intense rhythm. She'd deliberately done something she never did—set things up to *not* run entirely smoothly, so that each member of her team from her sous-chef to her pale but determined fifteen-year-old apprentice was working so hard to stay on top of the moment they could barely spare attention for worry.

But still they managed those flickering glances.

"We're open!" Vi called, and a cheer went up from the entire team. It vibrated through the kitchens, deep voices and high, mingling in a battle cry. *We're not afraid. You can't beat us.*

Lina's eyes stung with pride, and she shook herself so that no one could see her and mistake that stinging for any other kind of tears.

Out on the restaurant floor, the first people would be coming in, the tables booked solid from the seven-thirty open through the official last reservation at ten, which usually meant they cleared their last tables after midnight. In the time period between the attack and the re-opening, that space of time when feet got colder and colder, plenty of reservations had been canceled.

And the new requests to fill those spots had quadrupled. A different breed of Parisians rushing in. Not as many of those who had money to casually spend on Michelin-starred restaurants, but the ones who spent the money that they did have in order to make a point. Some of them were indulging in a starred restaurant for the first time in their lives, and they did it as a declaration. *We love you guys. We're here with you. And we're not afraid.*

Only Parisians could tell terrorists to go fuck themselves in quite this way. By hanging out with friends at a top restaurant, drinking fine wine over a long, delicious meal, and, Lina hoped to God, raising an eyebrow or two ironically at the faintest suggestion that anyone could ever make them do anything different.

Lina loved those people so much she wanted to kiss every single damn one of them. And since she couldn't, she was sending them a special dessert instead.

"I like the dragons," Vi said. She was not supposed to be on her feet all evening, and therefore her second, Adrien, was supposed to be in charge of the main side of the kitchens. Vi had had to come over to Lina's side of the kitchens to stop herself from second-guessing every single one of Adrien's calls.

"Yeah?" Lina studied the dessert, pleased with herself. It had been incredibly tricky to design a dessert of chocolate and spun sugar that looked like a dragon breathing fire. "I wanted it to be a hydra, but getting two necks on that thing was hell."

"What is it with you and this hydra obsession lately?"

"Long story," Lina said. "Let's say I respond poorly to people who try to cut off my head. Or make this city scared."

Vi grinned at her and held up a hand. Lina slapped it up high. "Fluctuat nec mergitur," Vi said.

Lina grinned back and nodded to a nearby rack. Where the chocolate hulls of her boat-themed desserts were prepped and ready to be finished on command.

"Shouldn't you sit down sometime?" Lina said to Vi.

"No. I respond poorly to people trying to cut my head off, too."

"Nevertheless." Lina grabbed the stool they had out here specifically for still-convalescing Vi and shoved it at her.

Vi sniffed. But she did lean her butt against it.

It sure as hell was good to see Vi back on her feet. Her hair washed and silky and currently knotted on top of her head, color back in her cheeks. Lina had noticed that Vi never strayed an arm's reach away from a possible weapon. Easy enough in a kitchen, where nearly everything was a possible weapon, but Vi kept an eye on that door into their kitchen worse than any of them. Ready to fight to protect them all.

Lina smiled at her. "Have I ever told you I love you?"

Vi looked startled, and then actually flushed. Then she got control of herself and sighed despondently. "Damn. I wish you'd told me sooner. I'm afraid I'll break Chase's heart if I dump him for you now."

"It's platonic," Lina said dryly. "Get over yourself, you vain woman."

Vi grinned at her, licked a finger, and touched it to her shoulder with a sizzling noise.

Lina laughed. Which felt so damn good. All the crazy moments of laughter they'd had in these kitchens, all the arguments and the victories and the slump-down-in-a-puddle moments of exhaustion and the pure *fun*, all flooded back in that laugh, knocking that ghost terror back into a corner to gaze at them sulkily.

"Have you told *him*?" Vi waggled her eyebrows.

Lina tried not to choke on a sudden onslaught of giggles. Stress was pretty high tonight, and when you added Vi's attempts to do weird things with her

229

eyebrows, the urge to act out silliness was strong. "Told who?"

"That wall of freckles who prowls around after you trying to pretend he's shy and geeky." Vi snorted. "Which is hilarious."

Lina grinned. "He's part of a book club."

And the women exploded into laughter. It rippled out from them through the kitchens, the solemn stress disturbed by it, eager grins breaking out here and there. In a moment, their usual pranksters were cutting up again, eddies of laughter and raucous humor breaking out around the kitchens.

"'Look! I can read! Doesn't that count as shy?'" Vi tried to make her voice ludicrously deep, and Lina burst into giggles again. "And did you see those glasses Ian uses?" Vi said. "Does he not even realize we know the lenses are fake?"

"The lenses are fake?" Lina said, indignant. She'd found it so endearing that such a cocky guy had a physical weakness like that. Ian had managed to play her!

"They can't go into special ops if they have any vision issues."

"Yeah, but they're civilians," Lina said very dryly.

Vi rolled her eyes. But then she sobered a little and gave Lina a quick look. "So how do you think you'll handle it when he's gone most of the year getting shot at?"

"The best I can," Lina said. "The same way I handle everything else." She focused on her dragon. Which could handle anything.

Vi nodded once, firmly. "That's what I figured I would do."

Lina wondered if she should tell Vi about Jake's talk of possibly getting out but wasn't sure. Seemed like the kind of thing he would want to break to his team in person, not through rumors spread by girlfriends. In any case, Lina held firm in her belief that she didn't get to dictate his decision any more than he could dictate hers about her career—she only got to decide whether he was worth sticking with, whatever he chose.

Steady. Strong. Patient. Persistent. All those beautiful freckles. The way his sly humor just slid into a moment and caught her by surprise, so that a laugh burst out of her when she least expected it.

It would be hard as hell to let him go for six months, to a place where she couldn't keep him safe. But it would be harder still to let him go forever.

Because it might still be scary to try to believe in a future. But she had to plan for one anyway. The one with him in it, somewhere in the world, thinking of her, always heading back to her as soon as he could. Or the one with him in it, the connection between them shattered by fear, trying to get over her while she crouched behind her bed and tried to get over him.

Yeah, fuck that last option.

The doors that led out onto the restaurant floor opened, and black-clad waiters came through with the first orders. Behind them, Jake slipped in and to the side of the door, the least in-the-way place in a restaurant kitchen in full swing. Lina glared at him, slipping the wannabe-hydra dragon dessert under the counter, and pointed out to the floor again, where he had a table with his buddies. The man sure was hard to prepare a surprise for. He liked to see things coming a *long* way out.

Jake grimaced, annoyed not to be able to stay and watch, and she pointed more firmly. He looked over everything—from the doors, to the windows, to the behavior of every single person in the kitchens—before he left. That was Jake.

"How do you think they chose which one of them had to sit with his back to the door?" she asked Vi wryly as Jake finally left. She and Vi had reserved them a table in the corner, with a good view of the doors, but the table was still round.

Vi shook her head. "I'm imagining them all clustered together to one side of the table, more willing to sit in each other's laps than not be able to see the rest of the room."

Probably. The waiters started to put up the first slips. Vi turned away, grabbing them, calling out. "Don't overdo it," Lina told her futilely, and focused on work.

It was about sixty minutes before she could send the first dragon out, and she'd calculated exactly right. Jake's table *was* the first one to finish the main course and order desserts. Americans. Seriously.

So he was the first to see it. The very first.

The dragon formed with such difficulty from red-gold blown sugar. The custard cream in its belly. The sparkle of gold dust over it, like freckles. The rosemary-scented smoke she pumped down into its throat just before the waiter carried it out—split second timing was crucial—so that it arrived at the table with plumes of smoke leaking out of its mouth.

Five dragons, one for each man at the table. But Jake's was the only one with freckles.

She smiled, watching the dragons go out, her hands resting for one tiny second on her hips. In about two minutes, all the other tables were going to see what Jake's table had received as their dessert, and her orders for more were going to explode past any ability to stop or do much but breathe and work for the next two hours.

And sure enough, they did, and she and her staff were deep into the rhythm when it penetrated Lina's attention that one of the waiters was standing awkwardly in front of the pass, his expression akin to a man being sent out as a sacrificial lamb.

"What?" she said impatiently. There was no time at this hour of the night for anything but lightning-fast communication.

Thomas, the waiter, cleared his throat. His head bent. "He sent it back," he whispered.

"What?" Lina rubbed an ear with the back of her wrist, to keep her hands clean. She couldn't have heard right.

"One of the clients sent his dessert back."

Every single member of her brigade stopped dead. Lina's middle congealed in one sick lump. "*What?*"

"I'm sorry." Thomas set the black plate on the pass and shoved it across.

Lina stared at it. The dragon was intact, but its smoke had all escaped. The guest hadn't even *tried* it. Her dragon. The dragon that was the freaking symbol of this whole evening, of Paris, of Jake, of *her*. And what was this—wait—

"What's that?" She touched the chocolate egg tucked up against the dragon's belly, her face scrunching. It was one of those shells of milk chocolate that little kids loved for the toys inside. It looked as if it had been broken and put back together again, too.

"Is he saying he'd rather eat *cheap candy*?" Lina asked incredulously. Thomas looked as if he was about to dig a hole straight through the kitchen floor and pull the concrete back over his head to hide from her. The egg cracked back open under the pressure of her finger.

A strip of white paper inside, and—

A ring.

A ring?

Not...not a cheap trinket you might find in candy either. Red gold. It looked like *real* gold. Delicately etched, so that as she looked at it, she realized that its form was the body of a serpentine creature—no. A dragon. No, it had two heads, one from each side, forming the setting of a ruby ringed with smaller orange-gold stones—topaz?

A double-headed dragon, breathing one strong fire.

Her heart caught. She turned the slip of paper over.

Be my dragon?

She looked up, tears sparking instantly.

233

Jake stood just inside the door to the restaurant floor, watching her, his face intense, alert. He always did like to see what was coming to him from a long way off.

And he never had quite understood that when he didn't eat one of her desserts she wanted to smack him.

"Jake." Somehow she made it around the frozen members of her brigade, who were starting to break out into delighted grins.

Vi, ever alert to what happened in her kitchen, was turning at the unexpected shift in rhythms, a hand lifting the nearest pan, ready to throw. She paused and lowered it. Mikhail, shaving tuna, set down the very same knife he had once had to throw at a terrorist and came closer to look.

Lina reached Jake. His hazel eyes fixed on her every step of the way.

"Egg for rebirth," he said. "Did you get that part? A dragon's rebirth."

She wrapped her arms around him and pressed her face into his neck, because she was crying, and that was embarrassing even in these circumstances.

All around them, the kitchen brigades and the wait staff were starting to cheer and clap. The door beside Jake opened, and his buddies poked their heads in, grinning. They must have been peering in the little circular window all this time. Elias ducked past them and stepped entirely into the kitchen, apparently too refined for crowding in a door.

"What?" someone called anxiously from the restaurant. "What's going on?"

"It's a marriage proposal," Chase told them cheerfully over his shoulder. "Shh."

"Did she say yes?" someone else in the restaurant called.

"Or he?" a male voice called, a rumor of laughter and pleasure rising out there.

"Did she say yes?" Chase checked with Vi.

234

"Not sure."

"Well, she didn't try to kill him," Chase said. "Which I just point out to you in case you want to learn from her example."

Vi made a pffing gesture of dismissal at him, as if he really should not be whining about a paltry few attempts at his demise.

"Did she say yes?" Ian asked Jake.

Jake looked down at Lina, their eyes meeting from so close, his hazel brilliant and rueful. "This is what I get for making this a public proposal. I think I imagined people in a respectful silence."

"Say yes!" someone shouted from the restaurant floor.

"Say yes!" someone else took it up. Within seconds, a rhythmic pounding started up on the tables, supporting the chant. "*Dis oui! Dis oui! Dis oui! Dis oui!*"

"Not to put any pressure on you, but I think all of Paris wants you to say yes," Elias said, amused.

Ian glanced back. "Yeah, they've got their phones up. You should come out to say it."

This was ridiculous. But Thomas the waiter caught up the plate with the dragon and its egg and carried it to them, and Vi pushed Lina toward the door, and Jake wouldn't let go of Lina, so he grabbed her hand and came with her.

The kitchen staff all crowded onto the restaurant floor behind them. The mostly strangers at the restaurant tables—all those strangers who had been brave enough to come, to make a point of coming, of saying *you can't beat us*—were clapping and chanting and stomping their feet. Célie and Joss were there, and Jamie and Dom, and Lina's family, all looking deeply intrigued. None of them were chanting, but Célie was clapping, and Lina's parents had their heads cocked as if they were considering whether Jake might have one or two points in his favor.

"Say yes! Say yes! Say yes!"

LAURA FLORAND

"Jesus, we're never going to be sent covert again in our entire lives, are we?" Ian muttered suddenly to Mark. "We're all on camera."

"Slouch," Mark retorted. "You know, act civilian."

"Say yes! Say yes! Say yes!"

"You must have been pretty confident about what I would say," Lina muttered to Jake for his ear alone. She knew she'd been very openly into him, but wow. This risk was *public*.

"I guess I was hoping you would seize me with both hands," he said quietly.

Their eyes held. He was so freaking beautiful, it was insane. Strong shoulders, hard abs, kissed all over by freckles. But his beauty came from more than that. It was that collected and concentrated determination of his, steady, persistent, fun to fluster and yet utterly sure.

She reached out and seized him with both hands. Damn, the resilience of his upper arm muscles felt good under her fingers.

He gave her that little lopsided smile. "Because I don't break. No matter how much pressure you put on me."

True. Her fingers kneaded into his muscles.

"And neither do you." He held her eyes as if he could see right through to the depths of her soul. And thought those depths were everything he'd ever craved. He reached out for the egg on its plate, that Thomas still carried with eager encouragement right by their elbows. "Even if the outside cracks under pressure"—he held the ring up—"the inside holds true."

"*Awww*," gushed the whole room. Lina's mother clutched her father's arm, going all mushy, too.

"Shouldn't he be down on one knee?" some stranger called.

"I can take a knee," Jake said, and started to bend a leg.

Lina smacked a hand on his chest. "Don't you dare."

236

He stilled, and they stared at each other a moment. Lina hesitated. "You're sure you don't want to date for twenty years or so to make sure we are compatible like most people do?"

"Your culture is insane," he said. "No. I knew what I wanted the first moment I saw you."

"Love at first sight?" Lina said, dumbfounded. Wait, hadn't he first seen her when—

"It was a telling moment. Your face was white, your eyes were huge, you had blood all down your chef's jacket, your own friend's blood. Your hair was tumbled over your face from fighting. And yet you had this tight grip on yourself, exuding calm because you knew you had to, sliding your shoulder under your friend's to help her."

Lina flinched. "I don't want you to have fallen in love with me *then*." It was the worst moment in her entire life.

Jake watched her a moment, with that steadiness of his that was like his own shoulder sliding under hers to help her. That secret humor curved his lips. "Okay. I guess it must have been when you asked to use me for sex, then."

"What did he say?" the woman at the nearest table asked the man beside her. A burble of laughter and encouragement ran through the room as people grasped it. Lina's mom clapped her hands over her father's ears.

Jake shrugged. "What? You really are fucking gorgeous. Don't know your own power, I'm guessing."

Lina had never met anyone who made her feel as powerful as Jake did.

"When did you fall in love with me?" Jake said.

She noticed he very deliberately didn't ask *if*. She considered him, so ridiculously masculine and beautiful that he kind of redefined what beauty was. And a little sigh escaped out of her, as if all her muscles just released her into happiness.

"I don't know," she said, and stretched out her hand, ring finger offered. "I just know that I am now."

The entire restaurant erupted into insane cheers. Even her grandmother grinned.

It went all over Paris, from all those phones held up to film them. Hell, it went all over the world.

To think that once upon a time, she had just been Lina Farah, top pastry chef. And now she was some kind of international symbol of courage and persistence and pursuing the beautiful in life no matter what. Like a tulip.

Or if necessary, a hydra.

Jake slid the hydra-dragon ring onto her finger.

"I'm going to get you a lion ring," she said, and wrapped her arms tight around him.

Cheers and cheers and more cheers. She wasn't the only one crying. Complete strangers were crying, actually.

Vi said something to the head of the wait staff, and in a couple of minutes, champagne bottles were popping at all the tables, and they didn't do what wait staff in a top restaurant were trained to do, discreetly pop them. They gave those bottles a little shake pre-opening and let the corks fly.

"If I become an international heroine because of a marriage proposal rather than for my career, I feel as if there's some kind of feminist issue here," Lina murmured to Jake wryly, resting her weight against his side.

He tightened his arm around her. "That's because you overthink things. You probably should join our book club. It's made for people like you."

"Only if you guys promise to read Simone de Beauvoir."

"Sure." Ian stopped beside her to grin at her and handed her a pair of black frames. "I'll even let you borrow my glasses."

Lina slipped them on and pulled them down her nose enough to give Ian a librarian's look.

TRUST ME

Ian winked. Chase laughed. Elias and Vi both shook their heads. Lina's parents looked at each other and smiled.

And all around them, people toasted them all through the night.

"And that," Jake told Elias with a great deal of relief and satisfaction a while later, as he took a sip of the champagne someone had thrust into his hand, "is what I call flirting. You should try it sometime."

FIN

Sign up to my newsletter to be the first to know when Elias's story is released and for a free copy of the novelette Night Wish, *the reader-requested story of Damien and Jess's first meeting in the Vie en Roses series. And as always, thank you so much for leaving a review, if you can. In the current publishing world, reader reviews have really become the lifeblood of authors.*

My next book will be Lucien's story in the Vie en Roses series. If you haven't tried that series, keep reading for an excerpt from the first book, Once Upon a Rose.

Website: www.lauraflorand.com
Twitter: @LauraFlorand
Facebook: www.facebook.com/LauraFlorandAuthor
Newsletter: http://lauraflorand.com/newsletter

OTHER BOOKS BY LAURA FLORAND

Paris Nights Series

All For You

Chase Me

Trust Me

La Vie en Roses Series

Turning Up the Heat (a novella prequel)

The Chocolate Rose (also part of the Amour et Chocolat series)

A Rose in Winter, a novella in *No Place Like Home*

Once Upon a Rose

A Wish Upon Jasmine

A Crown of Bitter Orange

Amour et Chocolat Series

All's Fair in Love and Chocolate, a novella in *Kiss the Bride*

The Chocolate Thief

The Chocolate Kiss

The Chocolate Rose (also a prequel to La Vie en Roses series)

The Chocolate Touch

The Chocolate Heart

The Chocolate Temptation

LAURA FLORAND

Sun-Kissed (also a sequel to *Snow-Kissed*)

Shadowed Heart (a sequel to *The Chocolate Heart*)

Snow Queen Duology

Snow-Kissed (a novella)

Sun-Kissed (also part of the Amour et Chocolat series)

Memoir

Blame It on Paris

ONCE UPON A ROSE

Book 1 in La Vie en Roses series: Excerpt

Burlap slid against Matt's shoulder, rough and clinging to the dampness of his skin as he dumped the sack onto the truck bed. The rose scent puffed up thickly, like a silk sheet thrown over his face. He took a step back from the truck, flexing, trying to clear his pounding head and sick stomach.

The sounds of the workers and of his cousins and grandfather rode against his skin, easing him. Raoul was back. That meant they were all here but Lucien, and Pépé was still stubborn and strong enough to insist on overseeing part of the harvest himself before he went to sit under a tree. Meaning Matt still had a few more years before he had to be the family patriarch all by himself, thank God. He'd copied every technique in his grandfather's book, then layered on his own when those failed him, but that whole job of taking charge of his cousins and getting them to listen to him was *still* not working out for him.

But his grandfather was still here for now. His cousins were here, held by Pépé and this valley at their heart, and not scattered to the four winds as they might be one day soon, when Matt became the heart and that heart just couldn't hold them.

All that loss was for later. Today was a good day. It could be. Matt had a hangover, and he had made an utter fool of himself the night before, but this could still be a good day. The rose harvest. The valley spreading around him.

J'y suis. J'y reste.

I am here and here I'll stay.

He stretched, easing his body into the good of this day, and even though it wasn't that hot yet, went ahead and reached for the hem of his shirt, so he could feel the scent of roses all over his skin.

"Show-off," Allegra's voice said, teasingly, and he grinned into the shirt as it passed his head, flexing his muscles a little more, because it would be pretty damn fun if Allegra was ogling him enough to piss Raoul off.

He turned so he could see the expression on Raoul's face as he bundled the T-shirt, half-tempted to toss it to Allegra and see what Raoul did—

And looked straight into the leaf-green eyes of Bouclettes.

Oh, shit. He jerked the T-shirt back over his head, tangling himself in the bundle of it as the holes proved impossible to find, and then he stuck his arm through the neck hole and his head didn't fit and he wrenched it around and tried to get himself straight and dressed somehow and—oh, *fuck.*

He stared at her, all the blood cells in his body rushing to his cheeks.

Damn you, stop, stop, stop, he tried to tell the blood cells, but as usual they ignored him. Thank God for dark Mediterranean skin. It had to help hide some of the color, right? Right? As he remembered carrying her around the party the night before, heat beat in his cheeks until he felt sunburned from the inside out.

Bouclettes was staring at him, mouth open as if he had punched her. Or as if he needed to kiss her again and—*behave!* She was probably thinking what a total jerk he was, first slobbering all over her drunk and now so full of himself he was stripping for her. And getting stuck in his own damn T-shirt.

Somewhere beyond her, between the rows of pink, Raoul had a fist stuffed into his mouth and was trying so hard not to laugh out loud that his body was bending into it, going into convulsions. Tristan was grinning, all right with his world. And Damien had his eyebrows up, making him look all controlled and princely, like someone who would *never* make a fool of himself in front of a woman.

Damn T-shirt. Matt yanked it off his head and threw it. But, of course, the air friction stopped it, so that instead of sailing gloriously across the field, it fell across the rose bush not too far from Bouclettes, a humiliated flag of surrender.

Could his introduction to this woman conceivably get any worse?

He glared at her, about ready to hit one of his damn cousins.

She stared back, her eyes enormous.

"Well, *what?*" he growled. "What do you want now? Why are you still here?" *I was drunk. I'm sorry. Just shoot me now, all right?*

She blinked and took a step back, frowning.

"Matt," Allegra said reproachfully, but with a ripple disturbing his name, as if she was trying not to laugh. "She was curious about the rose harvest. And she needs directions."

Directions. Hey, really? He was *good* with directions. He could get an ant across this valley and tell it the best route, too. He could crouch down with bunnies and have conversations about the best way to get their *petits* through the hills for a little day at the beach.

Of course, all his cousins could, too. He got ready to leap in first before his cousins grabbed the moment from him, like they were always trying to do. "Where do you need to go?" His voice came out rougher than the damn burlap. He struggled to smooth it without audibly clearing his throat. God, he felt naked. Would it look too stupid if he sidled up to that T-shirt and tried getting it over his head again?

"It's this house I inherited here," Bouclettes said. She had the cutest little accent. It made him want to squoosh all her curls in his big fists again and kiss that accent straight on her mouth, as if it was his, when he had so ruined that chance. "113, rue des Rosiers."

The valley did one great beat, a giant heart that had just faltered in its rhythm, and every Rosier in earshot focused on her. His grandfather barely moved, but then he'd probably barely moved back in the war when he'd spotted a swastika up in the *maquis* either. Just gently squeezed the trigger.

That finger-on-the-trigger alertness ran through every one of his cousins now.

Matt was the one who felt clumsy.

"Rue des Rosiers?" he said dumbly. Another beat, harder this time, adrenaline surging. "113, *rue des Rosiers?*" He looked up at a stone house, on the fourth terrace rising into the hills, where it got too steep to be practical to grow roses for harvest at their current market value. "Wait, *inherited?*"

Bouclettes looked at him warily.

"How could you *inherit* it?"

"I don't know exactly," she said slowly. "I had a letter from Antoine Vallier."

Tante Colette's lawyer. Oh, hell. An ominous feeling grew in the pit of Matt's stomach.

"On behalf of a Colette Delatour. He said he was tracking down the descendants of Élise Dubois."

What? Matt twisted toward his grandfather. Pépé stood very still, with this strange, tense blazing look of a fighter who'd just been struck on the face and couldn't strike back without drawing retaliation down on his entire village.

Matt turned back to the curly-haired enemy invader who had sprung up out of the blue. Looking so damn cute and innocent like that, too. He'd *kissed* her. "You can't—Tante Colette gave that house to *you?*"

Bouclettes took a step back.

Had he roared that last word? His voice echoed back at him, as if the valley held it, would squeeze it in a tight fist and never let it free. The air constricted, merciless bands around his sick head and stomach.

"After all that?" He'd just spent the last five months working on that house. Five months. *Oh, could you fix the plumbing, Matthieu? Matthieu, that garden wall needs mending. Matthieu, I think the septic tank might need to be replaced.* Because she was ninety-six and putting her life in order, and she was planning to pass it on to him, right? Because she understood that it was part of his valley and meant to leave this valley whole. Wasn't that the tacit promise there, when she asked him to take care of it? "*You?* Colette gave it to *you?*"

Bouclettes stared at him, a flash of hurt across her face, and then her arms tightened, and her chin went up. "Look, I don't know much more than you. My grandfather didn't stick around for my father's childhood, apparently. All we knew was that he came from France. We never knew we had any heritage here."

Could Tante Colette have had a child they didn't even know about? He twisted to look at his grandfather again, the one man still alive today who would surely have noticed a burgeoning belly on his stepsister. Pépé was frowning, not saying a word.

So—"To *you?*" Tante Colette knew it was his valley. You didn't just rip a chunk out of a man's heart and give it to, to...to whom exactly?

"To *you?*" Definitely he had roared that, he could hear his own voice booming back at him, see the way she braced herself. But—who the hell was she? And what the *hell* was he supposed to do about this? Fight a girl half his size? Strangle his ninety-six-year-old aunt? How did he crush his enemies and defend this valley? His enemy was...she was so *cute.* He didn't want her for an enemy, he wanted to figure out how to overcome last night's handicap and get her to think he was cute, too. Damn it, he hadn't even found out yet what those curls felt like against his palms.

And it was *his valley.*

Bouclettes' chin angled high, her arms tight. "You seemed to like me last night."

Oh, God. Embarrassment, a hangover, and being knifed in the back by his own aunt made for a perfectly horrible combination. "I was *drunk*."

Her mouth set, this stubborn, defiant rosebud. "I never thought I'd say this to a man, but I think I actually liked you better drunk." Turning on her heel, she stalked back to her car.

Matt stared after her, trying desperately not to be sick in the nearest rose bush. Family patriarchs didn't get to do that in front of the members of their family.

"I told my father he should never let my stepsister have some of this valley," his grandfather said tightly. "I told him she couldn't be trusted with it. It takes proper family to understand how important it is to keep it intact. Colette *never* respected that."

His cousins glanced at his grandfather and away, out over the valley, their faces gone neutral. They all knew this about the valley: It couldn't be broken up. It was their *patrimoine*, a world heritage really, in their hearts they knew it even if the world didn't, and so, no matter how much they, too, loved it, they could never really have any of it. It had to be kept intact. It had to go to Matt.

The others could have the company. They could have one hell of a lot more money, when it came down to liquid assets, they could have the right to run off to Africa and have adventures. But the valley was his.

He knew the way their jaws set. He knew the way his cousins looked without comment over the valley, full of roses they had come to help harvest because all their lives they had harvested these roses, grown up playing among them and working for them, in the service of them. He knew the way they didn't look at him again.

So he didn't look at them again, either. It *was* his valley, damn it. He'd tried last year to spend some time at their Paris office, to change who he was, to test out just one of all those many other dreams he had had as a kid, dreams his role as heir had never allowed him to pursue. His glamorous Paris girlfriend hadn't been able to stand the way the valley still held him, even in Paris. How fast he would catch a train back if something happened that he had to take care of. And in the end, he hadn't been able to stand how appalled she would get at the state of his hands when he came back, dramatically calling her manicurist and shoving him in that direction. Because he'd always liked his hands before then—they were strong and they were capable, and wasn't that a good thing for hands to be? A little dirt ground in sometimes—didn't that just prove their worth?

In the end, that one effort to be someone else had made his identity the clearest: The valley was who he was.

He stared after Bouclettes, as she slammed her car door and then pressed her forehead into her steering wheel.

"Who the hell is Élise Dubois?" Damien asked finally, a slice of a question. Damien did not like to be taken by surprise. "Why should Tante Colette be seeking out her heirs *over her own*?"

Matt looked again at Pépé, but Pépé's mouth was a thin line, and he wasn't talking.

Matt's head throbbed in great hard pulses. How could Tante Colette do this?

Without even warning him. Without giving him one single chance to argue her out of it or at least go strangle Antoine Vallier before that idiot even thought about sending that letter. Matt should have known something was up when she'd hired such an inexperienced, fresh-out-of-school lawyer. She wanted someone stupid enough to piss off the Rosiers.

Except—unlike his grandfather—he'd always trusted Tante Colette. She was the one who stitched up his wounds, fed him tea and soups, let him come take refuge in her gardens when all the pressures of his family got to be too much.

She'd loved him, he thought. Enough not to give a chunk of his valley to a stranger.

"It's that house," Raoul told Allegra, pointing to it, there a little up the hillside, only a couple of hundred yards from Matt's own house. If Matt knew Raoul, his cousin was probably already seeing a window—a way he could end up owning a part of this valley. If Raoul could negotiate with rebel warlords with a bullet hole in him, he could probably negotiate a curly-haired stranger into selling an unexpected inheritance.

Especially with Allegra on his side to make friends with her. While Matt alienated her irreparably.

Allegra ran after Bouclettes and knocked on her window, then bent down to speak to her when Bouclettes rolled it down. They were too far away for Matt to hear what they said. "Pépé." Matt struggled to speak. The valley thumped in his chest in one giant, echoing beat. It hurt his head, it was so big. It banged against the inside of his skull.

Possibly the presence of the valley inside him was being exacerbated by a hangover. Damn it. He pressed the heels of his palms into his pounding skull. What the hell had just happened?

Pépé just stood there, lips still pressed tight, a bleak, intense look on his face.

Allegra straightened from the car, and Bouclettes pulled away, heading up the dirt road that cut through the field of roses toward the house that Tante Colette had just torn out of Matt's valley and handed to a stranger.

Allegra came back and planted herself in front of him, fists on her hips. "Way to charm the girls, Matt," she said very dryly.

"F—" He caught himself, horrified. He could not possibly tell a woman to fuck off, no matter how bad his hangover and the shock of the moment. Plus, the last thing his skull needed right now was a jolt from Raoul's fist. So he just made a low, growling sound.

"She thinks you're hot, you know," Allegra said, in that friendly conversational tone torturers used in movies as they did something horrible to the hero.

"I...she...what?" The valley packed inside him fled in confusion before the *man* who wanted to take its place, surging up. Matt flushed dark again, even as his entire will scrambled after that flush, trying to get the color to die down.

"She said so." Allegra's sweet torturer's tone. "One of the first things she asked me after she got up this morning: 'Who's the hot one?'"

Damn blood cells, stay away from my cheeks. The boss did not flush. Pépé never flushed. You held your own in this crowd by being the roughest and the toughest. A man who blushed might as well paint a target on his chest and hand his cousins bows and arrows to practice their aim. "No, she did not."

"Probably talking about me." Amusement curled under Tristan's voice as he made himself the conversation's red herring. Was his youngest cousin taking pity on him? How had Tristan turned out so nice like that? After they made him use the purple paint when they used to pretend to be aliens, too.

"*And* she said you had a great body." Allegra drove another needle in, watching Matt squirm. He couldn't even stand himself now. His body felt too big for him. As if all his muscles were trying to get his attention, figure out if they were actually *great*.

"And she was definitely talking about Matt, Tristan," Allegra added. "You guys are impossible."

"I'm sorry, but I can hardly assume the phrase 'the hot one' means Matt," Tristan said cheerfully. "Be my last choice, really. I mean, there's me. Then there's— well, me, again, I really don't see how she would look at any of the other choices." He widened his teasing to Damien and Raoul, spreading the joking and provocation around to dissipate the focus on Matt.

"I was there, Tristan. She was talking about Matt," said Allegra, who either didn't get it, about letting the focus shift off Matt, or wasn't nearly as sweet as Raoul thought she was. "She thinks you're hot," she repeated to Matt, while his flush climbed back up into his cheeks and *beat* there.

Not in front of my cousins, Allegra! Oh, wow, really? Does she really?

Because his valley invader had hair like a wild bramble brush, and an absurdly princess-like face, all piquant chin and rosebud mouth and wary green eyes, and it made him want to surge through all those brambles and wake up the princess. And he so could not admit that he had thoughts like those in front of his cousins and his grandfather.

He was thirty years old, for God's sake. He worked in dirt and rose petals, in burlap and machinery and rough men he had to control. He wasn't supposed to fantasize about being a prince, as if he were still twelve.

Hadn't he made the determination, when he came back from Paris, to stay *grounded* from now on, real? Not to get lost in some ridiculous fantasy about a woman, a fantasy that had no relationship to reality?

"Or she *did*," Allegra said, ripping the last fingernail off. "Before you yelled at her because of something that is hardly her fault."

See, that was why a man needed to keep his feet on the ground. You'd think, as close a relationship as he had with the earth, he would know by now how much it hurt when he crashed into it. Yeah, did. Past tense.

But she'd stolen his land from him. How was he supposed to have taken that calmly? He stared up at the house, at the small figure in the distance climbing out of her car.

TRUST ME

Pépé came to stand beside him, eyeing the little house up on the terraces as if it was a German supply depot he was about to take out. "I want that land back in the family," he said, in that crisp, firm way that meant, *explosives it is and tough luck for anyone who might be caught in them.* "This land is yours to defend for this family, Matthieu. What are you going to do about this threat?"

Available now!

LAURA FLORAND

ACKNOWLEDGEMENTS

My many, many thanks to Virginia Kantra, Stephanie Burgis, and Mercy and Dale Anderson, for their early and invaluable feedback on this story. And a huge thank you, of course, to all my readers, as always, for all your support which has kept me motivated to write more books! Thank you all so much.

TRUST ME

ABOUT LAURA FLORAND

Laura Florand burst on the contemporary romance scene in 2012 with her award-winning Amour et Chocolat series. Since then, her international bestselling books have appeared in ten languages, been named among the Best Books of the Year by *Library Journal, Romantic Times,* and Barnes & Noble; received the RT Seal of Excellence and numerous starred reviews from *Publishers Weekly, Library Journal,* and *Booklist;* and been recommended by NPR, *USA Today,* and *The Wall Street Journal,* among others.

After a Fulbright year in Tahiti and backpacking everywhere from New Zealand to Greece, and several years living in Madrid and Paris, Laura now teaches Romance Studies at Duke University. Contrary to what the "Romance Studies" may imply, this means she primarily teaches French language and culture and does a great deal of research on French gastronomy, particularly chocolate.

LAURA FLORAND

COPYRIGHT